Her lips—soft pink, full and tempting—were parted, and, as rotten as he felt, still his loins stirred at the thought of tasting them.

He frowned, a memory floating a fraction beyond his reach.

Her lips. He could feel them, he knew their taste—silky as rose petals, sweet as honey. But how? He licked his own lips, paper-dry and sour. The answer eluded him as he continued his perusal of the woman by his bed.

Her hair. He paused, feeling his forehead pucker. Why had he thought her hair to be guinea-gold? It was not. It was more beautiful by far—the soft golden colour of corn ripening in the August sunshine. Not brassy, not a mass of curls, but soft waves where it escaped from its pins. He wanted to see it loose, flowing down her back.

He frowned again as he watched her sleep, striving to remember, fragments of memories teasing at his mind…

Janice Preston grew up in Wembley with a love of reading, writing stories and animals. After leaving school at eighteen she moved to Devon, and any thoughts of writing became lost in the hectic rush of life as a farmer's wife, with two children and many animals to care for. When her children left home for university she discovered a love of history, and of the Regency period in particular, and began to write seriously for the first time since her teens.

Janice now lives in the West Midlands with her husband and two cats. Over the years, apart from farming, she has worked as a conveyancer, a call handler for the police and an administrator for a teacher training programme at a local university. She currently works as an exam invigilator and has a part-time job with a weight management counsellor (vainly trying to control her own weight, despite her love of chocolate!).

This is Janice Preston's fantastic debut novel for Mills & Boon® Historical Romance!

MARY AND THE MARQUIS

Janice Preston

First published in Great Britain 2014
by Mills & Boon, an imprint of Harlequin (UK) Limited,
Large Print edition 2014
Harlequin (UK) Limited, Eton House, 18-24 Paradise Road,
Richmond, Surrey TW9 1SR

© 2014 Janice Preston

ISBN: 978-0-263-24002-3

Printed and bound in Great Britain
by CPI Antony Rowe, Chippenham, Wiltshire

Dedication

To Ian, for your unwavering support
and encouragement.

And with grateful thanks to
the Romantic Novelists' Association,
and in particular the organisers and readers
of the wonderful New Writers' Scheme.

Chapter One

September 1811

Mary clutched her cloak tighter around her and shivered as she peered through the gathering gloom. She hoped it wasn't going to rain. She felt a tug on her skirt and looked down.

'Mama.' Pinched features set in a face too pale stared up at her. 'Mama, I'm hungry.'

Mary summoned a reassuring tone. 'Hush, Toby; yes, I know, lovey. We shall have something to eat as soon as we find somewhere to shelter.'

Grimly, she quelled her rising panic and reached for Toby's hand as she hefted two-year-old Emily higher on her right hip, where she had fallen asleep, one grubby hand entangled in Mary's hair. They plodded on, following a muddy track that wound through dense woodland, the trees—a mixture of mature specimens and saplings—crowding in on either side, creating a claustrophobic atmosphere that had intensified as the afternoon wore on. No breath of wind stirred the limp foliage, not a bird sang and no woodland creature rustled amongst the undergrowth. The silence was unnerving.

Mary couldn't even be certain they were still heading north. She had become disorientated almost as soon as they had entered the wood. Such had been their weariness that the path, which had appeared to offer a short cut through the wood, had been accepted without thought. Now, however, Mary regretted her impulse. The track had twisted and turned like a serpent, until she no longer knew in which direction they walked.

For the past half-hour she had been on the lookout for something, anything—a woodsman's hut, perhaps, or even a fallen tree—that might provide shelter for her and the children, but there had been nothing. The afternoon was dipping inexorably towards evening. She knew she must find shelter for the night soon. Her arm ached with the effort of carrying Emily and Toby was tired and dragging his feet. She could hear his breath hitching and knew he was trying his hardest not to cry. She squeezed his hand and he looked up at her.

'It'll be all right, Toby. I promise.'

Suddenly, a deep, rasping groan sounded from

amongst the trees to her right. She whirled to face it, pushing Toby behind her and clutching Emily tight to her chest. She saw nothing. She took an uncertain step towards the trees, peering into the shadows.

'Mama?' Toby's panicky whisper sounded deafening in the eerie silence.

'Hush!' Mary hissed. Her eyes darted around, searching for the source of that groan. Nothing moved. She tightened her grip on Toby's hand. 'Come along, lovey, we must go.' She tugged him behind her as she hurried away, her heart hammering with the compulsion to put as much distance as possible between them and that unnatural sound. They reached the edge of a large clearing. It was lighter here, without the tree canopy, and Mary slowed, breathing a touch easier. As they neared the far edge of the clearing, however, a more familiar sound came to her ears—the jingle of a bit and the soft whicker of a horse.

Spinning round, Mary saw a large pale shape materialise from amongst the trees. The riderless horse walked on to the track, then halted. She looked around. There was nobody to be seen. A horse. Mary glanced down at Toby, read the exhaustion in his stance.

'Come, Toby.'

She led her son to a nearby fallen tree, then shook Emily gently.

'Emily…sweetheart; wake up, darling, there's a good girl.'

Emily opened her eyes a slit. Her face crumpled and she began to cry.

'I know, I know,' Mary soothed.

She lowered Emily to the ground before untying the knot that held the bundle of their worldly possessions on her back. She put the bundle down, then took her cloak off and lay it on the damp ground by the tree. 'There, sit on my cloak, sweeties. I won't be long.' She drew the cloak around the children for warmth.

The horse had reached the clearing and now cropped steadily at the grass. As Mary approached it, the grey stretched its head towards her, blowing softly through flared nostrils.

Mary slowly reached out to allow the animal to take in her scent. 'Hello, old fellow.' She stroked its nose, then took hold of the bridle. 'What are you doing out here all alone?'

The horse—a large, powerful grey gelding—relaxed, seemingly relieved to find some company in the silent woods. Mary examined him as best she could in the dim light. He was saddled and bridled and appeared unscathed, despite the broken and muddied reins trailing on the ground.

Mary gazed around again. There was nothing—nobody—to be seen.

'Is anyone there?' she called tentatively and listened.

Silence. She chewed at her lip, considering.

The horse had somehow appeared—at the exact time she needed it. Not that she believed in such things, of course. There was doubtless a perfectly reasonable explanation for the horse to be wandering loose in the woods, but she would be a fool if she did not take advantage of the opportunity he offered. He seemed placid enough and looked sufficiently strong to carry both her and the children. It wasn't as if she was stealing, she assured herself. She would leave him in the first village they came to, for his owner to reclaim.

Her one desire at the moment was to leave this dismal wood behind them and find some shelter for the night. Then they could have something to eat.

The last of the bread she had packed when they had left their home three days before was wrapped in a cloth in her cloak pocket. Her stomach rumbled at the thought of food. It would no doubt be dry and unpalatable, she thought with a grimace, but at least it was sustenance. Hunger had its own way of dealing with pernickety eaters. What they would eat on the morrow, she had no idea. She would face that problem when she must and she thrust the ever-present dread to the back of her mind. There was no sense in meeting trouble halfway. If she must beg for food to feed the children, she would do it. But, first, they must reach habitation and that, to her intense relief, was now possible, with the help of the grey.

'Come on, lad,' she said, urging the horse to follow her.

He dug his hooves in and shook his head with a loud jingle of his bit. Mary tried again, tugging at the rein. He did not move. Mary cursed under her breath. He did not look a flighty sort, but she would not risk her precious children on an animal that could prove dangerous. Decision made, she gathered the reins, hoisted up her skirts and reached for the stirrup, grateful for her misspent childhood riding astride before age and decorum had insisted she use a side-saddle. She had been an accomplished horsewoman once upon a time, although it was several years now since she had ridden.

Once mounted, the grey perked up and moved forward in response to the squeeze of her calves. Mary relaxed. He would be fine.

'Hi! Stop, thief!'

The sudden shout made her jump and the horse

shied sideways and lurched into a canter, almost un-seating Mary. Heart pounding, both from the shout and from the effort of controlling the horse, Mary pulled up the grey and looked over her shoulder, back across the clearing. Beyond its edge, and barely visible in the gloom, a man staggered from amongst the trees, halting a few paces shy of the track. He grabbed on to a tree, leaning heavily against it.

'Get back…here with…' His words slurred and faltered. His head drooped.

Heart in mouth, Mary urged the gelding towards the man. She wondered what he would do—if this was his horse, he must be a gentleman and, as Mary well knew, the richer the man the less forgiving he was likely to be towards someone who took what was his, no matter how great their need.

She halted by the man. His head lifted as if with a great effort, his eyes locking with Mary's. Even in the dusky light of late afternoon, she could make out his features, which stood in stark contrast to his ashen skin. His face was all hard planes and angles, with dark, dark eyes under scowling brows and messy, midnight-black hair.

He's very handsome. The thought came unbidden and Mary was shocked she would notice such a thing when she was in such a dire predicament. After all, this man now held the power of life and death in his hands. Were he to choose to turn her over to the authorities, she could be imprisoned, or transported, or even—and she quaked at the thought—hanged as a horse thief. She swallowed hard, controlling her fear. She must be at her most persuasive. She had the children to think of.

He reached out and curled long fingers around the rein.

'What…do…?' His voice tailed away.

His fingers slackened on the rein and he slumped heavily to the woodland floor.

'Sir?'

Leaning down from the saddle, Mary tried to make out further details. His clothing confirmed him as a gentleman, but it was too murky to see much more.

She could, however, smell the alcohol, even from this distance. Her nose wrinkled as she recalled his slurred words. A gentleman, in his cups. Memories of her father and his abusive ways when under the influence of drink awakened. She must get the children away before the gentleman came round.

There was no point in waiting, she persuaded herself. He could sleep off the effects of the alcohol here in the woods and, when he awoke, the walk back to wherever he had come from would do him good.

'Come on, lad, walk on,' she said to the reluctant

gelding, as she reined him away from the slumped figure and urged him on.

When they reached the children, Mary slid from the horse and hoisted Toby up to the saddle. It was a struggle. Toby, at five years old, was a sturdy little chap, but he took a pragmatic approach to life and, instead of making a fuss, he made every effort to help and scrambled on to the saddle. Emily began to wail and Mary hastened to pick her up and lift her in front of Toby. She put her cloak back on, re-tied her bundle, then positioned the gelding along-side the fallen tree and climbed on to it to help her to mount behind Toby.

She glanced back across the clearing, but could see no sign of the man. He was, presumably, still sleeping off the drink. She manoeuvred the grey on to the track leading from the clearing. No further shout sounded and Mary's tension eased a fraction. When they found a farm, or a village, she would release the horse and walk in with the children. No one would ever know she had 'borrowed' him. Like both her father and also her late husband she had no doubt the 'gentleman' would be unable to remember anything that had transpired that afternoon.

'Try to sit still, Toby,' she cautioned, as he squirmed in front of her, reaching to touch the horse's neck.

'I'm patting the horse to tell him he's being good, Mama.'

'He is, isn't he?'

'Mama? Look.' Toby held up his hand, showing fingers discoloured with a dark stain.

Mary took his hand and put her finger on the stain. It came away wet and sticky. She brought it closer to her eyes, but couldn't make out the colour. However, it smelled and felt suspiciously like…

'Toby! Are you hurt? Are you bleeding? Where did this come from?'

'Not me, silly Mama. The horse, I think he's hurt.' His voice wobbled.

'But…he can't be. I would have seen if there was blood on his neck.' A knot of dread formed in her stomach. If it wasn't Toby and it wasn't the horse, then it must be…

She reined in. What if he was hurt? Drunk or not, she couldn't leave an injured man lying in the woods all night. Muttering unladylike curses, she turned the grey. Immediately, his ears pricked up and his stride lengthened. To Mary's chagrin, they covered the distance back to the clearing in half the time.

'You old fraud,' she grumbled to the horse as she slid down from the saddle by the same fallen tree.

She tied the horse to a sapling. Injured or not, if the drunkard proved a threat they must be able to get away. Again, she went through the process of untying her bundle and spreading her cloak for the children to sit on. A breeze had sprung up, penetrating her thin woollen dress, and she shivered as she lifted the children down and sat them on the cloak, pulling the edges up around them once again.

'Don't move,' she whispered, 'and stay quiet. It's very important you don't make a sound. Do you understand?'

Both children nodded. Toby wrapped his arms around his little sister, who gazed up at Mary, her eyes huge in her face. Mary closed her eyes as the responsibilities weighing on her threatened to overwhelm her. Her stomach clenched, twisting into sick knots. What would happen to them all? She gritted her teeth and gave herself a mental shake. She forced a smile for the children as she stooped to plant a kiss on each of them.

'I won't be long,' she said.

Cautiously, she approached the track where she had left the man.

'You…you…came…' The voice rasped out from the shadows.

Mary gasped. The man had roused from his stupor and now sat facing the track, his back propped against a tree. She shot a quick glance over her shoulder to where she had left the children, but they—

and the horse—were safely out of sight. Warily, she picked her way towards the man, who watched her from under dark brows, his glittering eyes visible even in the gloom.

'Th...thank you. Shot...' His breaths were harsh and laboured.

'Shot? Oh, my goodness!' Mary forgot all caution and hurried to the man's side. 'Then it *was* your blood. Where are you injured?' She knelt by him.

'Shoulder...leg...careless...' He shifted and indicated his left shoulder.

'What happened? Who shot you? Was it an accident?' Mary glanced over her shoulder, at the surrounding woods. What if whoever had shot him was still out there?

He shook his head. 'Not here...safe here...please... take horse...get help...hurry...' Mary pulled his jacket open. 'No! Be careful! Aargh...' His right hand shot out and gripped her wrist with surprising strength, forcing it away from his shoulder. 'Just... go...get...help!' he gritted out.

Mary froze, her thoughts scrambling. The children! She couldn't leave them out here, alone with an injured man. She would have to take them with her, but they would slow her down. How long had he been bleeding?

'How far is it to find help?'

'Rothley…two miles…maybe more.' He seemed more alert, his breathing a touch easier.

Rothley. She knew the village, although not well. She had known it was on her route. She had her own reasons for avoiding it. 'Two miles? Is there nowhere nearer?'

He snorted. 'This is Northumberland. Sultan knows the way…won't take long…you can ride?'

'Of course I can.' Mary twisted her wrist, trying to work it free. 'But, first, I must look at your wounds. How long ago did it happen?'

'Not sure…lost track…but—' he squinted up through the branches overhead '—possibly…a couple of hours?'

'Are you still bleeding?'

'Never mind that…please…go…'

Mary eyed him with exasperation. If he was still losing blood, she must try to staunch the flow before leaving him. It would be an hour or more before help arrived. Three hours of blood loss could prove fatal.

'Please,' she said, 'let me see?'

He scowled, but he lifted his jacket away from his left shoulder. She leant over him, grasped the lapel and opened it wider, reaching inside and placing her hand on the huge patch of blood that stained the front of his white shirt. It was wet. He hissed with pain.

'Sorry,' she said as she lowered his jacket back into place. She had seen enough. He had lost a great deal of blood and she knew she must bandage the wounds before she left.

'You're still bleeding,' she told him. 'I shall have to remove your jacket, no matter how much it hurts, I'm afraid.'

'Any…other time…a pleasure.' His eyes glinted and a brief smile twisted his lips.

She narrowed her eyes at him, steadfastly ignoring the *frisson* of pleasure that skittered down her spine at his expression. A typical male, she thought. Not even a serious injury could curb his rakish tendencies.

'I'll need to check your back, too,' she said. 'If the bullet went straight through, you will need padding there as well. Have you a knife?'

'A knife? What…? You're not…?'

'No.' Despite the circumstances, she had to laugh. 'I only want it to cut your coat. I shall make no attempt to remove the bullet, if it is still in there. After all, you almost swooned when I barely touched your shoulder just now.'

His dark brows snapped together. 'I do *not* swoon,' he said. 'Passed out…pain…hardly the same.'

'Well, that's as may be, but removing your jacket will hurt a great deal more, I promise.'

'Hard woman…' he grumbled, but fumbled in his pocket and produced a clasp knife, which Mary took and opened, using it to hack at the edge of his jacket.

'Careful!' he gasped.

'The quicker I do this, the better,' she said as she grasped the cut edges of the cloth and ripped with a quick, steady motion. She repeated her actions with his blood-soaked shirt. 'Lean forward, if you please.'

He obeyed and she cut again, then eased the clothes away, exposing his left shoulder. His skin was warm to her touch, warm and smooth. She was close enough to register the male, spicy scent of him, overlaid with the coppery smell of fresh blood. She shook her head. What was wrong with her? *Concentrate, Mary*, she admonished herself.

'Good,' she said calmly, as if her thoughts hadn't been leading her in an entirely inappropriate direction, 'it seems as though the bullet went straight through. I'll…' She paused, thinking.

'You'll…?'

She looked at him and frowned. 'We need bandages.'

'Can use…shirt.'

'No, that won't do. Half of it is already ruined and you must keep warm.' There was no help for it, she knew. She must sacrifice her petticoat, although, heaven knew, she had few enough clothes as it was. Still, in an emergency...

'Stay there a minute,' she said as she got to her feet.

He looked up at her and his mouth quirked into a smile. His lips, she noticed with a flutter, were firm, shapely and very sensual. 'Going...nowhere,' he said. 'What's your name?'

'Mary. Mary Vale.'

She stepped behind the tree and lifted her skirt. She cut a slit in her cotton petticoat, then ripped a length from around the hem. She then repeated the action twice more, using the knife to cut one strip in half to pad the wound.

'What...you doing...behind my back...Sensible Mary?'

Mary's jaw clenched. Sensible Mary! The exact same phrase her late husband had used, taunting her for her practical outlook on life. Well, she might be practical, but that trait had kept her family together after Michael's drinking had spiralled out of control. Until he died, that is. Much use was practicality when the rent was due and you had no way of paying it. At least, no way she was willing to entertain. Resolutely, she forced her thoughts back to the matter in hand. There was much to do and, despite the sting of that name, she was grateful for her streak of common sense. Acting the lady and, yes, swooning would get them nowhere.

She came back around the tree and knelt again by his side. 'And you are?' she asked, as she folded one of the strips to form a pad.

'Lucas.'

'Mr Lucas?'

He eyed her, then sighed. 'Lucas Alastair. Rothley.'

She froze. 'Rothley? When you said Rothley before I assumed you meant the village.'

She knew of the Alastairs of Rothley. Her father and the Marquis of Rothley had once been friends who, in time, had become bitter enemies.

As she urged Rothley to lean forward so she could pad the exit wound, her mind whirled. The old marquis must have died and this would therefore be his eldest son. There had been two, as she recalled. The tales of their wild behaviour, recounted in whispers, had even penetrated north of the Border, where Mary had spent her childhood. Wild stories, half-remembered. She pushed her conjectures to the back of her mind. His past was of no immediate import.

'We are near to Rothley Hall, then?'

'Indeed…this…my land…' he gasped.

Mary studied him with concern. His eyes were screwed shut, his fine lips twisted in a grimace. He might be a wild, hedonistic rake—and drunk, to boot—but he was injured and in pain.

'Do you have a family?' she asked, in an effort to distract him as she pressed another strip of her folded petticoat against the hole where the bullet had penetrated his shoulder.

'Family?'

'Yes: a wife? Children?'

'No!'

Rothley's response to her idle question was swift, in a tone tinged with abhorrence, stirring Mary's curiosity. Why so hostile? Mayhap it was as well, she thought, as she continued to dress his wound. Better by far, to her mind, that the rakes of this world remained unwed and saved some poor woman, and their children, a life of misery.

She banished his attitude to the back of her mind and concentrated on the task in hand, listening with increasing anxiety to his shallow breathing. He groaned as she lifted his arm to pass the bandage beneath, wrapping it around to hold the pads in place.

'Why…do you…ask?'

'I beg your pardon?'

'Why ask…about…family?'

She smiled at his suspicious tone, secure in the knowledge he could not see her expression. Did he

imagine she wished to discover if he was wed? Did
he fear she might set her cap at him on the strength
of his title alone?

'I wondered if someone might be out searching
for you.'

'Not...' His voice faded.

Alarmed, fearing he was about to pass out, Mary
glanced up at Rothley. His eyes were riveted on her
chest. She glanced down and felt a blush rise as she
realised how much of her *décolletage* was revealed
to his gaze as she leaned forward to bandage him.
He glanced up and caught her eye.

'Merely...distracting...myself...S...Sensible
Mary.'

Mary felt a tingle deep inside at the heat she
glimpsed in those dark eyes. It had been a very long
time since a man—rake or not—had viewed her as
a woman and not simply as a burdensome wife.

'Let me see your leg,' she said, striving to sound
unaffected as she quelled her unwelcome response.
Rothley was a rake and a drinker. It was a combi-
nation she despised. How could she react to him in
such a way? It must be sheer animal attraction; he
was, after all, very striking: all brooding, sensual
masculinity.

She gently cut the material of his breeches away
from the wound, wishing she had some means of

cleaning the hole where the bullet had entered the fleshy part of the back of his thigh. There was no exit wound. That was bad. She bit her lip as she bandaged his leg.

Rothley groaned softly and Mary looked up with concern. His eyes were closed and harsh lines bracketed his mouth and furrowed his brow.

'My lord?' He did not respond. She laid her hand on his forehead. Not too much heat there. *Not yet, anyway*, she thought grimly, *but he needs a doctor. The sooner the better.*

'My lord?' Mary raised her voice, laying her hand against his cheek. His stubble scratched against her palm. She patted him, gently at first, then firmly.

He groaned again and opened his eyes. She could see the effort he made to rally, jaw clenched and nostrils flaring as he inhaled several times.

'Inside…brandy…' He indicated his jacket.

Mary felt inside what was left of his jacket. The muscles of his chest jerked in reflex as she brushed against them.

'Haven't you had enough of this already?' She retrieved a small flask, recalling the stench of alcohol she had noticed before. No doubt she had already become accustomed to the smell.

He thrust his hand out and, when she handed him the flask, he unscrewed the cap with his teeth and spat it out before taking a long swig. Mary shuddered, the smell again reviving unhappy memories. She forced herself back to the present, to the situation in hand.

'Which direction is Rothley Hall?' she asked. 'How shall I find it?'

'To right…follow path…turn left on road.' He paused, tensing, then raised dark eyes, racked with pain, to hers.

'Big gates…a mile…on right. P…please…Mary, be quick!'

'Don't fret, I shall go soon,' she replied. Taking his hand between hers she squeezed, her heart going out to him. 'But first, I shall fetch my cloak. It will keep you warm until help arrives.'

Toby and Emily were both awake and the relief on Toby's face when he saw Mary wrenched at her heartstrings.

'Stay quiet, both of you,' she warned as she raised them to their feet. 'I shall only be a minute, then we will take the horse. The man you saw before—he is injured. We must fetch help for him.'

'Are we rescuing him, Mama?' Toby asked in an interested voice.

'Yes, Toby, you'll be a real hero,' she replied as she pinched his cheek.

She hurried back to Rothley. He was drifting in

and out of consciousness, much as Michael had done on that fateful night when he had fallen from his horse in a drunken stupor on his way home. Simon Wendover, his drinking companion, had brought him home, leaving him on the doorstep for her to care for as best she could. Mr Wendover, Simon's father and Michael's employer, had sent the doctor the following day to see what could be done, but it was too late. He had died three days later.

Gently, she laid the cloak over Rothley.

'Angel...' he murmured, but did not fully rouse.

Mary studied his features. He looked younger in repose, his surprisingly long lashes dark against his pale skin, his lips relaxed and slightly parted. He looked nothing like the wild rake she knew him to be. She laid her hand gently on his forehead. The silky texture of his hair slipped through her fingers as she brushed it from his brow. His eyes flickered at her touch and she snatched her hand away, feeling her colour rise. She leant close and put her lips to his ear.

'I'll be as quick as I can,' she promised, sending a quick prayer that rescue would arrive in time, before heading back to Sultan and the children.

His angel was gone!

Lucas tried to rise, aching to follow her, to continue to bask in the glow of her comforting presence, but he was dimly aware his body would not obey his will. That he did not, in fact, move. He tried to call to her, but only a low moan sounded to his straining ears. The angel was no more, leaving a gaping void, as cold and as black as the loughs on the nearby hills, filled with pain.

He frowned, his thoughts slippery and evasive. *Who is she?* The wavering image of her face swam into view, reassuring yet tantalising: clear skin with a smattering of freckles, cornflower-blue eyes and soft lips, all framed by wayward wisps of soft gold, glimpsed as they escaped her bonnet. *Why is she here? In the woods?* The image of her face sank again, submersed in the inky black depths of his mind.

Julia!

The name surfaced, conjured up from the past, dragging the old feelings of hurt and rejection with it.

He muttered, uncertain of anything any more but the ever-present pain. *Was it Julia? How could it be? The face of an angel. The face that belied a heart as black as coal.*

He drifted, his mind a jumble of visions from his past: his father, face contorted with rage, roaring, arm raised; his mother, remonstrating, protecting, taking the blows meant for her sons; the gaming houses, the huge losses, drinking to deaden the blow; the opium dens with wild parties and orgies; friends, coming and going; Julia—her beautiful face and the sound of her scornful laughter as she rejected him.

My back! It hurts! With great effort, he forced his thoughts into some semblance of lucidity. The bark of the tree he leant against dug into his back. He shifted to ease the pressure and a white-hot spear of pain penetrated his thigh. As he sank into the void, he fought against it, vaguely aware he must not succumb.

Some time later—an hour, a day, a week?—he roused to the sense of a cool hand on his forehead. *Julia.* The name gained shape in his mind. He felt his lips move. Did he give voice to the name? He knew not. He tried to prise his eyes open, but the effort was too great. Then he felt hands take hold of him. The pain spiked through every nerve in his body and he sank—gratefully this time—back into oblivion.

Chapter Two

'Ah, there you are, Mrs Vale. Have the bairns settled?'

'Yes, thank you, Mrs Lindley. Susan did a splendid job with them. They are fast asleep,' Mary replied as she entered the huge kitchen at Rothley Hall. Despite the traumas of the past hours, her tensions melted away and she relaxed for the first time since she had left the cottage. At least, tonight, the children were safe and warm, with food in their bellies, thanks to Susan, the young housemaid, who had taken them under her wing the moment Mary and the exhausted children had arrived at the Hall.

Well, maybe not the exact moment, Mary reflected, recalling the scene with a wry smile. The Hall had looked deserted as she rode up the overgrown drive to the front of the house. She had ridden around to the rear and, spying a flicker of light in what she now knew was the kitchen window, she had pounded on a nearby door.

Mrs Lindley had responded, presenting a most intimidating appearance. She was almost as wide as she was tall, with arms as big as hams folded across her bolster of a bosom as she looked suspiciously from Mary to the children and stoutly declared her master was overseas and expected to remain there for the foreseeable future.

Her conjectures about Mary had been blatant, but Mary had taken no offence, instead silently admiring the woman for her devotion to Rothley. Upon hearing of her master's injuries, however, Mrs Lindley had swung into action, rallying the rest of the staff and begging Mary to return with the men to show them where Rothley lay.

Toby and Emily had been left in the care of Susan, with whom they had bonded immediately. Later, deemed too young and innocent to remain whilst the doctor ministered to Lord Rothley, Susan had continued in her role as nursemaid and settled the children in bed. Mary had not been as fortunate. It had been clear she was expected to play her part. The sound of Rothley's moans as the doctor removed the bullet from his thigh still echoed in her ears, sending shivers down her spine. He had thrashed around on the bed and, in the end, it had taken five of them to hold him still for the doctor. Mary's arms still ached with the effort.

'She's a good lass and a hard worker. She has to be, living here,' Mrs Lindley continued, as she turned to the kettle singing over the open fire and lifted it. 'I hope she's gone straight to bed, like I told her. It's going to be a long haul, I fear, till the master is up and about again, and we shall all have to pull our weight, even young Susan.

'Sit yourself down, Mrs Vale, do. Doctor'll be down in a minute, then we'll have some coffee and maybe a slice of my cake. I think we've earned it this night.'

Mary sank on to a chair next to the large, well-scrubbed table that dominated the centre of the room.

'May I ask where the rest of the staff are?' Mary asked. 'Surely a house of this size requires more than the few I have met here tonight?'

The house was huge and rambling, but the staff appeared to consist of a mere four souls, plus two stockmen-cum-grooms. Mrs Lindley had introduced herself as the cook-cum-housekeeper. It seemed to Mary almost everyone served a dual purpose in this house. No wonder it looked uncared for.

Mrs Lindley cackled. 'Bless you, dear. We're all

his lordship can afford and he can barely afford us, truth be told. Am I right, Ellen?'

Mary glanced round. The other maid had entered the room, followed by the doctor. Ellen was older than Susan, a cheery woman of around five and forty summers, as slim as Mrs Lindley was wide.

'You are indeed, Mrs Lindley, aye,' she said, then grinned at Mary. 'Worked to the bone, we are, ma'am, and no mistake. But, for all that, I wouldn't never leave 'is lordship and nor would any of us, and that's a fact. Started 'ere when I wasn't much older than Susan, I did. Seen 'is lordship grow up, aye. My, the tales I could…'

'Now, now, Ellen,' said the doctor. 'I am sure our visitor doesn't wish to hear all that old nonsense.'

Ellen coloured, but laughed, 'Right you are, Doctor, I was forgetting myself. I'll pour some coffee and take it to Mr Trant and then I'll take myself off to bed, if there's naught else you need me for, Mrs Lindley?'

At the shake of the housekeeper's head, Ellen bade them all a cheery goodnight and left the kitchen.

The doctor put down his bag and spoke to Mrs Lindley. 'I have asked Trant to stay with his lordship until someone can relieve him. It is imperative someone remains with him at all times in case of fever. It will prove a burden, I make no doubt, as short-staffed as you are, but you do at least have the benefit of... My apologies, ma'am,' he continued, now directing his attention to Mary, 'but I'm afraid, in all the excitement, I failed to catch your name?'

He was a spare man of around thirty years of age, of medium height, with close-cropped fair hair and grey eyes. He had a straightforward manner that Mary found appealing, although she was taken aback by his ready assumption she would help to nurse Lord Rothley. At first, she was inclined to resent such presumption but, upon reflection, it would at least provide her and the children with a welcome haven—a place, and the time, for them to recoup their strength before they must move on.

'I am Mary Vale, Dr...?'

'Preece; Robert Preece, ma'am, at your service.' He bowed, then rounded the table to sit opposite Mary. 'I understand it was you who discovered Lord Rothley in the woods this afternoon?'

'Yes, sir.'

'Did he tell you how he was shot? Or by whom?'

'I'm afraid not, Doctor. I did ask but, well...'

'Quite. You both had other priorities, I make no doubt.' He contemplated her in silence for a moment, then commented, 'It was most fortunate you were passing.'

Mary was thankful he dropped the subject; she

was altogether too weary to field questions about why she had been in the woods. Her eyes drifted closed, exhaustion near overwhelming her, as her mind travelled back over this most difficult of days.

'How has he been, Mrs Lindley? In himself?'

The quiet question penetrated Mary's reverie. She feigned sleep, shamelessly eavesdropping on the conversation. Her interest in the marquis was, she assured herself, transient.

'Oh, you know, Doctor. Much the same,' Mrs Lindley replied, her voice at the same low pitch as the doctor's. 'He drives himself relentlessly. Won't listen to no one: not his mama, not none of us. He's been a sight worse since she's been away.'

'When is she due home?'

'We're none of us sure. If his lordship knows, he's keeping it tight to his chest, that's for sure.'

'We have seen very little of him in the village in the past couple of years—he has become something of a recluse since his return. He would appear to have gone from one extreme to the other, if the tales of his time in London are to be believed. What I cannot understand, though, is his reluctance to socialise with his old friends.' There was a note of bitterness in the doctor's voice.

'No more can any of us, Doctor. When I think how much you two shared as lads...but he's changed, sir. You'd hardly recognise him. It's as if he cannot trust another soul. 'Tis a pity: he was always such a bonny, carefree lad, despite that father of his.'

'He was a harsh man, for sure, but that doesn't explain why Lucas has shut himself away.'

'It's my belief his lordship had no notion of how much debt his father was in. He came home, wanting to learn about the estate—a good five years ago, now—but his father were having none of it: sent his lordship off with a flea in his ear. Called him a no-account wastrel, he did. Eee, the look on his lordship's face when he walked out the door—I shall never forget it, as long as I live. And his poor mama, she near to broke her heart. He never saw his father alive again.'

'I wonder why his father rejected Lucas's help?' Dr Preece mused. 'One would have thought he would welcome it. Pride, maybe? Oh well, I dare say we shall never know the truth of it. And I,' he added in a brisker tone, 'should be shot for gossiping about your master in such a fashion, Mrs Lindley. Lucas would be quite within his rights to bar me from his threshold, were he to hear us. But I shall acquit myself, for I am genuinely concerned for him and it is a fact *he* will not confide in me.'

Mary had heard enough. She stirred ostentatiously and the quiet conversation ceased.

'Well, now, I must bid you goodnight, ladies,' the doctor said, rising to his feet. 'Don't forget: someone must sit with Lucas…his lordship…at all times. If he does develop a fever—and I shall consider it a miracle if he does not—I shall expect to be informed of it immediately.'

'Doctor…?' Mrs Lindley looked troubled. 'I'm sorry, Doctor, but your bill…?'

Dr Preece finished donning his greatcoat, then crossed to Mrs Lindley and placed his hands on her shoulders, peering into her face. 'Mrs Lindley, I forbid you to worry about my fee.'

As she opened her mouth, he continued, 'Leave me to thrash it out with Rothley. We will come to some arrangement. You are to send for me if I am needed, do you hear?'

Relief on her face, the cook nodded.

'Good. And as for you, ma'am,' he said, turning his attention to Mary, 'you have proved yourself already to be an oasis of calm in a crisis. I charge you with ensuring there is no silly hesitation in sending for me should Lord Rothley's condition deteriorate.

'Goodnight, ladies.' He bowed and left the room.

Mary sat alone by the side of Rothley's bed and studied the form lying in the huge four-poster, his complexion as white as the pillow upon which his head rested. His features were relaxed, the harsh lines that had bracketed his mouth and creased his brow had smoothed until they had almost disappeared, but, even in repose, he exuded danger. His dark, brooding features drew Mary's gaze like a lodestone. She conjured up the image of his body—large, muscular, inherently masculine—and felt her stomach perform a slow somersault as she allowed herself the indulgence of imagining his body covering hers, the weight of him on her, his hands and his mouth…

Pushing such thoughts aside, she rose from the chair and crossed to the fire to place a log on the flames.

What on earth is wrong with me, thinking of such things at such a time, when he is critically injured? But the feeling of him lying on her was so evocative, so familiar, she… Of course! With a surge of relief, she recalled the journey back to Hall on the flat bed of the cart that transported him home. She felt again his body, lying between her splayed legs, the weight of his head on her belly.

She was tired and her mind was playing tricks on her. She was not, after all, an immoral wanton, lusting after a man lying wounded in his bed—a man she was supposed to be caring for. She sat down in the chair again and studied her patient. He had suffered a great deal, but he was strong and would no doubt recuperate quickly. Then she could be on her way and these confusing sensations would be left behind, where they belonged. The thought of the journey still ahead of her and her likely reception raised old familiar doubts that pecked at her. Had she made the right decision? But what was the alternative? She could think of none.

It had been a grim few hours and Mary was exhausted. She leaned her head against the high back of the wing chair. Her eyelids drooped. Aware she was on the brink of sleep, she pushed herself back to her feet. She went to the window. Twitching the curtain aside, she peered out, but could see only the raindrops that spattered intermittently against the glass. Shivering, she let the curtain fall back into place, then crossed to the fireplace and placed another log on the fire. She glanced at the clock on the mantelshelf—nine of the clock. No wonder she was tired, for they had left the cottage before dawn, but she must remain alert. She must watch the patient. There was no sign of fever yet, but the doctor had said the next few days would be critical.

There was a faint sound and the massive form of Mrs Lindley appeared in the doorway. Mary went to her and stepped out into the hallway, that they might not disturb Rothley.

'I've come to apologise, Mrs Vale. I fear I mightn't have given you a very proper welcome at first.' Her eyes twinkled. 'I also must thank you again for all your help.'

'No thanks are necessary, Mrs Lindley. With hind-sight, it is fortunate I was in the woods this after-noon. I fear, otherwise, his lordship would still be out there.'

Mrs Lindley's expression became sombre. 'It don't bear thinking about, ma'am. We must thank the Lord He saw fit to send you through the woods today. Now, are you sure you don't mind watching over his lordship a while longer? You look exhausted. I'm worried we've taken your help for granted. I could stay—'

'I'm happy to help,' Mary interrupted, touching the other woman's arm. 'I am happy to take the first watch and then I shall enjoy some uninterrupted sleep so, please, do not tease yourself. I am grateful, to tell the truth, that we have a roof over our heads, if only for a short while.'

Mrs Lindley directed a long look of speculation at Mary. 'Well, if that's the case, I'll say goodnight. Ellen will relieve you at midnight and I'll take over at four of the clock. It'll be a hard task, keeping up with the nursing, I'm afraid, on top of everything else, but it'll be a boon having you here, ma'am, I don't mind telling you. And the bairns will be a tonic. Although it might be best...' her eyes slid past Mary, towards Rothley's door, before returning to Mary's face, '...it might be wise if they are kept away from this part of the house.'

'I shall ensure they do not disturb his lordship,' Mary said. 'I am sure the house is big enough for them to be kept well away. And I dare say we shall be long gone before he is up and about.'

'Thank you, ma'am. I can't say why he's set against having bairns around, but it is so. He's like to be a difficult enough patient as it is—' She stopped abruptly, her lips pursed. 'He's been under a strain, these last few years. I hope you've got a thick skin, but just remember his bark is much worse than his bite.' She grinned, then waddled away without another word.

Mary watched her retreat, thinking over her words. She shook her head as she opened the bedchamber door and went back into the room. Why would any adult feel such aversion towards innocent children?

'I thought I dreamed you.'

The whispered words made her jump and her eyes flew to the figure in the bed.

Chapter Three

Rothley was awake, his dark eyes open and riveted on Mary. She swallowed nervously.

'You're awake,' she said and then bit her lip. *Goodness, what a ridiculous thing to say.*

One corner of his mouth lifted. 'So it would seem,' he said.

'How are you feeling?'

'Sore,' he replied. 'Tired.'

Mary fussed about, a tremor in her hands as she straightened the covers on the bed, aware he watched her every move. He looked sinfully attractive, his black hair tousled and his dark eyes, under their heavy lids, appraising her. He had pushed the covers down almost to his waist and she pulled them higher. The top of his nightshirt lay unbuttoned, a sprinkling of dark hair just visible. She had seen him naked, whilst helping the doctor, and her blood quickened as she visualised his muscled chest, sprinkled with dark hair, glistening with sweat.

For goodness' sake! He's been shot and you're here to nurse him. What sort of a strumpet are you? She was ashamed of her physical reaction even as, contrarily, she relished the slow build of anticipation deep inside. *What he doesn't know, won't hurt,* she told herself.

'Why are you here? Not that I have any objection to a beautiful woman in my bedchamber, you understand, but…where is everyone else?'

'In bed, asleep, my lord. The doctor was here; he removed the bullet from your leg…'

'Hmmph, I remember.' He grimaced, stifling a moan, as he stirred under the bedcovers. 'What a butcher…never felt such pain. But that doesn't explain…'

'The doctor said we are to sit with you, my lord, in case you develop signs of fever. Ellen will take over at midnight and then Mrs Lindley will relieve her later on. I am taking the first shift.'

'With no chaperon? You are brave, my dear. Many a lady's reputation has been ruined for less.'

'I am a widow, my lord. My presence here is no different to Ellen, or to Mrs Lindley for that matter. And, might I point out, you are in no fit state to ravish anyone?'

'But I wouldn't be imagining ravishing Ellen or Mrs Lindley, now, would I? But a comely young widow—well, this is an unexpected turn of the cards.'

In the flickering light of the candle, Mary recognised the glint of admiration in Rothley's dark eyes as he looked her up and down. Resentment slid through her veins. It seemed as soon as a man learned she was a widow, his interest quickened. *And he's not mistaken, is he?* She felt the heat build in her cheeks as she recalled her earlier thoughts. She stiffened, stepping away from the bed.

A low chuckle sounded. 'There is no need to retreat. As you acutely observed, I am in no state to take advantage of anyone. At least, not at present,' he added, with a grin. 'It is possibly a touch late for formality, but I should introduce myself. Rothley, at your service.'

His attempt at a bow was no more than a bob of his chin as he lay in the bed and Mary bit back a smile at the absurdity. She relaxed. He was right. Despite his provocative words, he was no danger to her. Yet. And she would be long gone before he could make any serious attempt at seduction. She feared a Lord Rothley, in full health and vigour, might very well prove irresistible, despite her antipathy towards rakes in general.

'I know who you are, my lord. You introduced yourself when we met in the woods.'

He frowned. 'The woods, you say? What...?' His brow cleared. 'Yes. I remember now...vaguely. I owe you my gratitude for your help today.'

His lids drifted shut and he was silent. Mary approached the bed again and was about to sit in the chair by its side when he shifted in the bed. A moan, soon cut short, alerted Mary. She leaned closer and put her hand to his forehead. Still cool, but a touch clammy.

Rothley opened his eyes and regarded her ruefully.

'Never mind *your* reputation, this won't do mine any good at all,' he said, with a lopsided grin. 'Here am I, in my bedchamber with a beautiful woman for company, and the only moans to be heard are my own.'

Mary laughed at his disgruntled tone. 'You must console yourself, my lord, with the knowledge there is nobody within hearing distance, even were you to entertain a bevy of beauties within these four walls.'

'Indeed,' he murmured, capturing her gaze, his fine lips curving. 'My expertise would be for the sole appreciation of the recipient, would it not?'

One dark brow lifted. *He's testing me,* she realised, a slow blush heating her skin, unable—*or unwilling?* her inner voice teased—to tear her eyes from his.

As she froze, his gaze focused and intensified. His eyes gleamed and his sensuous lips curved as Mary, still bent over him, remained transfixed, her pulse racing as his masculine scent assailed her senses and pervaded her very being. She felt as she imagined a mouse must when confronted by a crouching cat, fearful of twitching the tiniest muscle lest it prove the wrong move: the move that would trigger the pounce. Every nerve of her being quivered, every sense was on heightened alert. The stillness of the house weighed heavily, the only sounds the soft crackle of the fire and the ticking of the clock.

The slow movement of his hand broke the enchantment for a brief moment, before he enmeshed her further in his spell. His finger touched lightly at her temple, trailed a path down the side of her face and followed the line of her jaw to her chin. It then lifted to caress her mouth, tracing the width of her trembling lower lip. Mary's lids fluttered closed as his hand cupped her chin and urged her closer, ever closer. His breath whispered across her sensitised lips as he feathered a kiss across her mouth. Desire snaked through her as his hand slid round to cradle her head. The moist heat of his lips as they moved against hers was an impossible temptation. Without volition, Mary's hand lifted to his cheek and she leaned into the kiss, lost in the moment, her whole body awakening and responding, every nerve tingling, anticipation flowing from a tiny pinpoint deep inside until it flooded every vein in her body. She trembled, the craving for more near overwhelming her, until the distant sound of a door banging roused her from her trance and, with a gasp of horror, she wrenched her lips from his. She scrambled away, her face aflame, her hands flying to her cheeks in a vain attempt to cover her shame.

'My lord...' she gasped.

The heat in those ebony eyes was undeniable. He smiled at her: a slow, seductive smile that set her quivering with desire. Her heart was pounding and she could feel the pulse jump in her neck. How had he captivated her so very quickly? How had one kiss resurrected those feelings she had thought dead and buried long since?

She stiffened, angry and ashamed that she had become so mesmerised by the touch of this stranger's lips that she had responded in a way no decent woman should. And she was *furious* she was now unable to conceal her embarrassment. Why should she make such a fuss over a stolen kiss that was no doubt a mere passing fancy to a rake such as he? She dragged in a deep breath to steady her nerves. It would test her ingenuity to its limit, but she must disabuse him of any notion she might be available for any sort of dalliance. Taking a moment, she smoothed her hands down her skirts. She then looked him in the eye, raising her brows in a way she hoped would make her appear unconcerned.

'Well,' she said, willing her voice to remain light and unconcerned, 'I cannot pretend you did not catch me off guard, or I would not have allowed that to happen. However, although your kiss was pleasant enough, my lord, I shall be obliged if you will restrain your...more *basic* urges in the future. I have no wish to be constantly on my guard if I am to assist in nursing you over the next week or so. As a gentleman, I am sure you will accede to my wishes.'

'Ah...but can you be certain I *am* a gentleman?'

Mary raised her chin. 'I make no doubt you were raised as such,' she said, 'and, no matter what direction your life has taken since then, I would urge you to remember that. I am here to nurse you, Lord Rothley, and that is all.'

Rothley's lips tightened a fraction, then a sudden gleam lit his eyes. Mary eyed him with suspicion.

'I'm so hot,' he murmured. 'My forehead is burning. I feel feverish.' His lids flickered shut.

'Hmmph!'

Mary's huff of disbelief was barely audible, but she caught the twitch of Rothley's lips, so it had been loud enough. Without approaching any nearer, she reached across and placed her hand on his forehead.

'Aaahh, so soothing, so comforting,' he murmured as his eyes opened and he captured her gaze again.

He grinned as she snatched her hand away, her insides melting anew. His masculine aura tugged at her senses, her body responding with a readiness she had never before experienced, even in the early days of her marriage.

He is a rake, she reminded herself. *Attracted merely because I am female and, seemingly, willing and available.*

'It feels quite normal to me, my lord,' she said, as she crossed the room to the washstand, which held a bowl and a pitcher of water, 'but I will bathe it for you, nevertheless. If—' she glanced over her shoulder at Rothley as she wrung out a cloth in the water '—you promise to keep yourself covered up.'

His lips twitched as she approached the bed. 'Does the sight of my manly chest bother you so?'

Mary tensed. She was a grown woman, not some silly innocent to be beguiled and misled by a silver-tongued rake, no matter how attractive. If she didn't take care, nursing the marquis would prove impossible. She must—for her own sanity—maintain her distance for, if she was honest, his flirtatious ways were proving hard to resist.

'It bothers me not one iota,' she said brusquely. 'I am simply concerned you do not catch a fever, for that would mean I am honour bound to remain here that much longer. The sooner you are recovered, the sooner I may leave.'

The amusement drained from his face. 'You are under no obligation to me, madam. You are not bound to remain here against your inclination.'

Mary felt a momentary qualm. Had she overreacted?

'My obligation is to my own conscience, my lord. I have experience of nursing and your staff, as far as I can ascertain, have very little. Besides, they are hardly under-employed in this household. An extra pair of hands will not come amiss, I am sure.'

'Indeed. My household, as you rightly point out, is staffed at a totally inadequate level. No doubt you are used to better.'

His voice was tight, his brows lowered, but Mary felt certain it was not anger that generated his response. Rather, she thought, it was worry creasing his forehead. She recalled Mrs Lindley's comments about the debts facing the estate.

'Once upon a time, maybe,' she said, as she applied the cool, damp cloth to his brow, 'but not in the past few years, I can assure you.'

His eyes sparked with interest. 'How so?'

'My childhood was carefree for the most part, but adulthood brings its own challenges,' she said. 'Hard work is not unknown to me.'

She sought to divert him. 'Do you remember what happened, my lord?'

His eyes glinted wickedly as he grinned up at her.

'I remember a beautiful angel coming to my rescue. I remember her ripping open my shirt—'

'I meant, what happened before,' Mary interrupted. The teasing, flirtatious Lord Rothley was back. Her diversion had worked only too well. 'Have you remembered how…why…you were shot?'

'Killjoy,' he murmured. 'I had much rather discuss the softness of your lap.'

Mary's face flamed. She had hoped he wouldn't remember the laborious journey home from the woods in the back of a cart—his head, heavy in her lap and her legs extended either side of his body in an effort to cushion him from the worst of the jolts. His eyes locked with hers and she felt again the slow, nervous trickle of anticipation deep inside. Her breath seized, her nerves all on edge, her legs suddenly weak.

'Your lack of denial leads me to assume my memories are not a wishful fantasy after all,' he said, with a lift of his brows.

Mary stepped back and sat in the chair by the bed, staring towards the fire.

'The doctor said you were very lucky,' she said, seeking to cover her confusion.

He snorted, but weakly. 'How so? I do not feel lucky right now.'

'The bullet went straight through your shoulder without hitting anything vital. He believes you will make a full recovery, in time.' Mary risked a glance at him. 'It could have been a great deal worse, my lord.'

'Time is what I don't have,' he muttered, as if to himself.

'I beg your pardon?'

His expression grew sombre. 'You asked me a question,' he said. 'The answer is yes. I remember every detail. Thieves...reivers...'

Mary's gaze flew to his face. Reivers was the old name for raiders along the border between England and Scotland. His use of the term revived memories of the dispute between their fathers.

'Surely,' she said, 'that practice died out long ago?'

'It's an old term, certainly,' he said. 'But where there is money to be made, some men will always take what is not theirs. Speaking of which...' He frowned, his eyes distant. Mary wondered what memory had nudged at him. Did he remember her taking his horse? Had he seen—or heard—the children?

'How did these reivers come to shoot you?' she asked, keen to distract him.

'I was checking my sheep, grazing up on the hills, when I came upon three men driving them away to the north. I tried to stop them. They objected. I was hit in the shoulder and lost control of my horse...' His gaze settled again on Mary, his eyes widening. Mary felt sure he now recalled her riding away on Sultan. He made no mention of it, however, continuing, 'Perhaps, with hindsight, it was fortunate. If we hadn't been moving when they fired the second shot, I fear I might not be here at all.

'And that reminds me,' he said, pushing himself up in the bed before collapsing back against the pillows with a moan, sweat breaking on his brow. Mary jumped to her feet and leant over him, fingers curving around the solid muscle of his uninjured shoulder.

'Please, my lord. You must remain still. Your wounds...'

'I must speak to Shorey—or Hooper. Immediately!'

Shorey and Hooper were the grooms who had driven the cart into the woods with Mary to rescue Lord Rothley.

'Can you not give me a message for them? It is late and I am certain they will be abed at this hour. I promise to relay any message to them in the morning.'

'I suppose there is nothing they can do tonight.'

He groped until he found her wrist. His touch set her skin aflame but he appeared oblivious to the effect he had on her.

'Tell Shorey and Hooper to go to the top pastures and bring the sheep nearer to home. They must go at first light.'

'The top pastures?' she queried. 'Not the hills? But what about the sheep the men were taking? Did they succeed? Are they all gone?'

'The men panicked and fled after they shot me. I managed to drive the sheep down...'

'*After* you were shot? What were you thinking? You should have ridden straight away for help.'

His expression was grave. 'Those animals will mean all the difference to the Hall this year. But they're not safe, all the way up there. You must tell the men. Promise me.'

'I promise. Please don't worry.'

Rothley released Mary's wrist, heaving a sigh as his lids closed. Mary rose and crossed the room to put the washcloth back in the basin.

'Who *are* you?' The soft query returned her attention to the man in the bed. His dark eyes glittered in the candlelight.

'Mary Vale, my lord.'

'Ah, yes, of course. I *do* remember. Sensible Mary.'

Mary turned away. How did that name still have the power to hurt? 'Sensible Mary'. What they really meant was Dull Mary. The name felt like an insult. Once upon a time she had been young and carefree, full of laughter. But now...

Rothley's eyes had closed once more and he appeared to be drifting off to sleep, to her relief. She settled back into her chair, raking through the happenings of the day. How did he elicit such a ready response from her, despite him being everything she feared and despised in a man? Was it lust over an arresting face and a tantalising body? She pictured his strong arms and shoulders, the hard, muscled planes of his chest, the long, lean legs and the taut buttocks, glimpsed as the doctor extracted the bullet from his thigh. He was a man any woman might desire, but she could not risk yielding to temptation again.

Experience had taught her the physical act of love was a mere fleeting pleasure if there was no emotional connection—no love—between a man and a woman. The marital act had left her feeling hollow and empty and used, and Michael had become increasingly disillusioned: resentful and angry at both her and the children. Mary had vowed never again to put herself in the position of being viewed as a burden, or to allow Toby and Emily to be resented as encumbrances. She had only to recall Rothley's strange antipathy towards children to know nothing could come of their apparent mutual attraction.

When she looked up, Rothley had roused—if he had indeed been asleep—and now watched her with that amused glint back in his eyes, as if he knew exactly what she had been thinking.

'Where did you come from, Sensible Mary?' he asked, when he saw he had her attention. 'And what were you doing in my woods?' He held her gaze for what seemed an eternity and then added, in a soft voice, 'And why were you stealing my horse?'

She felt herself grow pink. 'I thought it was a short cut,' she said, ignoring his other questions.

'To where, may I ask?'

'The north.'

'This is the north.' His eyes narrowed. 'Where did you say you had come from?'

She eyed him warily. Her instinct was to give as little information as possible. 'The south,' she replied, 'and I think it is time you rested. You look exhausted. You should sleep.'

'Mayhap you're right.'

As he settled down into the bed he grimaced.

'Are you in pain?' Mary asked. 'The doctor left some laudanum for you.'

A flash of alarm crossed his face.

'What is it? What is wrong?'

'Nothing's wrong. In answer to your first question: yes, I am in pain, but, no, I don't want laudanum. I found myself in thrall to the poppy's lure once before, in my youth. I shall never risk losing control in such a way again. Not unless I am desperate, do you hear?'

'I hear.' She pulled the covers up beneath his chin.

His lips twitched even as his eyelids drooped. 'Do not imagine I shall forget, Sensible Mary. My questions will wait until tomorrow, when I am stronger. And then, I shall insist on some satisfactory answers.'

'Mrs Vale! Mrs Vale!'

'What is it?' Groggy with sleep, Mary pushed herself up on one elbow. 'Susan?'

'Yes'm; Mrs Lindley sent me. It's the master, ma'am. She said can you please come?'

Fully awake now, Mary threw back the covers and jumped from her bed. Susan handed her a shawl.

'It's one her ladyship left behind, ma'am,' she said, in answer to Mary's lifted brow. 'Mrs Lindley said as how you didn't have much in the way of clothes with you. Sorry, ma'am.'

Mary threw her a smile. 'Don't apologise, Susan,' she said. 'I am grateful for the attention. Is his lordship fevered?'

'Oooh, yes'm. Tossin' and turnin' something awful, Mrs Lindley says.'

'Has someone been sent for the doctor?'

'Yes'm, Hooper rode out ten minutes since.'

They arrived at Rothley's bedchamber. Mary entered to see Mrs Lindley leaning over the marquis, trying to restrain him whilst he thrashed from side to side, muttering. The tangled bedclothes had slipped to the floor.

Mrs Lindley looked up, sweat dripping down her face, as she gasped, 'Thank goodness you've come.'

Chapter Four

Lucas opened his eyes and stared at the ceiling. His head hurt, his shoulder ached, his leg throbbed, his mouth tasted foul and his throat was as dry and rough as the bark of a tree. With an effort, he moved his head on the pillow, squeezing his eyes shut against the pain that speared through his temple.

When he opened his eyes again, she was there.

In the chair, by the bed. *His* bed.

She was familiar, but a stranger. How could that be? Where had she come from?

The south. But how did he know that?

He studied her, allowing her restful presence, her alluring features, to distract him from his aches and pains. She might not be a classic beauty, but she was enchanting. Her skin was smooth and creamy, with a smattering of freckles across her small, tip-tilted nose. The colour of her eyes was hidden, but he knew they were the deep blue of cornflowers. Her long, pale lashes rested on cheeks as lush and inviting as sun-ripened peaches. Her lips—soft pink, full and tempting—were parted and, as rotten as he felt, still his loins stirred at the thought of tasting them. He frowned, a memory floating a fraction beyond his reach.

Her lips. He could feel them, he knew their taste—silky as rose petals, sweet as honey. But how? He licked his own lips, paper-dry and sour. The answer eluded him as he continued his perusal of the woman by his bed.

Her hair. He paused, feeling his forehead pucker. Why had he thought her hair to be guinea-gold? It was not. It was more beautiful by far—the soft golden colour of corn ripening in the August sunshine. Not brassy, not a mass of curls, but soft waves where it escaped from its pins. He wanted to see it loose, flowing down her back.

He frowned again as he watched her sleep, striving to remember, fragments of memories teasing at his mind: the woods, a child's cry, Sultan, with a woman—this woman—astride, leaving him, deserting him. And something else. What else?

A pistol shot! Reivers! Stealing his sheep, his livelihood, his future!

Galvanised, he threw back the covers and made to rise. His torso barely cleared the mattress before he collapsed back in exhaustion, panting with the effort, as the pains racking his body intensified tenfold. He heard himself groan and stifled it, but it was enough to rouse the woman.

'Shh,' she whispered as she rose to her feet and leant over him, a smile on her lips. 'Lie still. You're still very weak.' She placed a cool hand on his brow; it was familiar, comforting. He looked up into her eyes—cornflower-blue, as he had known they would be—compassion shining from their tranquil depths.

'How...how long...?' His voice was croaky, as though it hadn't been used for a long time.

'It is five days now, since you were shot,' she said, pulling up the bedclothes, smoothing them. 'Do you remember?' He nodded. The faint scent of lavender assailed his senses. 'You have been in a fever. You have been very ill, my lord. You will need to rest, to recoup your strength.' She went to a table set up at the foot of the bed and returned with a glass. 'Here,' she said. 'You must be thirsty. Let me help. Drink this.'

She slipped her hand behind his head and supported him as she placed the glass against his dry lips.

He gulped the cool liquid, but she removed the glass before he had drunk his fill, saying, 'You shouldn't have too much all at once. Give your stomach time to settle. You may have some more in a while.'

He watched her, drinking in every detail of her as she replaced the glass. She wore a blue dress that matched her eyes and showed her figure to perfection, as it clung to the roundness of her breasts and her hips. Her manner and her movements spoke of neatness and restraint, calmness and competence. But her face and her body! He studied her with appreciation: her satiny skin, her eyes, her soft, lush lips, the thrust of her breasts, the sway of her hips. They proclaimed the exact opposite: wild abandon, passion, excitement.

He turned his head on the pillow, squeezing his eyes shut against the unexpected hurt that surfaced. He had known another such a woman. Her beauty had promised so much, yet it had been an illusion. Julia! How weak he must be, to allow that witch to affect him after all this time.

Had he really been so befuddled by his vice-ridden lifestyle? Had his senses been so dulled by the opium he had once blithely consumed, not to see through her looks to the reality? Not to see her for what she was—a greedy, grasping widow on the prowl, targeting naïve young bucks to fleece? He had fallen in love with an illusion of his own making.

Why think of her now, after so many years? He

had thought all memory of her long buried. He conjured up the image of her face: her white skin, guinea-gold hair and large cornflower-blue eyes. Of course! No wonder she had been on his mind—Mary's eyes were the exact same shade of blue as Julia's...

Mary!

Sensible Mary! He remembered. He frowned again. *At least, I remember some of it.*

He kept his eyes closed, struggling to recall. The quiet sound of her moving around the room brought him back to the present from time to time, even as, bit by bit, pieces of the puzzle fit into place. The sheep! The men and the dogs, driving them up the hill; the wild gallop after them; the shouts; the shots; the searing pain. His gut twisted and the fear that had plagued him for months reasserted itself as he realised the implications of losing those sheep. The estate simply could not afford...

'Shorey.' His voice, still weak, sounded no louder than a whisper. 'I remember...you promised...'

She returned to his side and lifted his hand, murmuring, 'Hush. Do not worry. I gave him your message and he and Hooper rounded up the sheep. They also brought the cattle closer to the Hall, in case the thieves try again. There are none missing and they are keeping a close watch on them until it's time to take them to market.'

He relaxed. The fear subsided but it did not disappear. It would not leave him, he knew, until he was free of his father's legacy of debt. He curled his fingers around Mary's hand, relishing the touch of her skin. He frowned. The skin on her palm and fingertips was roughened. She acted, and spoke, as a lady. But her hands—they spoke of work. He studied her face as she stood by the side of the bed, gazing down at him, her expression serious.

'All is well, my lord,' she said, releasing his hand and smoothing his brow. 'There is no need to fret. I am sure you will be up and about in no time.'

Her gaze was direct and reassuring. He was comforted by her presence. He closed his eyes, all at once exhausted.

The sound of the door opening caught his attention and he forced his eyes open. Mary was at the door, speaking in hushed tones to someone outside. Lucas strained his ears, but could not make out what was being said.

'What is it?'

Mary glanced back into the room. 'It's nothing, my lord.'

Was it his imagination, or did she sound furtive? He struggled to raise himself on one elbow.

'Go and ask Susan to come and sit with his lord-ship,' he heard her hiss. 'I shall be there as soon as I can.'

Lucas frowned. Who on earth was she speaking to? He didn't want Susan to care for him. He wanted Mary. He opened his mouth to object, but remained silent as he heard Mary's words. 'I know, lovey. I love you, too. Go on, quickly now.'

Lucas, an unexpected feeling of betrayal in his heart, fell back to his pillow. The words that had sprung to his lips remained unspoken.

It's you I want, Mary.

'Who is she?'

Lucas watched Trant as the valet finished putting his clothes away in the wardrobe later that day. Mary had not returned to his bedchamber since Susan had come to relieve her that morning and he was curious to discover more about her. He'd had little else to occupy his mind, trapped in his bed as he was.

'Who is who, my lord?'

'Mary Vale, of course. Who is she? Where did she come from?'

'I'm sure I couldn't say, sir.' Trant regarded Lucas with an impassive countenance. 'She has been a great help to the staff, though. She barely left your side whilst you were ill.'

'Come now, Trant. I'm sure you can tell me more than that.'

'I am not one to listen to the tittle-tattle of others, my lord.'

Lucas eyed Trant with exasperation. Was he being deliberately obtuse? Lucas had received a similar response from Ellen earlier and even young Susan had been no more forthcoming. Why were they all so reticent? Or perhaps it was Mary who was being secretive? All he knew for certain was that she was a widow who had been passing through his woods. And that she tasted divine—he could recall every detail of their kiss and it had awoken within him a hunger he'd been at pains to deny since his return to the Hall.

He'd been weak enough once to allow a woman to get under his skin. Julia's scornful rejection of him still galled him and the rage that had consumed him when he walked in on her and Henson still filled him with shame. No, Lucas would never again trust a woman. He would never wed, nor would he ever have children. In fact, it was safer not to have *any* children around him: he would not wish on any child the misery and the fear he had endured in his childhood. His attack on Henson had fuelled his fear that he was, as he had so often been told, just like his father, who had been unpredictable, with rage and violence constantly simmering just beneath the surface.

No, he must resist Mary. He had kissed her at a time when he was not himself, when he was weakened. Although…he recalled her assertion his kiss had been 'pleasant'. That rankled. Pleasant? Pleasant wasn't the word he would use to describe it. She was clearly too strait-laced to appreciate the sheer sensuality of such a kiss. He recalled the soft sweetness of her mouth with a silent groan and he knew he must taste her again.

One more kiss. It won't mean anything. What could be the harm?

After all, Mary Vale was not his type—far too sensible, except in her luscious looks, of course, but he had learned the hard way beauty was skin deep. He would not step into that trap again.

In the meantime he must be patient. There was no help for it—he would have to wait for the lady herself to return to his bedchamber before his curiosity could be assuaged.

His hunger, he had to admit, might have to wait a bit longer.

It was the following day before he saw Mary again. He was mentally alert, although physically still weak, and he chafed at his confinement.

Mary entered, carrying a covered bowl he suspected contained more of that disgusting gruel Mrs Lindley deemed suitable for invalids. He scanned her figure with appreciation as she walked towards him.

'I have decided,' he announced, in his loftiest tone of voice—specifically designed to needle her—'to take no further action over your attempted theft of my horse.'

Then he lay back to see what sort of reaction he provoked. He was bored and he was frustrated that Mary had been nowhere near him since the day before, when he had awoken. The servants were all too busy to pay him much attention and he was in desperate need of entertainment. He had decided teasing Mary would prove an enjoyable way to while away the time. He would prod at her self-control and goad her into revealing the real Mary Vale.

Mary's step faltered at his words. Then she straightened her shoulders and smiled.

'How very magnanimous of you, my lord,' she said, her tone one of warm honey, although her eyes flashed.

Lucas bit back his smile and continued to regard her, straight-faced. 'If, that is, you satisfy my curiosity. I have not forgotten you owe me satisfaction on several points.'

Not the least of which will be another kiss.

'Satisfaction, my lord? How so?' She eyed him coolly, chin in the air.

'For a start, I want to know who you are. Yes—' he added as she opened her mouth, '—I know you are Mary Vale, widow—although not of this parish—but knowing your name tells me nothing about you. Where have you come from? Where are you going? Why were you in my woods? Indeed, why were you stealing my horse? I am afraid, Mrs Vale, you owe me answers that are long overdue.'

'Goodness.' She laughed, although her expression was wary. 'So many questions.'

She walked to the table at the foot of the bed to place the tray upon it, before facing him again. 'You will have to sit up, I think, if you are not to make a mess with your food.'

She approached the bed and slid her arm behind his back, helping him to sit. A wave of desire crashed over him as her lavender scent enveloped him and her warm breath caressed his skin. She pulled at his pillows, plumping them behind him. He wanted nothing more this minute than to drag her down beside him and steal the kiss he had promised himself, to feast on those lush, provocative lips until she begged for more.

How could her mere presence provoke such a longing within him when he had sworn to never again fall under any woman's spell? He cursed his weakness—it must have affected his mind as well as his body. He focused on the window opposite the bed, willing his mind and body back under his control, before looking at her again.

'Prevaricating will not prevent me from pursuing answers to my questions, Mary,' he said. His voice sounded strained, even to his ears. 'I shall have my satisfaction sooner or later, you know.'

She coloured, her blue eyes falling before his steady regard, and her pearly teeth bit into her lower lip, sending his pulse rate soaring once more. It had been an unfortunate choice of phrase under the circumstances. All he had to amuse himself at the moment was his imagination and it was sending his thoughts in a very uncomfortable direction. He deliberately flexed his injured shoulder, using the stab of pain to remind himself that women could not be trusted. He was lusting after Mary and yet he knew next to nothing about her.

He thought back to that day in the woods: the bone-jolting fall from Sultan's back; the damp, peaty scent of the earth in his nostrils as he lay, winded, amongst the trees; drifting…so very tired…until he had been roused by a sudden sound. He had lifted his head to see Sultan being ridden away from him.

He had—somehow—gained his feet; had found enough breath to shout. The rest was a blur. But… that sound…

'There was a cry.'

'A cry?'

'That day, in the woods. It sounded like a child.'

'Are you certain?' Mary turned away, walking to the end of the bed.

Lucas hesitated. Was he certain? 'I thought…I seem to recall something…'

'Might it have been a local child, playing in the woods?'

Lucas stiffened. 'No children are permitted on my property,' he growled.

Mary stared at him, her eyes wide. 'Why so vehement?'

He shrugged. It was nobody else's business.

Mary carried the tray to his bedside. 'But what harm…?'

'The matter is not up for debate. It does not concern you.' Lucas was not about to discuss his reasons for banning children with a virtual stranger, particularly one as adept as Mary at keeping her own secrets. 'Where have you been, Mary?'

Mary stilled, her eyes guarded. 'What do you mean—where have I been?'

She placed the tray on Lucas's lap.

'Aaarrrgh!' Pain speared his thigh. *'Mary!'*

The crockery clattered as Mary snatched the tray away. 'Oh, no! I am so sorry! I didn't think.'

As the pain subsided to a throb, Lucas smiled ruefully. 'I cannot blame you, Mary, for I didn't anticipate that either. A lesson for us both, I think?'

'Yes, indeed. I shall take more care in future.' Mary placed the tray gently on the bed. 'There, although I fear it might prove more awkward for you.'

'I have you to help with what I cannot manage for myself, though, do I not?' Lucas grinned at the easily construed suspicion in Mary's eyes. 'So, I shall ask again, Mary. Where have you been, since yesterday, when I awoke.'

'Oh, since yesterday. Sleeping, for the most part,' she said.

'All day? Until now?'

'Well, not quite until now. I did eat. Speaking of which—' she removed the cover from the bowl on the tray '—you should eat this before it gets cold.'

Lucas peered at the contents of the bowl and grimaced. 'You must have been very tired.' He picked up the spoon with little enthusiasm.

'I cannot deny it was a relief to sleep in a bed again.' Mary cast a meaningful look at the chair by the side of his bed.

Remorse nudged Lucas. Hadn't Trant said that

Mary had barely left his side whilst he had been ill? He had been lying here, frustrated by her absence, without a thought as to what she and the rest of his household had been through.

'How often did you sit with me, Mary?'

'Every night, my lord.'

'For pity's sake, stop "my lord"-ing me. You are not a servant.'

'What should I call you then, my l…sir?'

'I should prefer Lucas, but I have no doubt you will deem it improper, Sensible Mary. And, in that case, sir will do.'

'Yes…sir,' she said, her lids lowering, but not before he glimpsed her expression. She clearly didn't appreciate the nickname as it wasn't the first time she had shown resentment at his use of it. But he had more pressing issues on his mind.

'You stayed here for four nights running? All night? With no relief?' he growled, vexed to think his servants would take such advantage.

'It was my idea to sit with you during the night,' she blurted out, with an anxious glance that piqued his curiosity.

Why was she suddenly on edge? Was she worried about his reaction to her answers? He knew she was not timid. What had he said to prompt this change?

As he watched she visibly took control of her emotions, drawing an audible breath before saying in a firm voice: 'It was the least I could do, with everyone else so busy every day. You are not to blame Mrs Lindley or the others, for I insisted.'

He raised a brow. *Come, this is a bit more feisty. Good for you, Mary.*

'And did you not sleep—in a bed—during the day?'

'I find it impossible to sleep in the daytime.'

Her lids drooped, concealing her thoughts again. Lucas suppressed his frustration. He could not fathom her lightning changes in mood. Why was she so guarded?

He turned his attention to his food. 'Do I really have to eat this…this…stuff?' He poked at the gruel with the spoon.

'The doctor said gruel is all you're allowed. For now,' she added quickly as she sent another anxious glance in his direction.

Why did she react as though she expected him to fly into a rage at any moment? What, or who, had caused her to view him with such trepidation? Had the servants warned her that his mood was, at times, on a knife's edge?

And can I blame them if they have? He was aware his temper had been unpredictable of late, despite his best efforts to conceal his worries.

Lucas forced the scowl from his brow and relaxed his jaw, determined to coax Mary into a more relaxed frame of mind.

He eyed the bowl of gruel again, then looked at Mary, raising a brow as he smiled his best winning smile. Mary returned his look, her suspicion again clear.

'It is too difficult to feed myself. I haven't enough strength,' he said, his voice a weak croak. '*Please* help me, dearest Mary.'

Mary pursed her lips, regarding him with narrowed eyes, then huffed a sigh as she sat on the edge of the bed and took the spoon from his slack grasp. Her wariness had vanished. His strategy had worked.

She dipped the spoon into the gruel and lifted it towards his mouth. Swiftly, he captured her hand, registering the tremor of her slender fingers as he did so.

'Take care, Mary,' he chided. 'You almost spilt some. I will steady your hand.'

He retained his hold as he guided the spoon to his mouth, relishing the sensation. As his lips closed around the bowl of the spoon, he looked at her, pleased with the success of his strategy as he saw the hint of a blush stain her cheeks and a smile hover on those luscious lips, although he still read caution in her beautiful blue eyes: caution and the merest hint of desire that promptly set his pulse soaring. He forced the gruel down, tearing his eyes from hers in an attempt to dampen his wayward urges once more.

Chapter Five

Mary's blood quickened as she fought to control her reaction to Rothley's touch. She felt the colour rise into her cheeks as her eyes met his and she was afraid he would read the desire the mere touch of his fingers had awakened deep within her.

She watched as he swallowed the gruel. The moment he released her hand, she snatched it away and replaced the spoon in the bowl.

'Perhaps if I hold the bowl for you?' she suggested, lifting it and holding it level with his chest.

Her eyes kept straying to the dark curls just visible in the open neck of his nightshirt. Determinedly, she fixed her gaze on his face. He appeared to have temporarily forgotten his questions, but she was sure he would revisit the subject sooner or later. Her brain scrambled in an effort to invent a convincing story that did not reveal the existence of her children, but it was hard to concentrate on anything other than Rothley.

'This is disgusting,' he said, as he pushed his bowl away. 'Have you tried it, Mary?'

'No, but it is not I who has been ill. You must know it is good for you—it is all your stomach can cope with, after eating nothing for days. And if you do not eat, your strength will take longer to return and you will have to remain confined to your bed. Please, try and eat a wee bit.'

As he ate another spoonful, Mary pondered her physical reaction to him. Why did she still desire him, despite the tales of his past? There was no room for such a man in her life, not even for a short time. She was a mother with responsibilities and she would not expose her children to another man who resented their very existence.

To be fair, although Rothley had been a touch tetchy—and could he be blamed after what had happened?—there had been no angry outbursts such as she had been led to expect. At least, not yet, but then her father had never been as bad when sober. It was only when drunk… Mary suppressed a shudder at the memory. She recalled the stench of alcohol when she had found Rothley. Had he been drunk that day?

She had, out of necessity, become adept at avoiding confrontation, whether with her father or, more recently, with Michael, whose temper had spiralled in tandem with his drinking. He had become ever more violent and the more Mary had been forced to adopt the role of appeaser, the more she had resented the necessity to repress her own feelings in order to pacify him.

Was the pattern set to continue whilst she remained at the Hall? And what about when she and the children arrived at her old home? Her father was unlikely to welcome her with open arms after she had shamed him by running away on the eve of her seventeenth birthday. Yet again she questioned her wisdom in going back, but what other choice did she have? Homelessness and starvation? The workhouse? No choice at all. At least she would be there to protect her children. There had been no one to stand between Mary and her father when he turned to drink after her mother had died.

Were there no men, she wondered, with something akin to despair, who did not believe it their right to intimidate and abuse those who had no choice but to pander to their every whim?

'Mary, Mary...'

The quiet words pierced her reverie and she came back to the present with a gasp.

'Will you tell me what you were thinking about?' he asked, then smiled ruefully. 'No, of course you won't. But you looked so very solemn, Mary, sitting there, your thoughts turned inwards, your face so very sad. Can I not help? What is it that fills your eyes with such dread?'

A lump formed in her throat, but she was determined not to cry. She stretched her lips in a smile.

'It is of no matter, my l…sir,' she answered. She glanced down and saw he had hardly touched his food. 'Please eat,' she said. 'It must be cold by now and that will not improve the taste, I can assure you. The doctor will be pleased if we can report you are eating well when he next visits.'

'The doctor? You mean Robert Preece? How many times has he visited?'

'Every day whilst you were fevered, sir.'

Rothley's jaw tightened as his brow lowered.

Mary tried to quell her trickle of unease. *Why should you imagine he's angry with you? For heaven's sake, stop being such a ninny!* Her disquiet remained, however.

'His last visit was yesterday morning, a short time before you awoke,' she added.

Rothley said no more, but finished his gruel, his expression growing more and more disgusted. He settled back with a sigh. Mary busied herself with clearing away the tray, her awareness of his dark gaze following her making her slow and clumsy in her task.

'Come, Mary, leave that and sit down—' glancing over, Mary saw Rothley slant a knowing grin at her '—on the chair, if you prefer. I would know more of the mysterious lady who happened to be walking through my woods at the very time I had need of her.'

His expression said it all: he knew precisely the effect he was having upon her. Her resolve steadied as she remained where she stood. Did he believe she would fall at his feet in response to his manly allure and handsome countenance? Mayhap he had reason to so believe, after that kiss, but he would find she was made of sterner stuff, she vowed. She would not allow her treacherous body to dictate her relationship with this man.

'There is naught to tell, sir. I was passing through. There is no mystery.'

'Where is your destination? Is there no one to worry over your non-arrival?'

Mary laughed and, even to her ears, it had a bitter sound. 'There is no one to worry over me. I am in no hurry to leave.'

Rothley indicated the chair by the bedside. 'Please...sit down, Mary.' He waited until she sat before saying, 'You still have not revealed your destination, which leads me to wonder why?'

Mary twisted her hands in her lap. How much could she divulge without letting slip the existence of the children? Mrs Lindley and Ellen had both urged her to conceal their presence from Rothley, but had not said why he was so opposed to the idea of children at the Hall. Nor was she inclined to reveal her family name, given the past acquaintance between their fathers.

'I do not go there by choice,' she said. 'I have no alternative.'

'You claim there is no mystery, yet I find myself more mystified every time we speak. If it gives you no pleasure to go to this place, why go? Why did you not remain in…wherever it is you have travelled from…and find employment there?'

'I could not remain there, sir.' It was a weak reply, but Mary could think of no other. She could read the scepticism in his eyes.

'If you will not tell me your destination, tell me where you have travelled from, Mary, and why.'

'I am a widow, sir…'

'That much I do know.'

'You asked me a question. Be pleased to permit me to answer.' She was determined not to be cowed by him.

He grinned at her, unabashed. 'My apologies, Sensible Mary. Please, do continue.'

Mary took a deep breath. She had nothing to be ashamed of. Why should she be ashamed of escaping the dreadful fate her father had planned for her?

'I come from a village close to Newcastle where...'

'But that is not where you grew up.'

'Well, no. How did you...?'

His lips quirked. 'I detected a hint of an accent, Mary. I guessed you were Scottish.' His face grew serious, his dark eyes narrowing as he stared at her. 'Have you really walked all the way from Newcastle to here?'

'No, not all the way, w— I encountered many generous souls along the way who offered to share their transport. I have been very fortunate.'

'Your husband failed to leave provision for you? How did you live, before he died?'

'He was steward to a gentleman and we lived in a cottage on his estate. Michael, my husband, died in a fall and his employer allowed u—me to remain at the cottage. I took in sewing for the household and I also helped with correspondence and other business in return for food and pin money. But then Mr Wen— the gentleman died unexpectedly...'

Mary faltered. They had been dark days, with two young children and losing the one hope she had of remaining independent. 'His son did not wish to continue his father's arrangement and I had no other way of earning money to pay rent. I had to leave.'

Rothley's dark brows drew together in a frown. 'His father's arrangement?'

'Yes. As I said, I did sewing and some letter writing. He entrusted me with both the household and the estate accounts. I have a good head for...' Mary registered Rothley's expression and his tone. She was momentarily lost for words. 'Oh!' She hauled in an indignant breath. 'You think...you think...!'

Words failed her. Belatedly, she understood precisely what Rothley implied.

'I do not condemn you, Mary. The father clearly had excellent taste, but I can understand the son's reluctance to take on his father's obligation. I see now the difficulty in obtaining further employment in the area.'

She leapt to her feet, her cheeks burning. Rothley's hand shot out and grasped her wrist. She twisted and pulled, but could not break free.

'Wait, Mary, please. There is no need to be ashamed. You said yourself you are only travelling from necessity and that your intended destination is not from choice. I can offer you an alternative. Stay here, with me. I will take care of you.'

He wants me as his whore. He is no better than

Simon. As his grip loosened, Mary snatched her wrist free and backed out of his reach. She whirled to face him.

'Just because I am a widow you *gentlemen* seem to believe I exist simply to slake your thirst. Well, I don't! Do you hear me? I shall never...'

She paused, willing her voice not to wobble. 'I am a respectable woman and I beg leave to inform you I resent your...your...insinuation...that I might have behaved immorally with Mr Wendo— with my employer. He was a lovely gentleman and extraordinarily kind to me and my...my...Michael. I...'

To her horror, tears blurred her vision. She had never imagined Mr Wendover's kindness to her could be so badly misconstrued. Her breath juddered, loud in her ears. She must get out of here. She ran to the door.

'Mary...wait...'

She ignored him, slamming the door behind her.

Chapter Six

Lucas tightened his hands into fists. What had possessed him? *Of all the cack-handed fools!* He didn't even want a mistress. The words had spilled out without thought. He had eagerly anticipated Mary's visit and now he had driven her away with his ill-considered words. Why had he blurted out his suspicions? Would it have hurt him to conceal his thoughts, at least until he could decide if there was any merit in them?

Her reaction had been an honest one, he felt sure, although it would not be the first time he had been taken in by a woman. But…Mary? Was she such a skilled actress, to put on such a convincing performance?

He was roused from his conjectures by the rattle of the doorknob. His heart leapt at the sound, but it was not Mary's expressive countenance that met his eager gaze, but the impassive features of Trant.

'The doctor is here to see you, my lord.' The valet crossed the room to pick up the tray discarded by Mary. 'Shall you require me to remain?'

'No, thank you, Trant, there is no need. Please send Dr Preece up.'

'Very well, my lord.'

'I showed myself up,' a cheerful voice announced from the doorway. 'No need for Trant to be put out, I know my way around well enough by now.'

Lucas experienced an unexpected spurt of pleasure at the familiar voice and features of his old friend, Robert Preece. He felt his heart shift in his chest. The burden that had weighed so heavily on him since his father's death eased a fraction.

'Rob…' he held out his hand '…it is good to see you.'

Why had he been at such pains to deny all his old friends and neighbours since his return to Rothley? Had he really convinced himself no one in this world could be trusted? That every person beyond the boundaries of the Hall was blighted by the same immoral bankruptcy as his erstwhile London intimates? Could he now put the past behind him and rebuild old friendships?

Robert approached the bed, a quizzical smile on his lips, and grasped Lucas's hand.

'It is a pleasure to hear you say that, Lucas. After

all, you have not been the most attentive friend and neighbour since your return from the metropolis.'

'*Touché*, my friend. As direct and to the point as ever, I see.'

'I have determined to make the most of your current weakened state, old chap, for I am persuaded that, once you are on your feet again, you will revert to that evasive fellow I have been trying to pin down these past two years.'

Guilt washed over Lucas at his treatment of his old friend. 'I fear I would have provided very poor company in those years.'

'That would make no difference to a true friend, Lucas. What happened in London to make you shun all company bar that of your mama?'

Despite himself, Lucas laughed. 'Goodness, man, you never hesitate to walk where others fear to tread, do you?'

Robert shrugged. 'You might bite my head off for asking difficult questions, but at least you are incapable of knocking my head from my shoulders at such presumption.'

He stood smiling down at Lucas for a moment, then turned away and placed his bag on the table at the foot of the bed. He removed his coat, then approached the bed, rolling his shirtsleeves to his elbows.

'Whilst you are deciding how little you can reveal in order to satisfy my curiosity, let us dispense with the tedious medical side of this visit,' he suggested. 'Then we can have a proper catch-up of all our respective news. For I, too, have led a full and active life since we were last confidants. You may therefore rest assured that my side of the conversation will not be confined to inane responses to your titbits...' His voice rose an octave, mimicking the tone of a gossiping woman. '"Did you *really*, Lucas?" "And *what* did you say then, Lucas?" "Goodness, whoever would have believed it?"'

They both laughed, then Robert sobered.

'No problem becomes easier by keeping it to oneself, Lucas. You would do well to remember that.'

'Who says I have a problem?'

'That is your pride talking, my friend.' Rob eased Lucas forward in the bed, helped him to take off his nightshirt and removed the bandage from his shoulder. 'It is no secret your father did not leave the Hall in the best of financial situations. Sir Gerald has made certain of that, gabble-mongering about his expectations, both in the village and all around the district.'

'Expectations?'

'The terms of his loan to your father are no secret.

He is convinced he will be in possession of that land of yours next to Dunwick by the end of the year.'

Lucas clenched his teeth, both against the stab of pain as Rob manipulated his shoulder and at the mention of Sir Gerald Quartly, a local landowner and mine owner who lived on the far side of the village at Dunwick Manor. The loan had been secured against the Hall's best pasture and arable land, and the next payment was due on the Quarter Day: Michaelmas, the twenty-ninth of September. Barely three weeks away.

Dread snatched at his insides, twisting his stomach into knots. Unless he obtained a good price for his livestock at Hexham market he would default on the loan and the estate would lose its most productive land. Thank goodness he had been in the right place to stop the theft of his sheep.

'That seems fine, all healing very nicely,' Robert said, rupturing the silence that had greeted his comment about Sir Gerald. 'You have a good range of movement in the joint, which is a positive sign. Now, let me examine that thigh.'

After more prodding, Robert declared himself satisfied with the healing process and he rolled down his sleeves and donned his coat, pulling the chair round to face the bed. He flicked his coat-tails out of the way as he sat down.

'Now my professional duties are fulfilled, I shall allow my curiosity full rein. What happened on that day, Lucas? Did you recognise the men who shot you?'

'No. I've never seen any of them before.'

'How many were there?'

'Three. On horseback. There was a dog with them, rounding up the sheep.' Lucas relived the moment he had come upon the gang: the agony as the first bullet had ripped into his shoulder; the struggle to control Sultan as he reared and spun; the white-hot pain as the second bullet speared his thigh. He gave a short laugh. 'It was fortunate, after the second shot, Sultan bolted *towards* them. They turned and ran, and I got my sheep back. If he had gone the other way...' He paused. That scenario didn't bear thinking about. If that had happened, he would now be fully immersed in the mire, with no way of paying his debt come Michaelmas.

'I'd recognise the dog again, though. It stayed working the sheep after the men had gone. A collie: wall-eyed, with half a black face and half white, and a merle ruff—very distinctive. Have you ever seen such an animal hereabouts?'

'Wall-eyed?'

'One brown eye and one blue, on the white half of its face.'

'No, I can't say I have, but I will pass the word around—the whole village is still abuzz with the news. I had half-expected to hear of others losing stock, but there have been no more reports.'

Thinking about that day brought Lucas's financial worries into sharp perspective. 'I need to get up,' he said, pushing the bedcovers away as he sat up. 'I must attend to the estate, Rob.'

'You are recovering from a debilitating fever, Luke. Do not expect too much—you must be patient until you regain your strength. If you try to do too much, too soon…'

Lucas levered himself round, swinging his feet to the floor. 'But you don't understand! I must…'

'Whoa! Steady!' Robert pushed at his shoulders and, to Lucas's chagrin, he subsided against the pillows, his energy all but spent.

'When can I get up?'

'My advice is to remain in your bed for at least another two days. You may then decide if you feel strong enough to rise. Your thigh will soon tell you how long you are able to sit in a chair without too much discomfort.' Robert folded his arms, head tilted to one side, as he studied Lucas. 'Can you honestly tell me—hand on heart—that you have the strength to get up at this very moment?'

Lucas wasn't about to admit how weak he felt. 'What about tomorrow?'

Robert sighed. 'Whatever I say, you are likely to do as you please. I know you too well. But I have no wish to be summoned because you have been stubborn and taken a tumble down the stairs. A broken neck will not help your cause, my friend. You must accept your strength will take time to recover.'

Lucas glared up at Robert, who chuckled.

'Do not think to intimidate *me* with your fearsome scowls, Lucas, for I know them to be pure humbug. Please; will you not humour me on this, even if my professional advice is not to your liking?'

'Speaking of which—about your bill...'

'Oh, no need to concern yourself with that, old fellow. Mrs Vale and I...'

Mary's stricken expression as she fled his bedchamber pricked at Lucas's conscience. 'Mrs Vale? What has your account to do with...?'

'Eminently practical lady, Mrs Vale,' Robert continued. 'As I was about to say, we have come to an agreement about payment in kind.'

Robert's words ignited Lucas's habitual distrust. He battled not to voice his immediate suspicions, conscious of his irrationality. Had he not known Rob since childhood? He was not of the same ilk as the London bucks Lucas had once thought his friends, men who thought nothing of stabbing one another in the back. And had it not been just such a suspicion—voiced without any consideration of the facts—that had upset Mary? He looked at his old friend, his familiar features. How could he suspect Rob of making some clandestine arrangement with Mary? Indeed, how could he believe such a thing of Mary, particularly after her earlier reaction?

Bitter with self-recrimination, Lucas began to see how badly Julia and Henson had soured his trust in those around him. It was time to change, to start to put his trust in people again and stop driving them away. Mary's face swam into view, before transforming into Julia's. He put his hand to his head, massaging his temple.

'Lucas? Are you all right?'

The concern in Rob's voice stirred Lucas and he squeezed his eyes shut against the unexpected moisture that gathered. He felt weak. Weak and stupid and humble.

'A slight headache, that is all. You were about to explain your arrangement with Mrs Vale?'

'Indeed. Mrs Vale has been overseeing both the estate and the household accounts...'

Lucas stiffened at the knowledge Mary was privy to his business affairs. 'She has no right! What business is it—?'

'Lucas, please calm yourself. She only offered in order to help. Mrs Lindley has been in one of her frets, not only about you and your health, but about the tradesmen's bills; do you not realise it is as much her home as it is yours? She cares very much about you as well, although who knows why when you have—by all accounts—behaved much like a rampaging goose since you came home.'

Lucas stared at Rob, then burst out laughing. 'A rampaging *goose*? Mrs Lindley described me as a rampaging goose?'

'Ahem. No, actually, they were my words.'

'I am stung, Robert. Could you not have found a more fitting analogy? A rampaging bull, perhaps? Or a marauding stallion? Yes...I like that last one. But a *goose*? Not even the courtesy of calling me a gander, I note!'

Rob laughed. 'Sorry, old fellow, but it had to be a goose. Do you not remember that time when...' and then they finished Rob's sentence in unison '...we were cornered in old Mrs Draper's orchard by her geese?'

'Yes, only too well,' Lucas said, memories flooding back. Good memories. 'And I still bear the scars to prove it! My word, but they were vicious, those geese. There was no reasoning with them, was there?'

'Reasoning? With a goose? I can see you've lost none of your nonsense, Lucas, despite everything. Can you deny your attitude over the past two years?'

'I may have been a touch prickly at times.'

Rob threw his head back and guffawed. 'A *touch* prickly? My dear fellow...' He sobered. 'I do hope we may now re-establish our old friendship.' His hand alighted on Lucas's uninjured shoulder. 'I have missed you. I must confess...when I heard what had happened...and then, when you almost succumbed to the fever...it was...' Rob faded as his fingers tightened their grip.

Lucas felt another shift inside, as though the solid ice in his heart had thawed some more. 'I hope so too, Rob.' He coughed to clear an unaccountable constriction in his throat. 'I have much to thank you for.'

'It is Mrs Vale who is most deserving of your gratitude, Lucas, for if she had not found you...indeed, had she passed you by then all the medical skill in the world could not have saved you. And, as I said, it was she who bartered for my services. She is a most resourceful young woman and a good one too.'

'I am well aware of the debt of gratitude I owe to Mary.'

'I hope you will keep it in mind, in the days to come.'

Lucas paused. What did Rob know that he did not?

'Why? What might happen, to prevent me from remembering it?'

'I…er…I meant…' Rob's cheeks reddened. 'Oh, you know what you can be like, Lucas. She has been a breath of spring in this household. Do not allow your pride to…to…' His chest swelled as he inhaled. 'I meant, I wonder if you will find it difficult to countenance a woman helping with estate affairs.'

There was more than that behind Rob's words, for certain. Ever since Mary's arrival, Lucas had the strongest feeling something was being kept from him. What it might be, to involve the whole of his household in the conspiracy, he could not begin to imagine.

'I will try to accept her assistance with my usual equanimity,' was all he said.

No doubt he would find out the truth of it in time.

Chapter Seven

Mary tilted her face towards the sun, lying low now in the sky compared to midsummer. She closed her eyes, its heat warming her skin, despite the sporadic breeze that punched at the ragged clouds and snatched at her skirt. The scent of late-flowering roses perfumed the air and the hum of bees lent a somnolent backdrop of sound to the vibrant chirrup of ground-hugging dunnocks and the intermittent, exuberant notes of a song thrush.

She could hear the children's excited chatter as they picked beans with Susan in the nearby kitchen garden and her heart swelled at the joyful sound. She would give anything to remain safe and secure at the Hall, where Toby and Emily were happy and thriving.

Her daydream slammed to an abrupt halt as reality intruded. She had seen the proof in the ledgers that the estate was barely able to support its existing occupants. Every extra mouth to feed would further diminish the scant resources. And she came with two additional mouths to provide for.

Then there was the danger Lucas posed to both her peace of mind and her self-respect. Even his name set a quiver dancing through her. Since his fever had abated, whenever she was in his presence she could sense his gaze upon her. She had glimpsed the desire in those ebony eyes, heard the undercurrent of seduction in his tone, had successfully parried the suggestiveness in his words.

But, oh, how she wanted him!

Despite everything: despite her common sense; despite him being all she despised in a man; despite her being, it seemed, exactly what he wouldn't want in a woman. But she knew from experience pure physical attraction would never be enough for her. And there was his antipathy towards children. In their short lives, Toby and Emily had already experienced the callous indifference of their own father.

She gave herself a mental shake and hurried towards the walled kitchen garden, to help gather the last of the beans for Mrs Lindley to salt for the winter.

'Good afternoon, Mrs Vale.'

Mary started and straightened up, peering through

the foliage to see the neat figure of Dr Preece on the far side of the row of beans.

'Good afternoon, Doctor.' She placed the beans she had picked into her basket and dusted her hands, then walked to the end of the row. Susan, Toby and Emily were at the other side of the garden and had not yet seen the doctor. 'How is his lordship?'

'He is recovering well, but is already bored with being confined to bed. You'll have quite some task in keeping him content, I fear, for he is already agitating to get up. It is vital he rests and recoups his strength, so I have advised him to stay in bed another two days, but it is imperative he does not attempt the stairs until he is much stronger. And I wish you luck in persuading him against *that*.'

He grinned and then fell silent.

'Have you more instructions?' Mary asked after a few minutes.

The doctor started. 'Oh, I do beg your pardon. Of course, you must wonder why I have sought you out. I saw you from the window as I made my way to the kitchen. I have come to ask you a favour.'

'A favour?'

'Yes, I…' The doctor looked around as Susan, Toby and Emily approached. 'Hello, young Toby, and how are you this fine day?' He squatted down to speak to Toby, who beamed.

'Hello, Mr Doctor. Look…' Toby thrust his half-full basket under the doctor's nose '…I've been working. Em'ly's too young.' He grabbed at his sister's basket and tipped it upside down, scattering the handful of straggly beans on the ground.

As Emily's face puckered Mary rushed to hug her into her skirts, muffling her cries.

'Toby, that is unfair. Emily has worked hard too. Pick them up and put them back into Emily's basket.'

'But, Mama…'

'Toby…' Mary bent a stern look on her son and he hastened to do as she bid whilst she hoisted a hiccupping Emily on to her hip, soothing her. She exchanged a rueful smile with the doctor.

'Do your children squabble, Doctor?' Mary asked as they started to walk back to the house.

'Indeed they do, they drive poor Jenny demented at times.'

'She is with child again, is she not? When is it due?'

'In November. And that brings me neatly back to that favour I would ask of you. I wonder, might you call upon Jenny, with Toby and Emily, some time soon? It would entertain the children to have new playmates and I am certain Jenny would welcome your company.'

'That would be delightful. I should imagine I, too,

will be in need of some female company after spending so much time with Lord Rothley.'

The doctor laughed. 'I should think you will. I will speak to Jenny and we will find a suitable time for you both.'

At the kitchen door, Dr Preece tipped his hat. 'I won't come in. Good day to you, Mrs Vale, Susan.' He smiled at Emily and ruffled Toby's hair. 'Goodbye, you two. Be good for your mama.'

Mary hesitated outside Rothley's bedchamber, reluctant to face him after the way she had fled earlier. One hand balanced his supper tray whilst the fingers of the other feathered the door handle. She inhaled, steeled herself, then opened the door and walked into the room. She pasted a smile on to her face and injected a cheeriness she did not feel into her voice.

'I have a treat for you, my lo— sir.'

'Do not speak to me as though I were a child to be cajoled or an invalid to be humoured.'

Mary put the tray down before facing Rothley. He was propped up against his pillows, arms folded. The candlelight reflected in his ebony eyes and flickered over his lean features, highlighting his dark-shadowed jaw. Nerves stirred deep in her belly, or was it the flicker of desire? She determined not to succumb to his allure. That would make her no better than a… She cut off that line of thought before it took hold.

'Mrs Lindley has prepared some chicken broth for your supper,' she said, ignoring his grumbled comment. She bustled towards him, careful not to meet his gaze. 'Let me help you to sit up straighter. I make no doubt you will prefer to feed yourself, now you are stronger.'

As Mary helped Rothley to lean forward so she could plump his pillows she heard a strangled noise. She peered into his face. 'Are you quite well?' At the sight of his expression she jerked back, a blush heating her cheeks. It was obvious he was stifling laughter.

He shifted himself back in the bed until his back rested against the pillows, grinning. 'You are as transparent as the air itself, Mary. Yes, I shall feed myself, if it will make you more comfortable.'

She was again aware he followed her every move as she collected the tray. This time she recalled his injured thigh and placed the tray next to him, on the bed. Before she could move away, he captured her hand, closing his strong fingers around hers. She stilled. She could not struggle without the risk of upsetting the tray. He squeezed her hand gently.

'Look at me, Mary. Please.'

Warily, she raised her eyes. His expression was contrite.

'Earlier today I implied something about your past that caused you distress. I have had time to consider my words and I apologise. I do not know you well, but that cannot excuse my suspicions or my voicing of them. I also regret the offer I made. I spoke without thought. I am sorry I offended you.' He cocked his head, raising his brows. 'Am I forgiven? If you are to continue to nurse me whilst I am confined to this accursed bed, it will be more comfortable for us both if we can cry friends.' He smiled winningly, then released her hand, picked up his spoon and began to eat.

Mary's stomach performed a slow somersault as she backed away. Rothley in a conciliatory mood was hard to resist. She almost wished for the flirtatious rogue again—it was far easier to harden her heart against *him*. But her innate honesty compelled her to meet his apology halfway, for she was aware her choice of words had been partly to blame for his interpretation of what she had told him.

'Of course we may be friends. I, too, have been thinking and I can see how my words might have been misconstrued and taken to have a different meaning to the one intended. I am sorry for my outburst, but I was upset that you might think me capable of…of…well, as you say, you barely know me, so why should you not wonder at my past? Please believe that my work for my late husband's employer was utterly legitimate. I would never…I wouldn't…' She faltered as her voice thickened and she turned away, wrapping her arms around her waist.

'I do believe you, Mary. I regret reviving such unhappy memories for you. It must be hard to lose someone you care for.'

She looked over her shoulder at Rothley, who was regarding her with sympathy. She swallowed past the sudden tears that threatened. She would never admit to another soul that she had grieved more for old Mr Wendover than she had for her own husband..

Nor would she reveal Simon Wendover's attempt to force her to become his mistress in order to keep a roof over her children's head and food in their bellies. He had not made his demand until three months after the death of his father, by which time she had owed him three months' rent, with no money to settle her debt. He had threatened her with debtors' prison if she didn't pay up—one way or the other.

The fear he might yet pursue her for the monies still haunted her. She had read the lust in his eyes whenever he saw her, even whilst Michael had still been alive.

'They were difficult times,' she admitted, facing

Rothley again. She garnered her strength. She was no longer the girl who had cowered before her father. She had coped with Michael as his body and mind had fallen victim to the lure of alcohol and she had resisted the lust-filled intimidation of her landlord. She would not be cajoled into talking about matters she would rather conceal. 'I should prefer not to dwell upon them, if you do not object.'

He did object. He wanted to know more. He wanted to know all about her late husband—Michael—and this employer. Had he coerced her? Or had he truly been a benefactor, as Mary would have him believe? With difficulty, Lucas stifled his instinct to probe further, recognising the finality in her tone, the determination in her stance. He directed his attention to his supper as Mary settled into the wingback chair by the fire. Not, he noted, next to the bed. She seemed determined to maintain a safe distance between them.

'I gather you have a talent for finance?' he said, between mouthfuls.

'I would not call it a talent, precisely, but I am good with figures. I...I hope you do not object, but I have been assisting Mrs Lindley with the household accounts. She was working herself into quite a fluster over them.'

'Hmm, so I understand.'

Mindful of Rob's earlier words, Lucas tamped down his irritation over Mrs Lindley involving Mary in his finances. He should forget his pride, for it was not *his* stewardship that had driven the estate close to bankruptcy and, against his natural instincts, he knew he must confide in Mary if he was to win her co-operation in overseeing the accounts during his recovery.

'I also understand you and the doctor have discussed the payment of his account. He was about to tell me about your arrangement, but somehow we were diverted from the subject and I still do not know the details.'

'Oh, yes. Well, I hope you will approve, but I suggested the estate might provide the doctor with firewood for the winter and, if that is insufficient, a supply of mutton until his account is settled.'

'Thank you, Mary. That is indeed a splendid suggestion.'

Lucas felt some of the pressure on him ease at Mary's idea. The approaching Quarter Day was never far from his thoughts—he would need all the coin he could muster to settle with Quartly. If only he could be up and about. There was so much to do. His nerves vibrated in frustration.

'As I am confined to this wretched bed for another day...'

'Another two days, the doctor said...'

'Hmmph. We shall see. Rob's an old woman, always fussing...and I'm bored.'

Mary frowned, her lips thinning.

'What have I said to displease you now, Sensible Mary?' Lucas could have bitten his tongue as soon as Mary's nickname passed his lips. He knew she disliked it. Why, at the very time he needed her goodwill, could he not have been more circumspect?

'Why do men always attribute undesirable characteristics to the female of the species? You might as well have said, *Rob's an old man, always fussing.* Women do not have a monopoly on fussing.'

Lucas stared at Mary in surprise as she sat poker straight in the chair, her lips tight.

'I apologise. You are correct, of course, but...I have to confess I am puzzled by your vehemence. It is a common enough saying. Did my words touch a raw nerve?'

Mary's cheeks bloomed pink and her shoulders slumped as a sigh huffed through her pursed lips. 'No, it is I who should apologise. I overreacted.'

'But why should those words anger you? I am aware I do not know you well, but I had not thought you to be of a confrontational nature.'

'I am not, in general.' She fell silent. Lucas watched as conflicting emotions chased across her expressive features. 'My late husband, he would often accuse me of being an old woman and of fussing over nothing, whenever I tried…if I tried…well, it does not matter now. It can be of no interest to you…'

Lucas wondered what she was not saying. It sounded as though she had not been entirely contented with her husband. A ripple of satisfaction coursed through him, to his surprise. Why should he care if her marriage was happy or not?

The silence yawned again between them and Lucas was aware that Mary, fidgeting with her fingers, was finding it awkward. It was a tactic that had stood him in good stead over the years: stretch the silence and you learn things you otherwise would not. Many people became uncomfortable with gaps in a conversation and felt compelled to fill them.

'Please do not call me that again.' Mary stood and crossed to the window. She stared out into the night for a moment or two, then turned to face Lucas.

'I beg your pardon? What is it you do not want me to call you?'

'Sensible.'

A laugh escaped his lips before he could stop it. 'I'm sorry, I didn't mean to laugh, but…are you not sensible? Would you rather be thought of as non-sensible?'

'That is not what I mean, as you are well aware. You are being deliberately provoking.' Mary approached the bed, determination in every line of her body, and stared earnestly at Lucas. 'I should prefer it if you would not call me "Sensible Mary".'

'You do not appreciate your nickname?'

'I do not.'

'Did your husband call you by it, as well as accusing you of fussing?'

'As I said before, I do not wish to dwell upon the past.'

'You do not consider the epithet "sensible" a compliment?'

'But it is not meant as a compliment, is it? It is uttered in a mocking tone and I am expected to laugh about it. Well, I am not laughing.'

Lucas remained silent, pondering her words as he finished his broth. How had he managed to upset her when his intention had been to try to coax her into bringing the ledgers to him? She had settled back into the chair by the fire and now gazed into the flames, her hands twisting in her lap.

'I apologise, Mary. I did not intend to annoy or insult you. I promise I will not call you that again.'

'Thank you.'

Lucas waited, but it seemed two could play at the game of silence and, eventually, he said, 'If you do not wish to talk about your past, will you tell me your plans for your future?'

'I do not have much in the way of plans. When you are recovered, I shall continue my journey. Now, if you are bored, I could read to you. Would you enjoy that?'

Lucas indicated the pile of books on his bed-side table. 'I can read for myself.' He might as well broach the subject. Delay would make it no easier. 'No, what you can do for me, dearest Mary, is bring the ledgers up here to me. I need to make sure...'

'The ledgers are all up to date and the doctor said you are to rest and not to be fretted over business matters.'

Lucas studied Mary's earnest expression as she sat forward in the wingback chair. 'Come and sit by me, Mary,' he said on impulse. 'We cannot comfortably talk with the width of the room between us.

'I promise I shall not take advantage of you,' he added, 'if that is why you are reluctant to sit by my side.' He indicated the chair by the bed.

She stood, then walked slowly towards the bed.

'That is better. Now we can talk in comfort.'

Mary raised her brows. 'My reluctance, as you put it, was not for the reason you imagine.' She removed the tray from the bed and placed it on the table. 'I chose the chair by the fire for reasons of pure self-indulgence.'

Lucas laughed. '*Touché*. That will teach me to make assumptions. If you are cold, you must of course remain by the fire.'

'Why, *thank* you, kind sir.' Mary smiled at him, a mischievous glint in her eye as her cheeks dimpled. 'It is very magnanimous of you, I am sure—' she pulled at the bedside chair as she spoke, swivelling it around so she was facing the bed '—but I now find this chair is more to my liking.' She sat and folded her hands in her lap.

He felt a warm glow inside at the return of Mary's usual good humour. 'Minx! Was that a subtle way of reminding me to consider the comforts of others when I make requests?'

'Requests?' Mary's fair brows arched further. 'I should rather describe them as demands. But it does remind me that *I* have a request to make of *you*.'

Chapter Eight

'Go on, Mary.'

She inhaled, then let the words out in a rush. 'As I said earlier, Dr Preece has advised that you remain in bed for a few more days, but he also admitted you are unlikely to heed his advice. He also stressed how important it is that you do not attempt the stairs before you are much stronger. Trant is already convinced you will refuse to listen and that you will fall and injure yourself all over again and it will be his fault.'

'How could Trant hope to stop me if I was determined to do such a thing?' Lucas demanded.

'Quite,' Mary replied. 'He cannot, but that would not prevent him blaming himself—or the rest of us for feeling some degree of responsibility, too. That is why I should like your word that you will remain in bed until the doctor pronounces you fit enough to rise.'

Her teeth worried at her bottom lip. 'Well?'

Why was she now on edge again? Fear over how he might react? No wonder she had gabbled her words. It had taken courage for her to speak out as she had.

'I cannot promise that, Mary. I am already sick of the sight of these four walls. Rob would have me cooped up here in bed for a month if he had his way. As I said before, he is like an old...' Lucas registered the snap of Mary's brows '...an old man, always fussing!'

Their eyes locked and they laughed in unison.

'At least give me credit for learning,' Lucas said.

'Oh, I always give credit where it is due,' Mary said. 'Now, about the doctor's instructions...'

Lucas laughed again. 'You are a determined negotiator, Mary, I grant you. Unfortunately, you have nothing to bargain with. I, on the other hand, do— for you have revealed your hand all too soon. I will promise to remain in bed until, say, midday tomorrow on the condition you bring the estate ledgers to me tomorrow afternoon.'

Mary's eyes gleamed and her lips twitched. She had the air of one who had won the point.

'You look entirely too smug, Mary Vale. What trick do you have up your sleeve?'

'I shall agree to bring you the ledgers if—and only

if—you give me your solemn promise not to even attempt the stairs until Dr Preece has agreed you are strong enough.'

Lucas gasped. 'I was right. You *are* a little minx. You tempted me to reveal my hand and all the while you had a hidden ace.' He shook his head in disbelief as her mouth stretched into a glorious smile. 'Very well, I concede. I shall give you my word, although I will not promise not to use every means at my disposal to persuade my *good friend*, Dr Preece, to see matters my way.'

'Hmmph.' Mary tried, and failed, to look stern. 'I shall bring the ledgers to you tomorrow afternoon, but I shall also reserve the right to encourage you to remain in bed for as long as possible...'

'And how do you propose to do that, sweet Mary?'

A delightful blush bloomed in her cheeks, but Lucas saw her bite back another smile.

'I might inform Mrs Lindley that the doctor has instructed you are to remain on gruel for the next week,' she said tartly.

'Trant would...'

'Trant can do nothing about the food you are offered, without Mrs Lindley's co-operation. And I can be most persuasive if I choose.'

'I have no doubt on that score, Mary, none at all,

but I ask again: how *will* you ensure I am fully en-
tertained whilst I lie in this bed?'

A variety of images chased through his brain,
none of which he could share with Mary. He held
her gaze, read the passion swirling in the depths
of her dilated pupils. His skin prickled as his loins
tightened. Curse his injuries! What wouldn't he give
to haul her into his arms right now and make love
to her?

Mary frowned, tearing her gaze away. 'We can
play cards,' she stated. 'And then there will be the
ledgers to occupy you tomorrow afternoon. We can
go through them together and, if you have any instructions, I will convey them to Shorey and Hooper.'

'Mary, sweet Mary, is a game of cards the only
way you can think of to save me from boredom? I
had thought a worldly-wise widow such as yourself
might—'

He stopped short, registering Mary's scowl.

'I told you this afternoon: I may be a widow, but
that does not mean I am available to pass the time for
a bored gentleman. Or for any man, for that matter.'

Lucas bit his tongue. Would he never learn? Had
he forgotten so soon the consequence of a similar
innuendo earlier that day? At least this time she
had stood her ground. That might be construed as
progress. He knew he was only teasing—*Are you*

sure?—but Mary clearly did not appreciate such banter.

He adopted a light tone. 'I seem doomed to spend my time apologising to you, Mary.'

Her brow smoothed. 'You do indeed. Mayhap you might claim your wits are still addled as a conse-quence of your injury?'

'Addled wits? Hmm, I am not sure I like the sound of that.'

'Temporarily, of course.' Mary chuckled. She paused, then said, 'I shall strike a bargain with you once more, sir, if you will? I shall agree to believe the addling of your wits is a result of your being shot—and thereby not your usual state of mind—if...' She paused, a speculative glint in her eyes.

'If...?'

'If I might borrow Trant in the morning?'

'Trant?' Lucas could not mask his astonishment. 'What on earth would you need Trant for?'

'Aaah.' Mary pursed her lips, her eyes sparkling as one brow arched. 'That is a surprise.'

'I do not care for surprises. What are you up to, Mary? And why ask my permission? Why not just ask Trant directly? How would I know what he is doing, confined to this prison of a bed as I am.'

'I have been here long enough to know Trant's

routine. The morning is for cleaning this room top to bottom.'

'I know it,' Lucas grumbled. 'I have no choice but to lie here with nothing to do other than watch him.'

'Ungrateful wretch,' Mary said, with a laugh. 'Trant takes great pride in looking after you and your belongings.'

She was right, Lucas knew. He acknowledged her scold with a wry smile. Mary took his hand and he fought to conceal his surprise, certain she had acted without conscious intent.

'Well? Will you tell him he must do as I ask tomorrow morning?'

'I can see my final hours stuck in this bed will be even more of a trial, if both you and Trant are off on some secret mission. Why can you not tell me?'

'I told you; it is a surprise.'

'Very well, I will tell him he is to put himself at your disposal.'

Lucas shifted lower in the bed in a bid to get more comfortable. He suddenly felt very weary. He felt a yawn fighting its way to the surface and struggled to suppress it.

'You are tired. I will leave you to rest.'

Lucas couldn't deny sleep sounded most welcome at this point, despite his enjoyment of Mary's company. His eyelids were getting heavier by the second.

He tried, and failed, to stifle another yawn. Mary's hand was still resting upon his and he turned his hand over and closed his fingers around hers.

He longed to gather her into his arms and hold her but he contented himself with a squeeze of her hand, which he then released. He shifted lower still in the bed, ready for sleep.

'Let me help.'

Her soft voice lulled him as her scent enveloped him. He lifted weighty lids a fraction to see her leaning over him, her eyes caring and kind. His eyes drifted shut as a gentle arm beneath his neck lifted him and his pillow was smoothed. He felt a cool hand smooth his hair from his brow and—though he could not be sure he did not imagine it—he tasted warm, sweet lips as they lightly brushed his.

The next morning he was no more certain whether or not that kiss had been a dream.

Trant had helped him freshen up and brought in his breakfast as usual, but had then disappeared. There had been no sign of Mary and his only other visitor had been Ellen, come to collect his breakfast tray. He had asked her where Mary was, but she had just shrugged, grinned and hurried away. As a distraction from the money worries he could do nothing to resolve at the moment, Lucas had set his imagination free to roam with the enigma that was Mary Vale. He revisited their conversations and relived the kiss he *could* be certain of: their kiss on the night he had been shot. The brush of her lips the night before, however, remained a mystery.

Then reality had returned with a crash—a literal crash that startled him out of his daydream.

'What the...?'

The door cracked open and Mary's face appeared.

'Good morning,' she said cheerfully. 'Sorry about the noise. Nothing to worry about. Don't forget your promise.' She gestured towards the fireplace, beamed and then disappeared before Lucas could gather his wits.

Promise? What promise? He glared at the fireplace as though it might provide some answers. What was going on? Listening intently, he caught whispered voices; scuffling and scraping on the landing outside; doors opening and closing. And, at one point, a man's hacking cough. That wasn't Trant, he was certain. He would never deign to cough in such an inelegant manner.

On the verge of shoving the bedcovers down so he could get out of bed and go and see for himself what was happening, Lucas paused.

His promise.

Midday.

The clock showed quarter past eleven. Gritting his teeth, he settled back to wait, arms folded across his chest.

Not knowing what was happening within his own household tested Lucas's patience to its limits, but the wait gave him time to think. Mary had told him it was a surprise.

For him.

That knowledge infused him with warmth and a sense of humility. Not so long ago his response would have been to snap at everyone, demanding to be told what was going on. Mary's occasional caution around him, however, had stirred his conscience. He already suspected the servants had warned her about his unpredictable temper. He reminded himself again that his father's debts were nobody else's fault.

On the stroke of twelve, the door opened again and Mary strolled into his bedchamber.

'Good gracious; still in bed, Lord Rothley?'

Her voice brimmed with suppressed laughter, her cheeks were flushed and her hair dishevelled.

He lifted his chin and deliberately looked down his nose at her. 'I never break my promises,' he said, in a superior tone. 'I said I would stay in bed until midday, did I not?'

Mary bit her lips, but was unable to prevent the corners of her mouth from curving up. 'Indeed. I am glad you take your word so seriously.' She glanced back over her shoulder. 'Come on in,' she called.

Trant came into the room and went to the wardrobe to fetch a nightgown and a pair of slippers. Mary walked over to gaze out of the window.

'Allow me to help you, my lord,' Trant said.

'Are either of you going to tell me what is going on?' Lucas asked, as Trant helped him to sit on the edge of the bed and put on his robe.

Lucas pushed his feet into the slippers as Mary crossed the room.

'Patience,' she said, before beckoning at someone outside the door. 'All right, we're ready now.'

Shorey and Hooper shambled into the room, looking slightly discomforted and out of place, bringing with them the smell of the stables. Lucas breathed in deeply. The mixed scents of horses and hay, leather and saddle soap prompted an urge to be out of doors and active. Lucas vowed there and then that, as soon as he was mobile, the stable yard would be his first point of call. Hooper carried a chair that Lucas identified as one of his dining chairs: a carver, with arms. But he was more interested at this moment in his men, whom he had not seen since his fever.

After exchanging greetings, he asked, 'How are the animals? Are they all accounted for?'

'Aye, milord. Looking bonnier by the day,' Shorey said, as Hooper set the chair down.

Trant and Mary placed themselves either side of Lucas and grasped one arm each. Lucas looked from one to the other and raised a brow.

'Do you intend to use words to communicate or am I expected to guess what happens next? Or is this, perchance, some modern game of charades designed to entertain me?'

Even Trant cracked a smile as Mary stifled a laugh. 'The chair is for you,' she said. 'We are merely here to steady you, as you have not been on your feet for several days. It would never do for you to fall.'

What on earth were they up to? Lucas eyed the chair with misgiving.

'Forgive me, but I quite fail to see the attraction of that chair when there is a perfectly serviceable—and far more comfortable—chair by the fire. I am certain I can walk that far, with a little assistance.'

'You will see the attraction in a very short while, I promise,' Mary said. 'Shall we see if you can stand?'

Lucas—to his annoyance—found it took two attempts to rise to his feet and, even then, he feared he might have toppled back on to the bed had it not been for Mary and Trant's support. The muscles in his legs quivered as he shuffled forward and it was with a sense of relief that he lowered himself into the chair. No sooner was he seated than the chair tipped precariously back and, before he realised their intent, Shorey and Hooper had hoisted both him and the chair into the air. He grabbed hold of the arms.

'*What?*'

He looked round wildly, ducking his head as they manoeuvred the chair through the doorway. Trant hovered on the landing, directing the two grooms. A glance over his shoulder revealed Mary, following behind, biting at her lip. Her sunny smile had faded and her brow was furrowed. Lucas had no time to wonder at her change in mood, for the men now carried him through the door into a disused bedchamber, always known as the Blue Room, along the landing from his own room.

He gazed around with a sense of wonder. It was no longer a tired, dust-covered, unloved bedchamber but had been transformed. It was fresh and clean. The windows sparkled and every surface was polished. A fire burned merrily in the grate. No longer dominated by a huge four-poster bed and a monstrous wardrobe, it now boasted two comfortable chairs, set either side of the hearth, and a *chaise longue* had been placed by one of the windows. The men carried him across to the *chaise longue*—

which he now recognised had come from his mother's private sitting room—and lowered the chair to the floor.

'There ye be, milord,' Shorey panted. He nodded at Mary. 'Just send word when ye need us to take his lordship back to his bedchamber, ma'am,.'

'Thank you, Shorey, and you, too, Hooper.'

'Yes, indeed, thank you both,' Lucas said, still in a state of disbelief.

He pushed himself out of the chair and, with Trant steadying him, he sat on the *chaise longue*. 'And thank you, too, Trant. You have worked miracles in here.'

He lifted his legs up and Trant produced a blanket to cover him.

'It was a joint effort, my lord. Now, if there is nothing further you need, I will go and see to your bedchamber.'

Finally, Lucas was alone with Mary. She stood rigidly in the centre of the room, her blue eyes filled with doubt, her slender fingers twining together in front of her. He longed to sweep her into his arms and reassure her. He felt a surge of…what? Not lust, although that lurked ever-ready below the surface. Protectiveness: that was it. It was an uncomfortable realisation. He could barely protect those who were already his responsibility. He had no wish to add to their number. But…she had done all this…for him. She had seen his need and had set out to satisfy it. That knowledge did, indeed, humble him.

'I have changed my mind,' he said. 'I have decided I do like surprises after all.'

Mary felt her tension dissipate. She had been so sure Lucas would like her idea, right up until the time Shorey and Hooper had been carrying him, like an ancient king upon a litter, along the landing. Then the doubts had assailed her. What if she had misread him? What if he was furious? What if he objected to her rearranging his house and interfering with the servants' chores?

'I am glad you approve.'

She had so wanted to do something special for him, to help relieve his boredom. She felt a warm glow at the undisguised pleasure on his face. She moved nearer to him and looked out of the window.

'I chose this room because it is a corner room and you have a choice of views.'

She was standing so close she could hear the steady huff of his breathing and his scent—male, familiar, exciting—pervaded her senses. Unable to resist, she stroked her hand across his shoulder as she leaned forward to indicate the landscape: the Cheviots—dark and threatening under the clouds—

loomed in the distance. He started at her touch and she quickly tucked her hand down by her side, flattening her palm against her skirt.

'It is a pity the weather is not better.' Her throat felt tight and her voice was strained.

'You cannot help the weather, Mary. I do not mind. I love the changeable moods of the hills—the very best days are the showery ones, with the sun breaking from behind the clouds. The shadows on the hills make a dramatic moving picture—vastly more entertaining than the wallpaper in my bedchamber.'

Mary turned the carver chair around so she was facing Lucas and sat. He reached out and took her hand, tracing lazy circles on her palm with his thumb. Pleasure shivered across her skin, raising the fine hairs on her arms. His eyes—jet-black and intense—searched her face as she fought to hide her reactions.

'Thank you.'

Her erratically beating heart leapt, feeling as though it was lodged in her throat.

'To think you have done all this…' Lucas tilted his head, indicating the room '…because I complained I was bored. Really, Mary—I do not know how I can ever thank you.'

He raised her hand. Mary focused on his lips, her insides clenching as desire spiralled through her.

Every nerve tingled and sang. His warm, moist mouth pressed against her inner wrist, where the skin was thinnest and the blood beat close to the surface. For sure he would feel her racing heart, recognise her mounting need. Her innate caution burst to the surface and she pulled her hand from his grasp, hardening her heart against his hurt expression.

'There is no need to thank me,' she said. 'It was my pleasure.' Goodness, how formal she sounded. But what was the alternative? She was in danger, she knew, of being sucked into an affair that could only end, for her, in tears and self-recrimination. 'I will go and find out if your luncheon is ready.'

Lucas turned his gaze to the window, acknowledging her words with a nod. She left the room, feeling, somehow, that she had let him down.

Cowardly it might be, but Mary delayed her return until well after luncheon. She had spent the interval with Toby and Emily, using the time to mentally reiterate all the—very sensible—reasons why she must resist Lord Rothley. And the two biggest reasons were right there, before her eyes. Her children.

Ultimately, however, she could no longer put off returning to the newly refurbished Blue Room. Her end of their bargain had still to be honoured. The ledgers were in the library. They were not too heavy for her to manage so, rather than ask for help from one of the servants, she carried them herself.

Chapter Nine

The instant Mary entered the room her stomach swooped in that now familiar way, despite Lucas's cool welcome. She kept her focus on the pile of ledgers, which she put on the table.

'Which would you like to see first?' she asked brightly.

'You.'

Mary started at his blunt reply. What…? She looked directly at Lucas for the first time since she had entered the room. His dark eyes appraised her, heating her skin wherever they lingered. The silence stretched until Mary could stand it no longer.

'What…what do you mean?'

She clasped her hands in front of her, gripping tight. Why didn't he say something? She realised she was holding her breath and she let it go in a rush. The sound seemed to break the spell and Lucas visibly relaxed.

'Never mind,' he said. 'I'll check the estate ledger first, then we can look at the household accounts. Mayhap you can advise me of any further economies you can identify.'

Mary wondered what Rothley had been about to say, or do. Her imagination ran riot, prompting her nerves to skitter pleasurably, even as she scolded herself for being a hypocrite. Why was she incapable of deciding upon a course of action and staying true to it?

She selected the required ledger and handed it to Lucas before sitting down.

'That's no use,' Lucas said matter of factly. 'You'll have to sit here if we are to look at the figures together.'

He patted the narrow *chaise longue* as he shifted to one side to make room for her. When Mary hesitated, horrified yet enthralled by the prospect, he continued, 'Come on. I won't bite, I promise.'

He grinned and the effect was like the sun coming from behind a cloud. A playful gleam lit his eyes and Mary's pulse quickened as she sat by him. Heat radiated from his body as his masculine scent enveloped her. Every sense quickened, tempted by his nearness, but her brain—sensible as ever—rang with caution. She took the ledger from his hands and rested it on her lap, riffling through the pages to find the most recent entries.

'I doubt I can be of assistance in finding any economies in these figures,' she said, striving to keep her voice level despite the leap of her heart as her arm brushed against his. 'I can work with numbers, but I do not have experience of agricultural matters.'

'No matter,' he muttered, as he scanned the page. His hand—strong, with long fingers ending in square, well-trimmed nails—traced the neat column of numbers she had transferred into the ledger from the scrappy notes Shorey had left in Rothley's study. She stared at his hand, mesmerised. *How would it feel...?* She tore her thoughts away from that direction to concentrate on his murmurs as he checked the entries. His deep voice spread over her like warm honey, doing nothing to distract her from the intimacy of their position. His breathing was steady in the quiet of the room, punctuated only by the tick of the clock on the mantelpiece.

Gradually, Mary realised Rothley was totally immersed in the accounts. She was the only one affected by their nearness. Resentment simmered. How dare he disturb her sanity so? He teased her one moment and then behaved as though she were not even there! If it wasn't for the fact she would die rather than give him the smallest inkling of how he affected her, she would…

She bit her lip against a self-deprecating giggle. In her imagination, she had flounced out of the room. Her! Sensible Mary! And now, here she was, thinking of herself by that loathsome nickname. Whatever next? Determinedly, she settled her thoughts. She was Mary Vale, a penniless widow with two young children: a woman of no importance. He was the Marquis of Rothley, an arrogant aristocrat with a shrouded past and an aversion to children.

Hmmph!

Lucas stirred. 'Sorry? Did you say something?' His attention was still riveted to the page.

'No. Sir.'

Her brusque reply gained his attention. She could feel the ever-ready blush heat her cheeks.

'Call me Lucas. Please.'

His wistful tone made it hard to refuse. 'I cannot, it would not be right.' The words were uttered, but she did not—if she was honest—believe them. She longed to call him by his name, but she was afraid it would be the first step towards what she really coveted and she knew she must erect every barrier possible against that.

'Mary, surely you cannot believe calling me by my given name would be so very wrong? Look at what we have been through together, the intimacy, how we sit together right now. Your use of my name cannot be deemed improper in comparison to that.' He nudged his shoulder against hers and smiled at her, his brows raised. 'Please?'

'I must not,' she replied, hardening her heart even as she thought, in near despair, *How am I to resist him?*

Lucas abandoned his struggle to concentrate on the estate accounts.

How could he attend to dry-as-dust ledger entries when Mary sat so close her every breath whispered through his senses, rendering his brain to mush? He was acutely conscious of her presence: the delectable fragrance of woman, overlaid with the now-familiar lavender notes; the heat of her body where it touched his. How would it feel to hold her in his embrace? To lie with her? To feel the silk of her skin pressed against his? Oh, how he longed to taste her again... and again...deeper...the very essence of her.

How can I resist her?

But he must. He must strive to keep their relationship on an even keel. She had been adamant: she was not a woman to embark upon a casual liaison and he could offer her nothing more. He felt again the pounding of her pulse against his lips when he had kissed her wrist that morning. She was a passionate woman, but she had decided—for whatever reason—to deny her needs and he must respect her wishes, as he respected her.

Besides—he forced his attention back to the ledger—his business affairs were in such a dire state, he could not in all conscience offer...

No! Where had that thought been heading? *No! No! No!* Had Julia taught him nothing? Women could not be trusted. They wanted one thing from a man—a life of luxury. Julia had been brutal—rejecting as worthless his offer of his hand in marriage, his heart. And she had scorned him whilst standing in the embrace of another man.

A man he had thought his friend.

His vision blurred. He could make no sense of these figures.

'Are you feeling unwell?' The soft voice broke into his reverie.

'I am tired,' he said abruptly. 'Will you ring for Trant? I want to go back to bed.'

Mary's face fell as she jumped to her feet. 'It was too much for you. All this, it was too soon after your fever.' She put the ledger on the table and crossed the room to the bell pull. 'I am so sorry. I should have waited, I was excited and was so looking forward to seeing your reaction, I didn't think...'

'Mary!'

'I should have noticed...'

'Mary!'

It took a few attempts to stem the flow of her determined self-recrimination. Lucas reached out his hand and Mary clasped it, her touch triggering a rush of desire that he quickly suppressed. 'It was not because of this. It was my own stubborn insistence that I was ready to concentrate on the ledgers. If anyone should be apologising, it is me.'

Trant came, together with Shorey and Hooper. By the time Lucas was back in his own bed he was utterly exhausted.

When Lucas awoke it was dark. Mary was in the fireside chair, sewing by candlelight. He spent a few contented moments watching her, then frowned as he saw her stifle a yawn before rubbing her hand across her eyes.

'Why are you sewing in that light? It will hurt your eyes.'

She looked round and he was struck by how careworn she looked. Then she smiled and her face lit with that familiar inner radiance.

'I like to keep occupied,' she said as she put her sewing to one side and stood up. She poked at the fire, coaxing a flame from the embers, before adding more wood. She crossed the room to Lucas's side and perched on the bedside chair. 'You are right, though,' she continued. 'It is far more comfortable, not to say efficient, to set stitches next to a window in the daylight. How are you feeling now?'

'I feel...tired.' He couldn't believe it. Had he not just slept away the afternoon and half of the evening? 'How on earth can I still feel tired after all this time spent sleeping?'

She laughed. 'Why so condemnatory? You sound positively affronted that your body has the temerity to need time to recover. Must I remind you that you were shot seven days ago, you have grappled with a debilitating fever and you have hardly regained your appetite as yet? It is no wonder you are exhausted.'

'Hmmph. But there is so much to be done, Mary. I...'

'And it is all being done. All you need to concentrate on is regaining your strength. Speaking of which, there is some soup in the kitchen. Would you like me to heat some for you?'

His stomach roiled in protest at the thought of food. 'I am not hungry.'

Mary sat on the bed and reached out to feel his forehead.

'I am not fevered,' he grumbled. 'Just tired. And not hungry.'

'You need something to eat and drink. I thought you were eager to recover your strength?'

He turned his head to one side. He knew she was right, but he could not garner any enthusiasm.

'Tell me, if you cannot stomach soup, what might tempt you? Shall I make you a posset?'

Lucas grimaced. 'Invalid food.'

'And you, Lord Rothley, are an invalid, are you not?' Mary stood up. 'The milk will nourish you and help you to sleep.'

'As if I need any assistance with that.'

She shook her head at him, smiling. 'Stop complaining. I won't be long.'

Lucas suspected he must have dozed off again, for it seemed barely a minute before Mary was back, helping him to sit up and encouraging him—in a way that brooked no argument—to drink the warming, milky posset and to eat a small slice of plum cake she had brought up from the kitchen. When he had finished, he smiled at her.

'You were right, I do feel better. How could I have questioned you?'

'Mayhap you will remember that, the next time you are inclined to doubt that I know best,' she replied, laughing.

He remembered how weary she had looked, sitting by the fire. 'You need to look after yourself, too, Mary. You should go to bed. Get some rest.'

'I cannot deny I am tired,' she said, 'but there was something I wished to ask you first, if I may?'

'Of course. What is it?'

'When we were looking at the ledgers, you spoke of finding further economies. I have identified a few possibilities and I wondered if you might agree to a few changes around the house?'

'Changes?'

'Yes…' Mary leaned toward him '…the Hall takes a great deal of cleaning and, with so few servants, the result is that it looks dull and shabby.'

Lucas had to laugh. 'You do not pull your punches, do you, Mary? I cannot take on more staff. You have seen the accounts; you know my circumstances.'

'I do know, but why can some of the seldom-used downstairs rooms not be shut up for now? There are plenty of dust covers in the attics.'

'You have been wandering around in the attics?' Lucas was uncomfortable with the idea of a near stranger poking around in the far-flung corners of his home.

Mary laughed. 'Of course not. Mrs Lindley told me, when I asked. But she refused to close off any of the rooms because she said you would not allow it.' She cocked her head to one side. 'Surely it cannot matter to you one way or the other? You are one man. The small parlour could be used as a dining room. After all, you don't…that is…' She faltered.

'Do not be bashful now, Mary. Say what you were about to say. I don't have any guests, is that it? I can see you and Mrs Lindley have had plenty to discuss.'

'It is true.' Mary reached for his hand and clasped it warmly. Lucas was sure she had, once again, acted without conscious intent. 'Do not be angry. Mrs Lindley is only concerned about you and I have overheard the servants. There is nothing underhand or…or…*nasty* about it, I assure you. They say the only guest you ever entertain is your mother and she—I am sure—would not object to dining in a more intimate fashion than using that huge, formal dining room. And then,' she rushed on, 'if the music room were to be made into a small sitting room and with you spending much of your time in your study, well…' She paused for breath.

'Well…?'

'It just makes sense,' she declared.

Sensible Mary is back, Lucas thought, although he did not say it. *At least I have learnt that lesson.* 'Does it indeed? How so?'

'Not only will it save time, but it will also save on firewood as there will be fewer rooms to heat.'

'Firewood is free, Mary. It is cut from fallen and diseased trees on the estate.'

'But the labour to cut it and transport it is not free; at least, not in terms of time. If your men are not spending time hauling wood, they can spend more time with your animals. And it takes Susan time to clean and lay all those fires every morning, not to mention keeping them alight.'

Lucas couldn't believe his ears. 'Do you mean to tell me she is continuing to light all the fires even now, when I am confined upstairs?'

'Yes.'

'But why? Why have you not told her to stop?'

'I did try. But I have no authority, you know…not that I think I should have any, you understand… and Mrs Lindley's stock reply to me is: "It's always been done this way, ever since her ladyship's day." It seems, in the absence of any direction from you to the contrary, the staff have continued in the same routines they followed when your mother lived here.'

'But why did they not ask me?'

'I think they did not dare.' Mary smiled, lifting her brows. 'Have you been an easy man to approach over trifling matters, would you say?'

'I…' Lucas paused, searching for the words to convey how he felt. 'I find it hard to believe, Mary…

that it has taken a stranger to point out something so fundamental… Have I really been walking around with both my eyes and my mind shut?'

'It is small things such as this that could make a difference to the comfort, and the expenses, of your household. But do not be too hard on yourself, Lucas, for you have had more serious matters to grapple with since your father died.'

Lucas wondered if Mary was aware she had used his name. Studying her earnest expression, he thought not, but the fact she had done so kindled a pleasurable glow inside.

'Thank you, Mary. I see I shall have to pay more attention to household matters in future. I suppose I had thought—if I activated my brain at all in the matter—that the staff would run the domestic side without any need for guidance from me. I can see I was wrong. Send Mrs Lindley to me in the morning, I shall tell her she is to take her orders from you.'

'Goodness, no! The last thing I want is for her to resent me. Please don't be angry with her,' Mary said. 'It is not her fault, you know. She is only doing as she has always done.'

'I shall not upset her, Mary, I promise. And, talking of upsetting people, will it upset you if I thank you again for what is, if I may say this, a very *sensible* suggestion. And that *is* meant as a compliment.'

'I am not upset,' Mary said, her voice suddenly shy. She blushed, gazing down at their clasped hands. 'I am pleased to have been of use. I have some experience of managing on a small budget.'

Lucas felt his heart constrict in his chest. He longed to gather her into his arms and comfort her but he contented himself with a squeeze of her hand, which he then released. Their conversation had livened Lucas up, but he was determined not to keep Mary from her sleep and did not demur as she settled him down for the night. He was certain he would lie awake for hours, but he drifted into his dreams without hesitation.

The next day Ellen handed Mary a letter as she breakfasted in the large formal dining room for what she hoped was the last time. After breakfast she had every intention of persuading Mrs Lindley to close up the room and to serve meals in the small parlour at the back of the house. It was nearer the kitchen and, with a good clean, would be a cosy, welcoming room—far more pleasant than dining alone in this barn of a room, with its oppressive décor and huge table, large enough for four-and-twenty settings.

Mary opened her letter. It was from the doctor, inviting Mary and the children to call upon his wife later that morning. Her spirits rose at the prospect.

It had been a very long time since she had made a social call of any description. And it would be good for the children to meet some playmates.

'Ellen,' she called, as the maid opened the door, 'how far is the village?'

Ellen retraced her steps to Mary's side. Mary waved the notepaper.

'I have an invitation to visit Mrs Preece this morning, with the children.'

'Ah, bless 'em, ma'am, they'll have a lovely time playing with the doctor's bairns, they will, aye. 'Tis a tidy step, though. I'm thinking young Emily will find it a mite far for her little legs. I'll speak to Shorey. The hosses could do with the exercise, he's forever complaining they grow fat, with too much grass and not enough work.'

'Oh, no, please, Ellen. I have no wish to be a nuisance. Shorey and Hooper were planning to sort the sheep for market—they have enough to do.'

'Nonsense. It'll be no bother at all. They can sort the sheep this afternoon. What time will you be wanting the carriage?'

Mary hesitated and Ellen tutted. 'Mrs Vale, with all you have done for us, dinna be feeling guilty for needing a favour. Will eleven o'clock suit?'

Mary capitulated. 'Thank you, Ellen. Could you also tell Mrs Lindley I wish to speak with her?

I'll come to the kitchen as soon as I've finished breakfast.'

'As you wish, ma'am. I might warn you—she's not in the best of takes this morning. The master called her to his room first thing. Happen you'll know what that was about, aye?' Ellen left the room without waiting for a reply.

Mary was not looking forward to tackling Mrs Lindley about changes to what was, after all, her domain. Although the cook was welcoming in very many ways, she had made it clear from the start she did not appreciate advice from anyone, no matter how well meaning. Mary was not surprised to find her at the kitchen table, massive forearms coated in flour, pummelling bread dough whilst she muttered under her breath. She shot a look at Mary from beneath lowered brows as she entered the room.

'Morning, ma'am,' she said. 'Got to make sure all the air's knocked out.' She pulled the dough towards her, stretching and folding it before slamming her fist into it.

'Indeed.' Mary hovered by the door, whilst Mrs Lindley pointedly ignored her, until she realised delay would not improve the cook's mood. 'I understand you have spoken to Lord Rothley this morning already, Lindy?' She used the pet name the children had coined for the cook and was rewarded by a slightly less hostile glance than before.

'I have.' The cook's tone was still grim. 'Seems I'm to take my orders from you now. ma'am.'

'No, no, that is not the case at all. I have no wish to interfere with your day-to-day running of the household, I only thought to lighten your load. Can we not give my way a try and you can see what you think? Just think of the benefits: fewer fires, less dusting and polishing, less sweeping. Would that not help all of you?'

'Hmmph!' Mrs Lindley shaped the dough before placing it on a tray near the fire to rise. She dusted her hands, then wiped them down her apron.

Mary walked over to her. 'Come on, Lindy. Give it a try. What do you say?'

'Seems I've got no choice in the matter seein' as you saw fit to go to his lordship over my head. Where is it you want us to start?'

'I am going out this morning, to visit the doctor's wife. Mayhap we could start with the dining room this afternoon?'

Mrs Lindley glared at Mary. 'I should prefer to get on with it. There's no need for you to help. The dining room it is, then. I'll ask Mr Trant to help get the dust covers from the attic. Now, if you'll excuse me, some of us have work to do.'

She marched over to the larder and disappeared inside. Mary could hear her rattling and banging around. She had asked Lucas to intervene with Mrs Lindley on impulse and now she had offended her. She hoped the housekeeper's wrath would not last too long, or her last few days at the Hall could prove most uncomfortable.

Chapter Ten

'Good morning. Have you finished your breakfast?'

Lucas opened his eyes as the door to his bedchamber opened. It was Mary. He forced himself more upright in the bed, causing the crockery on his tray to clash as the mattress dipped. He had been on the verge of dropping off to sleep again, but he would not admit that to Mary. He would far rather have her company than yet another doze.

'I understand from Trant that you do not wish to go to the Blue Room until after luncheon?' Mary went on as she picked up the tray.

She made no attempt to place it on the table, instead standing with it in her hands whilst she studied Lucas, her head tilted to one side. Then she glanced down at the tray.

'Excellent,' she said, smiling at the sight of two

empty plates and an empty cup. 'Your appetite appears to have perked up since last night.'

'Indeed.' What was she up to? She was behaving most oddly and looked positively on edge. 'Do you intend to hold that tray indefinitely, Mary? Why don't you put it on the table? You look as though you cannot wait to scurry away.'

'Very well.' She walked to the end of the bed and deposited the tray before returning to Lucas's side. 'Is that better?'

'What are you up to this time, Mary? Are you planning another surprise? Incidentally, I've spoken to Mrs Lindley this morning about your plans.'

Mary's fair cheeks turned pink. She looked even more furtive than before. 'I know,' she said. 'I have just spoken to her in the kitchen.'

'Has she demanded your help?' Lucas would not allow his staff to bully Mary. 'If she has, you must tell me. I will—'

'No, no, quite the contrary; in fact, she doesn't seem to want my help at all. I would appear to be quite redundant. And that is why—if you do not object, that is—I should like your permission to use the carriage to go into the village this morning.'

Her blue eyes were fixed on a point by his right ear. She looked secretive and guilty, and…

'Who are you going to meet?' he growled. Quite

apart from the unexpected flare of jealousy, he was dismayed he would not see Mary for the rest of the morning.

'Mrs Preece.'

Her blue eyes were wide and innocent and Lucas felt a slap of shame that he had instantly imagined the worst of her motives. He hoped Mary had not noticed his suspicions.

'I received a letter this morning, inviting me to call.' She pinned him with a piercing look. 'You can ask Shorey where he takes me, if you do not believe me.'

'Why should I not believe you?' he asked, in what he hoped was a nonchalant way.

'Doctor Preece told me the other day that his wife would appreciate a visit. She is...she is unable to pay social calls at the moment.'

'She is with child, is she not?'

'Yes.'

The furtive look was back. Lucas could not fathom it. Mayhap Mary was embarrassed discussing such intimate matters, but it seemed unlikely. She had gone to collect the tray again and was standing looking at him expectantly.

'Of course you may use the carriage.'

What else could he say? He could hardly keep her prisoner at the Hall, much as that idea appealed whenever he thought about her leaving to continue her journey.

Mary beamed. 'Thank you. I shall see you later.'

After she had gone, Lucas pondered his growing reliance on her. True, he looked forward to her visits but, surely, only because he was still weak and convalescing? Once he was up and about, he would resume his old life and would no longer crave her company and, with his friendship with Rob rekindled, his life would be less lonely than before. His thought processes seized as he considered that last sentiment. It was true: he *had* been lonely, particularly since his mother had been away, but it was a state of his own making. He had, quite deliberately, eschewed all company since his return to the Hall. In fact, he had kept all his acquaintances at arm's length since Julia...

With a muttered exclamation he pushed the bed-covers back and eased his legs over the side of the bed. He was beggared if he was going to lie in bed, useless and helpless, whilst that witch invaded his thoughts. Her image floated into his consciousness...wavered...shimmered...and transformed into another. Mary! A curse on all women! They played havoc with a man's peace of mind until he could no longer think straight.

He pushed back against the bed, levering himself

to his feet, giving his shaky muscles time to become accustomed to his weight. As soon as he felt steady he shuffled towards the fireside chair. His legs and hips were stiff from lack of use and his thigh grumbled in the background, but it was not the red-hot agony that had tormented him when he had awoken after his fever. He must take that as a good sign. He lowered himself into the chair gingerly. Not too bad. At least he had managed to walk, an improvement on yesterday.

Mary invaded his thoughts once more. He could not fathom the effect she had on him. She was an enigma, presenting her calm and sensible face to the world, but he had caught glimpses of a different person beneath the surface—a complex mix of fear and courage, virtue and passion, uncertainty and fun.

Where was she heading? What were her secrets? And why did he sometimes catch a hint of fear in those beautiful eyes of hers? What was she scared of? Him? Surely not, for she had shown she was unafraid to stand up to him when necessary. Mayhap she feared the passion within her? For passion there was—passion he longed to sample—but his Mary evidently considered it wrong to capitulate to her base feelings.

His Mary? He stared into the flames. He wanted her, but did he want more than a dalliance? No! His every fibre screamed denial. He had sworn to never surrender his heart to another woman. Restless, he stood up and limped over to the window. Bracing his hands against the frame, he gazed unseeingly through the glass until he heard the door open behind him.

'My lord!'

With a sigh, Lucas turned from the window and allowed Trant to help him back to bed. He was no closer to understanding his true feelings—or intentions—towards Mary. Exhausted, he rolled on to his side and closed his eyes.

'You've been gone a long time. Whatever can you find to talk about all this time? How long have you been back?'

Mary glanced at Lucas as she closed the door, gauging his mood. He sounded irritable. His expression was not encouraging. She heaved a silent sigh. She had spent a wonderful few hours with Jenny Preece, whilst the children played together.

Since then, however, she'd had to endure the cold shoulder from Mrs Lindley who had underlined her displeasure by serving a particularly lavish luncheon to Mary in the morning room, because the dining room was now under wraps and the small parlour was not yet ready to take its place. Together with the constant reproachful looks from Ellen, Susan and Trant—all of whom had spent the entire morning on the receiving end of Mrs Lindley's bile—Mary had been relieved to escape to the Blue Room, where Lucas was, once again, ensconced on the *chaise longue*.

Judging by his growled interrogation, however, the bad humour seemed to be infectious.

'I returned to the Hall just before luncheon,' Mary replied, vowing to ignore his disgruntled tone, 'as you must know, for I am aware Shorey came straight up here to help move you to this room. And I had a delightful time visiting Mrs Preece, thank you so much for asking. Are you acquainted with her?'

'I've not had that pleasure,' came the sardonic reply.

She had known what his answer would be, having been told the same by Jenny, who had wasted no time in detailing Rothley's reclusive behaviour over the past two years and in speculating as to its cause. Mary had been fascinated by her tales of the Rothley family, much of which tallied with the stories she had overheard in her formative years. Any guilt she felt in indulging in such gossip had been allayed by convincing herself the more she heard of Lucas's debauched lifestyle, the less likely she would be to succumb to his allure.

That now seemed a forlorn hope. The instant she had set eyes on him her stomach had performed its now-customary swoop as her heart skipped behind her ribcage. She was now so used to his effect on her that she could at least be confident of hiding her reactions.

'What would you like to do? Do you want to finish looking at the ledgers? I cannot promise any further ideas, but you may at least set your mind at rest that all is up to date.'

He was appraising her, sweeping her with his black eyes and her skin tightened into goosebumps. 'Shall I bring...?'

He pushed the covering from his legs and swung them over the side of the *chaise longue*. A fleeting frown crossed his face. Mary hurried to his side.

'Be careful. You mustn't aggravate your injuries.' She began to push him back, but he resisted.

'I walked without any help earlier.'

Mary bit back a gasp. 'All the way from your bed-chamber?'

'No,' he admitted. 'Earlier, in my room. I walked to the window on my own.'

Mary frowned. 'Was Trant there in case...?'

'I am perfectly capable of making it to the table without making a song and dance about it,' he growled as he stood.

Mary jerked back as if scalded. Why so venomous? She had only been trying to help.

'Please,' she said. 'Just for me?' She nudged into position, by his side. 'Please?'

He sighed, slinging his arm over her shoulder. She nearly buckled under his weight and suspected he was making his point. They shuffled slowly across the room. She sighed with relief when they reached the table and he sat down, pulling the ledgers towards him. Mary fetched another chair and sat beside him, waiting for him to open the ledger.

He made no effort to get started. Instead he looked sideways at her. Sighed.

'Sorry,' he said in a gruff voice. 'That was not very handsome of me, was it?'

Mary shrugged, pretending nonchalance.

'I'm pleased you spent a pleasant morning with Mrs Preece. Truly. It has done you good—put the roses back in your cheeks. You don't get enough fresh air.'

She laughed. 'That is because I am here to care for you. And that means staying indoors.'

The instant the words left her lips she realised her mistake. She stole a look at his puzzled frown.

'But what about the times you are not with me? You do not spend every minute of the day up here. What do you do then?'

'Oh,' she said airily, 'there is always something to be done: mending, paperwork...speaking of which...' She flipped open the ledger.

'What did you talk about this morning? Did I figure in your cosy chat? Did Mrs Preece spill my secrets?'

Laughter bubbled to the surface. 'I dare say she might have, if they were not secrets,' Mary said. 'To set your mind at rest, yes, you did figure in the conversation, but only long enough for us both to admit we knew nothing about you.'

'Hmmph.' Lucas slid the ledger closer and bent his head to peruse the columns of figures.

Mary studied him surreptitiously. She had been a touch economical with the truth, for they had discussed Lucas for longer than she had suggested, but it was rumour and innuendo, not facts, they had dealt in. How little she knew of him. She could not even be sure the man she was coming to know revealed his true nature. His behaviour did not tally with his reputation as a dissolute rake. Had the tales of his past been wildly exaggerated, or was he a changed man?

They sat close, not quite touching, heat radiating from his body. One touch and she could melt in his arms. But she wouldn't. She remained outwardly still, not wanting to draw his attention, but inside she quivered like a bow that had been drawn tight, ready to snap back and let its arrow fly. The room was so silent she could hear the faint shouts of the men outside as they handled the sheep. After several minutes, Lucas lifted his head.

'I have had enough of these. Everything seems in order. Thank you.' Mary's breath caught at his smile. 'I can hear Shorey and Hooper outside.' He pushed back his chair. 'I have a yen to look out and see what they are about. Will you help me, Mary?'

Mary shot to her feet and fitted her shoulder beneath his arm to help him rise. They moved slowly towards the window overlooking the side of the house. When they reached it Lucas braced his other hand on the windowsill, easing his weight on her, leaving his other arm across her shoulders. Shivers spangled her skin as he toyed with a tendril of hair behind her ear.

After several minutes watching the men herding the sheep, separating them into two flocks with the aid of dogs and hurdles, Lucas tightened his arm, hugging Mary briefly against him.

'I will rest now, Mary. Thank you for your help.'

She felt awkward, acutely aware of the undercurrents. There were so many words and emotions flowing beneath the surface it was nigh on impossible to act, or even breathe, normally. Her heart beat a frantic tattoo as she helped him back to the *chaise longue*, every step an agony of apprehension, every breath a ragged triumph.

When he was at last settled, the blanket pulled up to cover his legs, she said, 'Is there anything else you would like me to do, sir?'

He captured her gaze and raised one brow. She felt the ready blush rise up her neck and scorch her cheeks.

'You called me Lucas last night.'

'What? I mean, I beg your pardon?'

He was playing that silence game again. 'I did not! No, I would not…I am certain I did not…you are saying that to tease me. I would…' the words dried up as Mary registered the desire that flared in his eyes.

She tore her gaze from his.

You are an available female. He is interested only in the flesh, in the physical. He does not want love, or a companion. He has no need of you, Sensible Mary!

'If I did indeed do so, I did it without intent or realisation.'

She provoked mayhem inside him. As they stood at the window it had taken an iron will not to haul her against him for that kiss he had promised himself. His eyes had been on the activity outside, but every other sense, his mind, all his attention, had been on Mary. He had felt her tremors and heard the fractured breathing that chimed with his own. Passion simmered in her depths, but she had made it clear she was no lady of easy virtue.

And now she was quibbling over the use of his name. Lucas eyed her with exasperation. Why was she being so stubborn over such a small detail? He cast around for a less contentious subject.

'I half-expected the doctor to call at the Hall this morning,' he said. 'I wonder if he might come later this afternoon?'

'I do not believe so,' Mary said as she sat down. 'Robert arrived home as I was leaving and mentioned he had been called upon to visit a patient on the other side of the village. He told Jenny not to expect him home until late.'

A shaft of pure jealousy impaled Lucas. *Robert?* He skirmished briefly with his inner demon not to voice that jealousy. He lost.

'Robert?' The abrasive voice sounded quite unlike his.

'Doctor Preece, I mean,' she said, a laugh in her voice and her eyes.

'I know who Robert is! You call him by his name and yet, not two minutes since, you deemed it improper to call me Lucas. You barely know him. You spend many hours a day, and night, with me…'

'And that is precisely why it is improper for me to call you Lucas.'

Lucas held his silence. He did not understand.

'It is because we are in such close proximity… in such intimate surroundings…can you not see? This—' Mary swept an agitated arm aloft '—is not normal life. It is not real. It encourages…it invites…'

She took a deep breath, pressed both hands against the arms of the chair and pushed herself up. Lucas watched as she paced the room. Her bosom heaved as her fingers twisted and untwisted. Finally, she halted at the foot of the *chaise longue.*

'Can you not say something? I am persuaded you know exactly what it is I am struggling to say, yet you leave this…this wretched silence, in the hope I shall make a fool out of myself. Hoping I will reveal more of myself than I otherwise would.'

She was right. He did use the silence in that way, although he had never wished for her to make a fool of herself.

'You are right. And I do understand what you are trying to say, Mary. You believe the fact I am wounded and you are nursing me could lead to a false intimacy that might otherwise never have oc-curred.'

'Indeed.' Mary's voice rang with relief. 'You do understand and that is why I cannot call you Lucas.'

Thoughts chased each other around Lucas's head. Did that mean she was developing feelings for him? Triumph surged through him, despair close on its heels. What did it matter? He knew she desired him, but had he not just articulated the very reason why any apparent emotional closeness was false? To his mind, however, it was the situation they were in that fostered such emotions, not whether or not they called each other by their first names. Whatever the truth of it, the sooner he was back on his feet and could return to his accustomed life, the better for them both. Then these yearnings would be exposed for what they were: base sexual urges he might satisfy with any lightskirt he chose.

'I understand your point of view, but I do not agree with you,' he said. 'You would have me believe that, by using my name, you would be in danger of developing feelings for me that otherwise would not exist? I am sorry, Mary, but that does not make sense. Not to me.

'I am tired,' he added brusquely. 'Do you mind leaving now? I need to rest.'

The flash of hurt in her eyes stabbed at him, but he closed his own and kept them closed until he heard the door shut behind her.

Chapter Eleven

As she climbed the stairs, Mary wondered what mood she would find Lucas in this evening. Would he still be angry at what he clearly saw as her obstinacy over the use of his name? She was in need of congenial company, now the children were asleep, for they were the only occupants of the Hall who were not in a bad mood with her. She opened the door to his bedchamber, balancing a tray on one hand.

'More infant pap?'

The sardonic comment assaulted her ears before she had even set foot inside the room. Lucas sat in the wing chair by the fire, glowering at her, his legs propped up on a stool. Setting her teeth, refusing to be cowed by him, she crossed the room, pasting a bright smile on her face.

'As it happens, Mrs Lindley has prepared a stew for you this evening.' The cook had handed it to

Mary with a scowl and a muttered, 'You can tell his lordship if it's not up to my usual standards. I'm sorry, but I've been extra busy.'

'Well, I suppose it makes a change from gruel and broth,' he grumbled, but his eyes brightened and she recognised his frustration over his continued confinement.

'You should be grateful she cares enough to tempt your appetite.'

As Mary set the tray on a table next to Lucas, he murmured, 'Are you chastising me, Mrs Vale?'

Mrs Vale? Was this his attempt to prove to her that it made no difference which names they used?

She glanced sideways at him. He had an unmistakable glint in his eyes and a teasing smile hovered on his sensuous lips. Her mouth dried and her pulse accelerated as their gazes collided. His hair was damp, the drier ends curling over his ears and she could detect the smell of soap over his customary male, musky scent.

'I don't know...' Lucas heaved a theatrical sigh '...here am I, a poor invalid, and my nurse—my only comfort, I might add—needs must chastise and censure me the moment she steps into my bedchamber.'

Mary pulled the table closer to his chair.

'I am sorry to prove such a disappointing companion,' she said. 'You are clearly in need of more congenial company than I am able to provide. You can reach your food now. Should I leave you in peace? I could ask Trant, or Mrs Lindley, to bear you company this evening if you prefer?'

'You shameless tease, Mary. You are in a mischievous mood tonight. You know very well I shall beg you to stay, if that is what you want?'

Mary laughed. 'There will be no need to beg, Lucas.'

He stilled. 'Lucas? Was that another unintended slip of your tongue, Mary?'

Mary bit at her lower lip. She had thought long and hard about their earlier conversation.

'No. I decided you were right and I was wrong. I will call you Lucas, but only when we are alone together.'

He pretended to choke on his food. 'Might I request that in writing?'

'I beg your pardon? Request…what? That I have agreed to call you Lucas?'

'No. That I was right and you were wrong. It is a most pleasing concept.'

Mary laughed with him, then busied herself with plumping the pillows and straightening the bed.

'Mary.' The softly spoken word caught her attention. 'Come here. Please.'

He held out his hand, fingers crooked. Heart in

mouth, Mary crossed to his side, but did not take his proffered hand.

'Thank you. The matter of my name might have seemed a trivial matter to you, but my life is full of people who call me "my lord" and "sir". It is nice, even for a short time, to have someone call me as an equal. To feel maybe we are friends.

'I miss you when you are not here, Mary,' he added, his voice deepening as he held her gaze.

Mary's nerves jangled. Her pulse—already unsteady—lurched into a mad gallop and her dress seemed to tighten, constricting her chest. Had she made a serious error of judgement? Was this not what she had feared all along?

She stepped back, conscious of his sheer size and of his raw masculinity as he lounged at his ease in the chair. Desire smouldered, his words fanning the lick of flame into a conflagration. She fought to conceal her reaction, her eyes riveted to his as he studied her face.

He smiled knowingly as he reached for the plate of stew. She took advantage of his distraction to watch the play of the firelight over his lean features as it accentuated the strong jut of his nose and the enticing curve of his lips. Her stomach performed a slow, sensual somersault as Mary relived the moment those same lips had caressed hers.

A yearning ache, deep in her core, nagged at her as she watched Lucas chew his food and swallow, the movement of his throat intensifying the lump that unaccountably obstructed hers. Aware she was standing mesmerised, Mary gathered her wits.

'You have had a bath?' she asked. As soon as it left her lips, she knew the question would not serve to distract her. Her imagination ran riot as she conjured the picture of a naked Lucas in a bathtub: large, wet, glistening, the soap lathered all over his body. The same body she had no need to imagine. Her memory provided her with all the detail she cared to recall.

'A bath of sorts,' he replied, between mouthfuls of stew. 'Unfortunately, Trant is as unbending as you when it comes to what he considers appropriate for an invalid. He wanted to wait to ask the doctor if a bath would damage the wounds. In the end we compromised. I stood in the bath whilst he soaped me down...' He paused, then directed a provocative look at Mary as she stood, transfixed. 'I suggested he might leave the task of bathing me to you, as you are my chief nurse, but my pleas fell, I am sad to say, on deaf ears. Pity.'

Mary felt her face flame as her fevered imagination conjured up an even more potent image of his lordship, standing upright in his bath, his lean body gleaming as water cascaded down his torso and legs.

She battled to suppress her mounting desire, tearing her eyes from his face, desperate to distract herself from her salacious thoughts and rampant urges. The strength of her desire for him took her unawares and it both horrified and enthralled her.

It was not what she wanted, not what she had intended, not what she had planned. She felt the shackles of despair close ice-cold jaws around her heart. It was clear she must leave Rothley Hall soon if she wished to retain her pride. She had never been in love before and she could not tell if her growing obsession with Lucas was the first green shoots of that emotion, or merely lust, but suddenly she was unable to consider the prospect of never seeing him again without feeling the urge to weep. No, she could not stay. She could not risk her heart, or her children's happiness and future, by becoming embroiled in a relationship that could have no happy ending.

Gritting her teeth, she battened down her emotions, casting around for an innocuous topic, keen to avoid any of the numerous contentious subjects between them.

'It must be a relief to have some real food to eat, after all that gruel,' she commented, her voice sounding, to her own ears, cold and strained.

She didn't wait for his reply, but bustled around the room: drawing the curtains, refuelling the fire and tidying the dressing table. She doggedly avoided eye contact and made no effort to speak again, vowing to take her cue for any conversation from Lucas and to keep any ensuing subject impersonal.

As he ate his supper, Lucas watched Mary fuss around the room, sensing her mood had changed, but not sure why. Her burgeoning desire had been clear to see, but a shutter had now slammed shut and the view through the window of her eyes was obscured. He frowned, thinking back. What had he said to cause her withdrawal? Had he gone too far, too quickly? After all, it would not be the first time his teasing had caused her abrupt retreat.

He held his tongue whilst she drew the curtains and added logs to the fire, but when she began to straighten the items on his dressing table—items that were kept meticulously neat by Trant, who had left the room only minutes before—his impatience got the better of him.

'For goodness' sake,' he bit out, 'stop fussing and come and sit by me.'

Mary flinched and Lucas immediately regretted his harsh tone. His confinement had given him time to think, for the first time in many months, if not years, and the conclusions he had reached about himself were not pleasant. Deep down, and with a mounting sense of shame, Lucas knew he had been guilty of increasing carelessness in his treatment of others. Would he never learn? The last thing he wished was for Mary to be wary of him.

He kept his attention on his food as, from the corner of his eye, he saw Mary sit on the chair next to his, smoothing her skirts as she did so. When she had settled he noted the slight blush staining her cheeks as she avoided eye contact. He had seen her passion and her growing desire, but now all he could read was fear. Of what, though? Him, for his brusque manner? Or of her body's response to him? But why should a widow fear what was, after all, a natural urge? Fearful she was, though, and he cautioned himself to moderate his tone of voice.

'I was teasing, Mary, about the bath.'

Her cheeks reddened further. Lucas decided to confront her.

'Are you afraid of me?'

A muscle at the side of her jaw bunched. 'No.'

'Are you certain? This is not the first time you have flinched when I have spoken. I am sorry if my words sounded harsher than they were intended.'

Mary did not look convinced. 'You have a ready temper,' she said. 'That is undeniable. How am I to know if you are liable to lash out?'

Lash out? Where would she get such an idea? He had never…

What about Henson? his inner voice whispered. *You half-killed him.*

But Mary could not know about that shameful episode. It was years ago. He had worked hard to put it behind him, to avoid treading the same path as his father, who had used his fists whenever life did not go his way. Since Henson he had never even come close to physical violence, no matter how angry and frustrated he had become with his life.

'Why on earth would you think I might lash out at you? Or anyone? What in the world have you been told to believe me such an ogre? Do not think I haven't seen you when you recoil from me. When have I given you cause to fear me?'

'I do not fear you. I—'

'Do not lie to me. I have seen it in your eyes. More than once. Why, Mary? What is it you think me capable of? Why are you so wary around me? You kissed me…'

Her gaze shot to his face, her blue eyes burning in their intensity.

'I did not kiss you! *You* kissed *me*; you took me by surprise. What kind of woman do you think I am?'

'You are a widow, Mary, not a naïve virgin. It was only a kiss.'

'Oh, yes, I am well aware of that,' Mary hissed as she surged to her feet and glared at him, her small fists clenched at her sides. 'For you, it was only a kiss. It was nothing, it meant nothing…less than nothing, for that matter.'

Mary's voice shook with rage and Lucas stared at her aghast. Where had this wildcat come from, slashing at him with unsheathed claws? What had happened to Sensible Mary?

Oh, but she's magnificent when she's angry.

'I cannot stay. I must…'

Mary started for the door and, without volition, Lucas's hand shot out and grabbed her wrist. She gasped and twisted her arm, trying to free herself. Lucas pulled her closer. Her thighs bumped against his.

'No!' She twisted, trying to break free. 'What are you doing?'

'You're wrong, Mary, that kiss did matter. It meant a great deal.'

He stared up at her distressed face, his gut wrenching at the sheen of tears in her eyes. 'Don't go, Mary, not like this. Please.'

Lucas tugged until she sat with a bump in his lap. He winced as pain stabbed at his thigh, but he did not loosen his hold. One arm was wrapped around her waist and, as she slapped and pushed at that arm, he captured both her hands in his much larger fist. She froze. She sat rigid on his knee, her ragged breathing loud in the quiet of the room, her whole body quaking.

'Mary?' His voice was a harsh whisper.

She kept her face averted.

'Please, let me go,' she whispered.

His mood swung instantly from exasperation to guilt. What on earth did she think he was going to do? The answer came with an explosion of shame. She thought—she *really* thought—he was capable of taking her against her will? Abruptly, he released her hands and took his arm from around her waist.

'I am sorry, Mary,' he said. 'I didn't mean to scare you. Again.'

She remained seated on his lap, but twisted to face him. The wary expression was back.

'And you were right, too,' he said, with an attempt at a self-deprecating smile. 'It was I who kissed you, not the other way around. And it mattered enough for me to long to kiss you again, but you must trust me when I tell you I will never take anything from you that is not freely given.'

Mary's eyes searched his. The caution had retreated, their blue depths now dark and luminous as he felt her stiff body relax.

'Do you trust me, Mary?' he whispered, staring

at her lush, moist lips as they parted. Blood pooled, hot and heavy, in his loins.

Her lids lowered as she swayed towards him. His skin tingled as her hand rose to caress his cheek. He responded without conscious thought, his arm wrapping around her waist as their lips met, his wits scrambling to catch up with this change.

Passion ignited, exploding between them as she melted against him, winding her arms around his neck and threading her fingers through his hair. Her mouth was all soft, moist heat, her lips moulding sweetly to his. Their tongues tangled as he cupped the soft fullness of her breast, his thumb flicking at the hard bud of her nipple through the thin fabric of her dress.

Impatient for naked skin, he slid his hand inside her neckline. The weight of her breast, her satiny-smooth skin, her heat and the unique feminine scent of Mary fanned the flames of desire. The throb of his arousal, trapped and tortured beneath her squirming bottom, drove him mindlessly on. He tore his lips from hers and nudged under her chin, seeking the sensitive skin of her neck. He pressed hot kisses to the delicacy of her collarbone, then traced a path to her ear, licking and nibbling at the lobe before pushing the tip of his tongue inside, eliciting a gasp from the writhing woman on his lap.

He eased her breast from the restriction of her dress, trailing his lips down the slender column of her neck and laving the hollow at the base, before kissing his way to his goal. He drew her nipple deep into his mouth, sucking and nibbling and flicking, and Mary cried out, twisting towards him, easing his access with her movement, as she clasped his head to her.

Her whimpers of pleasure were a rich enough reward, but he longed for more. He must have all of her. He needed everything she had to give. He yearned to hear her screams of ecstasy as he plunged deep inside her moist heat. His hand skimmed down the fabric of her skirts to the hem and lifted, exposing the smooth skin of her thighs to his touch. His hand traced a meandering path, circling and stroking, ever higher, until his fingers brushed against the curls at the apex of her thighs. He stifled a groan as he parted the swollen folds and relished in her sharp intake of breath as he touched the sensitive flesh within.

His world rocked on its axis as he fought to restrain the powerful urges threatening to overcome his self-control. Mary's scent, her taste, her silky skin beneath his questing fingers—they enveloped him, pervaded his very being and soothed his soul even as they drove him onwards and upwards to seek ecstasy. He was possessed by her, lost in a glorious swirl of desire. He did not want it to end. Ever. It felt right. But despite his need, although he fought hard to ignore it, the real world impinged, slashing through the intense erotic haze that had invaded him.

The pain in his thigh had yet again become a red-hot spike of agony. His shoulder throbbed, gradually drowning out the infinitely more pleasurable throbbing in his loins. He was jerked back to reality and, reluctantly, he took his hand from between Mary's thighs and removed his mouth from her breast. As he smoothed her skirts back in place, he took her lips in a long, soothing kiss, before resting his forehead against hers. He was not ready for this, not yet. He shifted uncomfortably. Mary leaned back to look into his face.

'I'm sorry, Mary,' he said. 'I can't do this. I...'

She jumped from his knee as if scalded, tugging at her clothing until she was covered. 'Of course not,' she said. 'I understand. I should not have kissed you; I don't know what came over me. It won't happen again, I promise.'

'No!' Lucas stretched to take her hand, but she moved sharply away. 'You don't understand. It was...'

'Please, Lucas. It doesn't matter, do not try to explain. It is unnecessary. It will just embarrass us both. We must pretend it never happened…'

There was a knock at the door and Trant entered.

'I have come to help you to bed, my lord.'

Chapter Twelve

In utter turmoil, Mary fled to the sanctuary of her bedchamber, shut the door behind her and leaned back against its solid strength as she tried to make sense of what had happened.

Her initial relief—for she trembled to think of the consequences had Trant walked in earlier—was soon overtaken by mortification. What on earth had come over her? How had she gone from happiness, to anger, to fear, to desire within such a short time? She could not deny she had instigated *that* kiss. Nor could she pretend she would have gone no further, for she had been totally, and willingly, enmeshed in a sensual web of her own design.

When Lucas pulled her on to his lap her imagination had run riot and she had been sure he was about to force a kiss, or more, but his prompt release of her had disarmed her. The feel of his hard thighs and the evidence of his arousal under her buttocks had excited her; his clean, male scent had enticed her; the sheer size and strength of him, holding her close, had made her feel secure.

How long has it been since someone held me and comforted me?

She had forgotten the sheer joy of simply being held.

When he took his arm from her waist she had wanted him to hold her again. She had wanted to feel safe. She frowned. *Safe?* But, yes. Despite her beliefs about the type of man he was, she trusted his word he would never take anything she was not willing to give.

Her blood heated as she felt again his mouth at her breast, his questing touch at her most intimate place. She had given more than she meant to, but she had not been rational at the time, whereas Lucas...

Nausea rose. What must he think of her? Had he kissed and caressed her because she had offered herself to him? He had admitted he wanted to kiss her again and she had felt his arousal under her, so he had wanted her. But he had stopped. What were his words?

'I'm sorry; I can't do this.'

How could she face him again?

Impatient with her circling thoughts, Mary pushed away from the door and sat on the bed, considering her options. There were only two. She must either leave Rothley Hall straight away, without even saying goodbye, or she must accept the humiliation of his rejection and continue to nurse him.

The former was unthinkable. Having made up her mind, she decided to act. If she hurried, mayhap Trant would still be with him and she could make her peace without even mentioning that disastrous kiss.

She tapped at Lucas's door. 'May I come in?'

A quick glance around the room ascertained Trant was not present and Rothley was now back in bed. A half-empty glass of amber liquid stood on the bedside table. Mary eyed the glass with misgiving, recalling the stench of alcohol when she had first encountered Lucas in the woods. She had not seen him touch alcohol since he had been shot. Was he reverting to type, now he was on the road to recovery? She glanced around again. A bottle of brandy stood on the table at the foot of the bed.

'Mary.' The relief in his voice was unmistakable.

She walked in and stood by the bed, her emotions churning, but she was determined not to behave like a hysterical female, despite the temptation to do so. She was an adult, the kiss was at her instigation and Lucas had every right to stop kissing her any time he wished. She had repeated that mantra time and time again as she had traversed the corridors between her bedchamber and his, in an attempt to ensure she would remain calm and collected. In an attempt, she realised with a wry smile, to be Sensible Mary.

'I have come to apologise for rushing off in such a way, sir.'

'Sir? I thought we had an agreement, you and I, Mary? Did you not agree to call me Lucas?'

There was a pause as he studied her face and she fought to keep her expression blank.

'Please?' He cocked his head to one side and raised his brows.

Mary felt the corners of her mouth tug into a reluctant smile. How could she resist that look? He managed to appear both contrite and seductive at the same time, his allure as strong as ever as his dark eyes cajoled. She longed to cast aside her doubts, to throw herself into his embrace, to kiss his mouth, to run her fingers through his ruffled hair...

Oh, dear, was I responsible for that? She returned to reality with a jolt as she recalled his freshly washed—and combed—hair when she had come to his room earlier. What must Trant have thought?

'Lucas,' she acknowledged. It was ridiculous to insist on calling him 'sir' when his hand had so recently... Mary felt her cheeks heat. She must not forget Lucas did not want *her*.

Lucas picked up his brandy glass and drained the contents in one gulp. Hardly aware she did so, Mary stepped back. Lucas focused on her and frowned.

'Do not run away, Mary. We have some unfinished business.'

Mary felt her colour flare. He couldn't mean...?

A sarcastic bark of laughter stopped her torrent of thoughts in mid-flow. 'Not that! Are you aware, my sweet Mary, that every thought you have is writ large in those beautiful blue eyes of yours? I shall put your mind at ease. I am devastated to inform you, much as I long to finish what we started earlier, I am afraid my body has other ideas. That is, certain parts of my body—to whit, my cursed thigh, which still pains me, and my shoulder.'

His voice softened and deepened. 'Come here, Mary.'

He held out his hand out, long fingers beckoning. As if in a dream, she moved close enough to put her hand in his. His gaze caressed her face as his thumb traced lazy circles on the sensitive skin of her inner wrist, setting her pulse racing again. Anticipation smouldered deep within her belly.

'That is the reason I stopped, Mary, not because I did not want you. The rest of my body, I am pleased to report, is eager and ready. In fact,' he added, wrapping his fingers around her hand and pulling her gently towards him, 'I am finding it hard to resist trying again, even though I know the same thing will happen.'

It took all her resolve but Mary pulled her hand from his grasp. 'You mentioned unfinished business?'

His eyes crinkled at the corners. 'Transparent as ever, my dear. Yes, we shall change the subject, if you wish.

'I have realised, Mary, despite several attempts on my part to discover your destination when you leave the Hall, you have deliberately diverted my attention. You must have a plan? Some destination in mind? Or am I to believe you intend to wander aimlessly for the remainder of your days?'

A direct question; one she would struggle to answer honestly, for she would then be forced to reveal her father's betrayal and the reason for her elopement. She sat on the chair by the bed, fussing over her skirts whilst she tried to order her thoughts. How well did Lucas know her father? He would recognise his name, for certain. Would he send word to her father that she was here, at the Hall? How could she justify her willingness to go back to a man such as her father without revealing the existence of her children? Her mind whirled, but she could think of no way of further diverting Lucas.

'You are inventing a story again. I can see it in your expression. You are wondering what you can say to prevent my probing further. Why the big secret, Mary? What are you ashamed of?'

'I am not ashamed,' Mary retorted, stung. 'There is no secret. I am returning to my family home. You are making a mystery where there is none. The reality is humdrum, of no interest to anyone, least of all you.'

'I should like to be the judge of that. Where is your home? How far?'

Mary chewed her lip. Rothley waited. Finally, she could bear the silence no longer.

'Linburgh.'

'Linburgh? Who is your father? I may know of him—my father had many acquaintances over in that part of the Borders.'

'My father is William Cranston,' Mary bit out.

'Sir William Cranston? I have not had the pleasure myself, but….' His voice tailed away and Mary stiffened. How would he react, when he remembered? 'As I recall, Mary, there was no love lost between our respective sires.' Rothley's expression revealed nothing of his thoughts. 'If I were a suspicious man, I might wonder at your presence on my land at the same time an attempt was being made to steal my sheep.'

Mary gasped. He could not believe? Surely…?

She had wondered if Rothley might bear any animosity towards her family from the time his father had accused hers of stealing his cattle—despite having no proof—but it had not occurred to her he might construe her presence in such a way.

'No! You must not—'

'Relax, my dear.' Lucas laughed, grabbing her hand as she started to rise. 'I am teasing. Although… if I remember rightly, you did attempt to steal my horse on that occasion. Like father, like daughter, mayhap?'

Mary eyed him doubtfully. 'You *are* still teasing me, Lucas?'

'Do you really need to ask? I hope I am a better judge of character, Mary, than to believe you have a dishonest bone in your body. Tell me, is that old feud the reason you have been so reticent about your past?'

Mary nodded.

'You silly goose. You are not your father, as I am not…at least…' Lucas paused, frowning. Mary wondered what new thought troubled him. His chest rose as he inhaled '…at least, I have no interest in perpetuating my father's old feuds,' he finished.

Did that mean he was his father's son in other ways? There was a faraway look in his dark eyes and Mary wondered what memories stirred, prompted by this talk of their fathers? She longed to smooth his furrowed brow. A few moments passed, then Lucas seemed to shake out of his reverie.

'What I cannot understand is why your father did not send you the means to travel home, Mary?'

Mary stared down at her clasped hands.

'Is he even aware you are on your way?' From the corner of her eye, she could see him study her, another frown creasing his brow.

'No.'

'Would you care to explain why?'

She would prefer not to, but the stubborn set to his mouth persuaded Mary that Lucas was not to be deflected.

'I married against his wishes.' He did not need to know the full story of her father's betrayal of her. 'I wrote to him after Michael died last year, but I received no reply.'

'And your husband's family?'

'He had none.' She looked down at her lap, smoothing the fabric of her dress over her knees. 'He was working for my father when we met. My father was...my father would never have sanctioned our marriage and we eloped.'

It had not been, strictly, an elopement. Mary had enlisted Michael's help to run away, intending to find work and support herself. He had turned up that night with his bags ready packed, full of plans for their future together and she—unworldly, vulnerable and barely seventeen—had bowed to his judgement.

'How very romantic,' Lucas said.

Mary flinched at that dry observation. Romantic was the last word she would use to describe that midnight flight, but Lucas did not need to know it had been born out of pure desperation. And for all Michael's faults in the latter years of their marriage, he had, she was aware, saved her from a far worse fate. For that, and for her beautiful children, she would always hold gratitude in her heart.

'You are clearly a lady and well educated. Why did you not seek further employment in the Newcastle area? Why did you choose to embark on such a long and difficult journey to a place where your welcome is by no means assured?'

Why indeed?

He sounded suspicious and she sensed his withdrawal. Mary paused, searching for the right words.

'I wanted to make my peace with my father. I am an only child. I am all he has since my mother died. I thought…' She trailed into silence, conscious how insincere she sounded. 'I have nowhere else to go.'

'Was your childhood a happy one, Mary?'

His tone was brusque and she felt her cheeks heat. She concentrated on her hands, fisted in her lap.

'I have heard past tales about your father. They did not flatter the man and they did not—despite what you may think—all originate from my own father's opinion of him.'

She could not dispute that. She had no need of tales. She had lived the reality. She pushed herself up from the chair. 'Please excuse me, Lucas. I am very tired. I wish to go to bed now. Is there anything I can get you before I go?'

His eyes were distant and he made no attempt to dissuade her from leaving. He indicated the empty glass on the bedside table.

'Please refill that before you go, if you will. Or, better still, pass me the bottle.'

Mary handed the bottle of brandy to Lucas and he murmured his thanks as he refilled his glass. She shuddered in distaste at the pungent smell.

'You reeked of brandy when I found you in the woods,' she blurted out.

Lucas paused in the act of raising the glass to his lips. He raised one brow. 'And?'

'Were you drunk, when you were shot?'

He laughed. 'No, *Suspicious* Mary, I was not. I

poured brandy on my wounds. Hurt like the very devil, too.'

Mary released the breath she hadn't realised she was holding. Mayhap Lucas was not as in thrall to the bottle as she had feared. It changed nothing, though. She walked to the door.

'Was Cranston a kind father to you, Mary?' Lucas asked as she reached for the door handle. 'Is he likely to prove forgiving?'

She bit her lip as she considered her reply. 'Kind? Not in later years. Forgiving? I doubt it.' She would not lie.

'And yet still you are going back.'

She bowed her head. She could offer no further explanation. 'Goodnight, Lucas. Sleep well.'

Lucas was awoken by Trant early the following morning. He had a thumping headache from lack of sleep and a sour mouth from the brandy he had drunk in an effort to dampen his unfulfilled desire for Mary. He had barely drunk two glasses, but felt more like he'd imbibed a couple of bottles of the stuff. He ran his tongue over his teeth and grimaced, then winced as Trant opened the curtains, flooding the room with light. Squinting, he watched as the valet rekindled the fire and approached the bed holding a breakfast tray. Lucas sat up, then groaned as the room spun like the whirligigs that inhabited the loughs in the summer.

'Are you in pain, my lord?' Trant's eyes flicked towards the bottle and glass on the bedside table.

Curse the man. Trant had seen him too often in his cups in his wild youth. Lucas did not want him to think he was sliding back into old habits.

'I had but two glasses, Trant. I slept badly, that is all.'

Going over what he had learned about Mary. Not liking the conclusions he had come to.

'Should I send for the doctor?'

'That will not be necessary, thank you. I will eat breakfast and then try to catch up on my sleep.'

'Very good, my lord, I shall ensure no one disturbs you.'

He had started to believe Mary might be different, that he could trust her, but the long hours of the night had fuelled his doubts. He could come up with only one explanation for her going back to her father rather than seeking employment and it threw a harsh light on her character.

He finished his breakfast, then lay down and tried to sleep.

Mary's image shimmered on his eyelids: the curve of her cheek; the sweep of her lashes; her collarbone, so delicate under his caress. His heart squeezed in his chest. Could she really be as idle and selfish as Julia? Yesterday he would have said no, but now...

Lucas rolled over and thumped the pillow that now felt full of lumps.

He had never felt more the need to confide in someone. Ironically, the first person who came to mind as a trusted confidante was Mary herself. How could that be? Despite the suspicions that had plagued him through the night, she remained the person he wanted most to open his heart to. He longed to trust her, but could he?

He forced himself to lie still, but sleep continued to evade him.

He dredged up every story and titbit of gossip he could remember about William Cranston. Mary's father had visited Rothley Hall on a number of occasions during Lucas's childhood, before his relationship with the old marquis had turned sour over an allegation of cheating at cards. Lucas had been away at Oxford at the time. The occasional story had filtered down south since then: tales of drunkenness, violence and—according to his father—theft. A charming individual if even half the tales were true. Why on earth would Mary voluntarily return to such a despot?

Eventually, a tap sounded at the door and Mary's voice announced she had brought his luncheon tray.

He abandoned any thought of sleep. He needed to understand, but hesitated over how best to broach the subject.

He would eat his food and then he would try to find out exactly why Mary sought protection from a man she should despise and fear.

Chapter Thirteen

As soon as she set foot in the room, Mary sensed Rothley's constraint. She was surprised to find him still in bed, but made no comment as she laid the tray across his lap. She had heard Trant tell Ellen his lordship had been at the brandy. In her opinion, it served him right if he had a sore head as a consequence. She would not waste her sympathy on someone whose ills were self-inflicted; neither did she excuse his bad manners in not acknowledging her beyond a muttered 'Thank you'.

The intimacy they had shared last evening might never have happened. How she wished she had not gone back to his bedchamber afterwards. He would still be ignorant of her identity and would not now be treating her as an unwelcome intruder. She choked down the threat of tears. She could not bear this atmosphere.

As soon as Lucas began to eat, Mary headed for the door.

'Don't go, Mary. Stay and bear me company.'

His tone was brusque. Mary hesitated, unsure how to deal with this new Lucas. She forced a smile. 'Is that an order?'

His dark brows contracted. With his unshaven jaw and tousled hair he looked dangerous—piratical almost—but also sinfully attractive. Her heart beat faster against her ribcage as she imagined caressing his stubbled cheeks and tasting his lips. Despite his less-than-welcoming mood, she still tingled at the memory of his touch, still yearned for him to hold her. She tensed, feeling her false smile fade.

'No. If it sounded like one, I apologise,' he said.

Mary hovered near the door until Lucas beckoned to her. 'Come, Mary. Sit here. Please.'

For one brief moment she considered leaving, but what would that achieve? She must face his questions at some point. Better to get the worst over with, than to fret about what was to come. She crossed to his side and sat by the bed, watching as he continued his meal. He concentrated on his plate, shooting an occasional brooding glance in her direction.

'I understand you've been unwell this morning,' she said, more to break the silence than from a wish to know how he felt.

'Not unwell, merely tired. I didn't sleep well last night.'

Neither did I. She had been thinking about her father and worrying over Lucas's reaction to their conversation of the night before. Rightly so, it seemed. It had, as she had feared, affected their relationship—their growing friendship, she told herself firmly—and not for the better. Still, what did it matter? She would have to leave soon. The day was drawing ever closer—the day when she could no longer delay setting off on the final leg of her journey to her childhood home.

'What do you do with yourself, when you are not here pandering to my whims?' Mary jumped as Lucas's voice interrupted her thoughts. 'I feel very isolated, stuck up here whilst everyone else is going about their daily business.'

It was not the subject he wished to debate, she knew. That—the matter of her father and why she would choose to return to such a man—loomed large and unspoken between them.

'I help Mrs Lindley and the others where I can,' she said.

Silence reigned once more and Mary could feel his eyes on her. She tightened her lips and plaited her fingers in her lap, squeezing until the skin over her knuckles shone white.

'What is it you are not telling me? I can hear in your voice you are hiding something.'

She couldn't tell him the truth. When she wasn't with him, she was with the children. The old nursery at the top of the back stairs had been utilised as a temporary schoolroom, where she sometimes played with and read to the children and taught Toby his letters and numbers, and helped Emily with her speech. She was improving all the time, but still Mary worried over how little time she spent with them. When she was with Lucas the children spent their time in the kitchen with Mrs Lindley or accompanied Susan on her lighter duties.

Mary sighed. She could tell by his expression he wasn't about to drop the subject.

'It has been difficult, since you spoke to Mrs Lindley about making changes.' That, at least, was the truth. 'I appear to be in everybody's bad books,' she went on. 'I have tried to explain, but they cannot—or will not—see their workload will be vastly improved with the changes being made. But I cannot blame them altogether. From their point of view, I instigated the changes and then I was unavailable for most of yesterday, leaving them with all the extra work. By the time I visited Jenny and then came up to see you in the afternoon, they had finished and were busy in the kitchen.'

'You are not a servant. You should not be doing menial tasks.'

'I am no delicate flower, either. I am happy to help out where I can. I have become used to it, over the years. Do you not turn your hand to so-called menial tasks on occasion? When there is too much work for your men to handle?'

Lucas shrugged. 'Once in a while,' he acknowledged. 'I take your point, although how my household is run is not your concern.'

'Is that a reprimand?' The old Mary—conciliatory and cautious—would never have confronted her father or her husband in such a way, but she had no qualms about challenging Lucas in the face of such an unfair comment. She had asked for his support in changing the routine of the household and he had given it, even to the extent of instructing Mrs Lindley about them.

He looked directly at her for the first time since she had entered his room. 'It was not meant to be.'

He ran one long-fingered hand through his hair, ruffling it even further. Mary's thoughts flew to the night before, feeling again the silkiness of his black locks slipping through her fingers. An unbearable ache squeezed her chest.

'I chose my words badly,' he was continuing. 'What I meant to convey is that you are not responsible for the household in the same way in which I am responsible for the estate. I am sorry. Blame it on tiredness. I am not myself this morning.'

'Well, that is good news,' Mary said with an attempt at levity, 'for it is now the afternoon and I shall expect an immediate return to the jovial, articulate Lord Rothley I have become used to.'

'Minx!'

He smiled at her, but it appeared forced and, all too soon, he lapsed once more into brooding silence, his full attention on his food.

Despite his current mood, she realised her original wariness of Lucas had vanished, to be replaced by...? Here her newfound insight collapsed. She glanced at him. He was staring at the window, arms folded, his mouth a hard line, his dark brows lowered. As she watched, his chest rose and he moistened his lips.

'Should I call Trant?' she said quickly, keen to delay the dreaded conversation about her father. 'Would you like to go to the Blue Room?'

'No. Not yet.'

Silence reigned once more, the tension in the room palpable. Nerves churned her stomach and she felt her heart thump against her ribcage. She thought frantically for some way of diverting him from the subject of her father.

'Mary…'

Mary looked up and their eyes fused. Her name hung in the air between them. Desire curled deep within her as awareness flared in his eyes. Her blood quickened and fire coursed through her veins. She licked at dry lips. Dark eyes followed the movement, then lifted to penetrate, it felt, deep into her soul.

Distraction.

That would work and she had no need to pretend. She dropped her gaze, fixing hungrily on those smooth lips that could tantalise and tease in a way she had never felt before, nor imagined could exist.

Without volition, she reached out, touching his cheek, the stubble prickling her skin. His breathing suspended as she feathered her fingertips along his jaw, lingering over the strong cleft in his chin. She raised her eyes to his as her fingers inched upwards until they lay against his firm, beautiful lips. Warm air moistened her skin as he exhaled. As she watched, his lids lowered and he kissed her fingertips, each in turn, his lips soft and gentle.

His hand lifted. Long fingers threaded through her hair and cradled her skull as he eased her closer, angling her head. Her hand moved to his chest, the hair at the open neck of his nightshirt rough to her fingertips. She felt his heartbeat, strong and fast, as their lips met. She leaned into the kiss—a slow, sensual caress of the lips. A gentle nip to her bottom lip, followed by the soothing sweep of his tongue encouraged her to open to him and he explored her mouth with leisurely strokes. Her breasts were heavy and tender, craving his touch, and hot desire pooled deep in her belly but, all too soon, he took his lips from hers. She whimpered in protest. He bent his head, resting his forehead against hers, and gazed deep into her eyes.

'What is happening between us, Mary Vale? Are you a sorceress sent to bewitch me?'

His breath caressed her sensitised lips. Mary suppressed the shiver of her response.

'I do not know,' she whispered. 'I only know it cannot be.'

He straightened, his hands on her shoulders, pushing her from him. There was vulnerability in his expression: vulnerability and pain. She had no time to wonder at that, for he was speaking, a new determination in his voice.

'Your father...our conversation last night... I need to understand why you are going back to a place where it seems you were unhappy.'

What could she say? She was going back purely for the sake of her children. She had no other choice. It was that, or the workhouse. But she couldn't tell him that. Not for the first time, she wondered at his aversion to children. It still made no sense to her. To hide her consternation, she went to the fireplace, fussing around, poking the fire and adding more fuel.

'Leave that!'

Reluctantly, Mary returned to the side of the bed, determined to mask her discomfort as he scrutinised her from head to toe. That loving moment between them might never have happened. Mary's head reeled. No words would come.

'I will repeat my question,' Rothley said in a soft voice. 'Why do you go to him, when it would seem you are unlikely to be made welcome? Why not get a post? You could be—oh, I don't know: a governess? A housekeeper maybe? You have been used to work. Or is that the reason?' His eyes narrowed and his voice hardened. 'Have you had your fill of working hard for a mere pittance and long for a life of idleness and riches?'

Mary was left confused and floundering as she tried to adjust to this mercurial change in Lucas. One moment he was full of sympathy, the next he was condemning her. Perhaps she had given him cause, after the way she had behaved.

Let him believe the worst of me. I shall be gone soon and his opinion of me will no longer matter.

To her dismay, the thought of never seeing Lucas

again—to never again feel his lips take hers or experience the sensual, urgent craving they invoked—twisted like a knife in her heart. In near despair, she tried to deny those thoughts: they were false, conjured up by her weak body and its base needs, masquerading as true feelings.

If that is true, a small voice of dissent whispered inside her head, *and what you feel for Lucas is purely physical, why did you not accept Simon Wendover's offer?*

She had no answer to give, neither to her conscience nor to Lucas. She remained silent, lowering her eyes before the accusation burning in his.

'Well?' he snapped. 'Is that it? Are you as fickle as the rest of your sex, wanting a man for the sole purpose of keeping you in luxuries?'

Stung, Mary glared at him. Why was he attacking her?

'You must know that is not true! If I was such a woman, would I not have accepted your offer?'

'You have been at the Hall sufficient time to realise there are no luxuries to be had,' he said bitterly. 'Hard work and going without awaits any soul who allies themselves to me.'

'How little you know me, if you believe riches and an easy life to be my goal. I am not afraid of hard work.' She took his hand, gripping it with the urgent need to convince him. She could no longer deny her growing feelings. She could not bear his bitter tone. 'You know…I have read it in your eyes…my feelings…how I feel…' Her voice faltered. How could she even think of saying such a thing? Could she really admit to her growing regard for him? Would that not be the same as throwing herself willingly upon his bed?

His dark brows scowled, but his eyes still exuded pain. A memory surfaced. The memory of a name, uttered in despair, cried from the hot, dark depths of fever.

'Who is Julia?'

His eyes flashed and his face darkened. Mary's courage almost deserted her, her stomach twisting as she fought against her instinct to retreat. She needed to understand why he was so ready to believe the worst of her motives. His feverish mutterings had revealed enough for Mary to know his memories of Julia were not happy ones. She couldn't deny it had piqued her curiosity. And stirred her jealousy. Had Lucas been in love with Julia?

'What did you say?' he growled. 'Where did you hear her name?'

Mary gritted her teeth. 'Julia,' she said. 'I asked who she is. You spoke her name in the woods and during your fever. I have told you of my past; now I am asking about yours.'

A part of her stood aside, marvelling at her own courage. Again, this was not the Mary of old. She realised with pride that, having relied on her own resources for some time, she had grown stronger. She lifted her chin, holding his gaze, seeing beyond the fury in his eyes and his lowered brow.

'It is a reasonable request.'

'I am entitled to know about *your* past. You are a part of my household...'

'But I am not in your employ. I am not a part of your household in the sense you imply,' Mary pointed out, determined not to be intimidated. 'Why should I not ask you a question? If it causes you pain...'

A loud wail suddenly rent the air, then was cut short. The house fell silent, almost as though it held its breath.

'What the...?' Lucas half-rose from his bed, twisting awkwardly, then flopped back again with a curse. 'A thousand curses, that hurt!' he groaned as he clutched at his shoulder.

Mary stood frozen, shocked into temporary immobility by the sound of Emily's cry.

'What on earth was that?'

Mary was spurred into action. 'Nothing,' she

gasped as, frantic, she rushed for the door, visions of her beautiful daughter, crumpled in a heap at the bottom of the stairs or flattened by falling masonry in this ruin of a house, crowding her mind.

'Mary! What...?'

She slammed the door shut behind her and looked up and down the landing outside his bedchamber. The cry had sounded close. Biting back a sob, she headed for the stairs. There, at the top of the staircase, stood a guilty-looking Toby, with Emily clutched in his arms, her sobs muffled against his chest. Susan, looking frantic, was hurrying up the stairs towards the children.

'Toby!' Mary gasped. 'What happened? Is Emily all right? What are you doing up here?' She took Emily from Toby's grasp and folded her young daughter into her arms, comforting her.

'Ooh, ma'am, I'm sorry. I turned my back for a moment and they were gone. Is Emily hurt?'

Toby's head hung whilst he scuffed his foot against the bare boards of the landing floor.

'I'm sorry, Mama,' he said as a lone tear trickled down his cheek.

Mary was overcome with remorse at the sight of her forlorn little boy. She had been neglecting her children again whilst caring for—and lusting after—Lucas. Despite their welcome at the Hall, the servants were still virtual strangers to two young children who had only ever been used to the care and nurture of their mother.

'Toby, lovey, it's all right, I'm not cross with you. Why are you up here?' She crouched down and wrapped her arm around Toby, who nuzzled into her shoulder.

'I wanted to see where you were, Mama,' he said, his voice muffled. 'I was scared the bad man will hurt you. And Em'ly followed me!' He lifted his head and bent an accusing stare on his sister. 'I told her to go back to the kitchen, but she followed me up the stairs, so...'

'He pinch me!' Emily's voice rose into another wail. 'Toby pinch me, Mama!'

'Hush, Emily...'

'Be quiet, Em'ly!' The panic in Toby's voice was clear. 'Stop it or the bad man will hear you...'

'Too late.' The sardonic drawl sounded from behind the small group clustered at the top of the stairs. 'The bad man has already heard.'

Chapter Fourteen

Lucas stood on the galleried landing, leaning against a wall to take the weight off his injured leg, and glared at the group gathered at the head of the staircase.

'Would someone care to tell me what is going on?'

The small boy took one look at him, screamed and then clutched hold of Mary, whilst the child in her arms cried even harder. The children, no doubt, were the product of her marriage to Michael Vale. A shaft of jealousy ripped through Lucas, shocking him with its strength. He clenched both his jaw and his fists against the unaccustomed emotion. Out of the corner of his eye he noticed Susan back away from him, her face pale.

As well she might, he thought with bitter self-loathing. *After all, I have been, it would appear, cast as the Bad Man in this scenario. And perhaps with good cause—my temper has not been the sweetest since I came home. But then, what else do they expect? I am, as they are so fond of telling me, just like my father.*

Mary stared up at him from where she crouched on the floor, rebellion in her eyes. Seeing beyond the defiance, though, he glimpsed trepidation.

'Well?' he bit out, irritated at the prolonged silence that greeted his question and even angrier at the memory of Mary's caution around him.

Her reticence now made sense. He had recognised her passionate nature from the first but, until last night, something had held her back, erecting a barrier that prevented her fully responding to him as her body clearly wished. There had been no logical reason for her to deny her desires—she was a widow, not some wide-eyed innocent with dreams of love.

'Well?' he repeated, his temper continuing its climb.

Mary glared at him, before bending her head over the children once more, murmuring. As the child's cries quietened, she rose to her feet, pushing the children behind her.

'The children were looking for me, my lord. I am sorry they disturbed you. It won't happen again.'

She was back to 'my lord'-ing him again: a sure sign of her anger.

'The children are yours?' It was obvious, but he asked anyway.

Before she could reply, there was a bustle on the stairs and Mrs Lindley panted into view, followed by Ellen and Trant.

'Oh, wonderful,' Lucas muttered in exasperation. 'Now we have the entire household disrupted. And, as you are now all here, can someone please explain why I wasn't informed of the presence of children in my house? You are all aware of my views on the subject, are you not?'

'Of course the children are mine,' Mary snapped. 'And the reason you weren't told they were here is precisely because of the unreasonable way you are reacting now.'

There was an audible gasp from Susan but, out of the corner of his eye, Lucas was aware of Mrs Lindley nudging Ellen, identical amused expressions on their faces.

Curse all old family retainers! 'Unreasonable? And why, might I enquire, do you deem it unreasonable for a man to dictate his own lifestyle in his own household, Sensible Mary?'

Her colour rose and he saw the familiar flash of hurt anger in her direct gaze. Well, if she was going to 'my lord' him…! He quashed his shame over the pettiness of that thought.

'Of course, it is not unreasonable to have your own views. I apologise,' she added stiffly. 'But might I remind you I have helped that same household in caring for you whilst you were indisposed and where I am, my children are. We shall gather our belongings immediately and...'

The small boy stepped from behind Mary's skirts and stood at her side, clutching at her hand. He was trembling, Lucas could see, but he glared up at Lucas nevertheless.

'I found your blood,' he announced in an accusing tone. 'We rescued you.'

Despite his fury at having his orders overridden—and, astonishingly, his hurt at being excluded—Lucas experienced a sneaking admiration for the way the boy, despite his obvious terror, stood up for his mother. He had done much the same for his own mother, until he had learnt that any defiance of his father resulted in more punishment for them both.

'Hush, Toby.' Mary cast an apprehensive look at Lucas. 'Susan—please will you take the children downstairs whilst I speak with his lordship? I shall be down very shortly.'

'Yes, you can all go,' Lucas said. 'The spectacle is over. The bad man is not going to hurt anyone. Not this time anyway.'

'Noooooooo, Mama, noooo,' the boy wailed,

clinging to Mary's arm, his eyes glued to Lucas as tears streamed down his face. 'Come with me, Mama, pleeeease. I don't want you to stay with him.'

Mary cast Lucas a fulminating glare before kneeling by her son. She folded him into her arms and rocked him whilst she murmured in his ear, words too quiet for Lucas to make out. Lucas stood his ground, staring stonily at the tableau before him, until Mary planted a kiss on the boy's cheek, then urged him towards Susan, waiting at the head of the stairs.

Susan gathered the children and ushered them down the stairs, followed by the rest of his household, but within seconds Trant was back.

'Doctor Preece, my lord,' he announced, then promptly disappeared again.

'Well, well, well—' a jovial voice could be heard from below '—no wonder I couldn't make myself heard at the kitchen door, for here you all are. I let myself in.' He climbed the last of the stairs and then stopped short. 'Lucas!' he exclaimed. 'What are you doing? Mrs Vale, I am surprised at you. I had thought you to have more sense than to allow—'

'Do not place any blame at Mary's feet, Robert.' Lucas pushed away from the wall he had been leaning against. 'I was anxious to find out what was going on in my household.'

'Going on? What do you mean?' The doctor turned his puzzled frown from Lucas to Mary and back again.

'His lordship is referring to the fact that I have had the temerity to conceal my children in his household,' Mary said acerbically. 'However, my lord, you need concern yourself no longer, for I shall leave immediately and take my two dangerous, undesirable children with me.'

Her voice trembled over her final words and Lucas saw the sheen of unshed tears in her eyes. Shame at being the cause of her distress swamped him. He looked at Robert, whose bewildered expression did nothing to make Lucas feel any better.

'There is no need for that, Mary,' he said. 'You do not need to leave. As you said earlier, an extra pair of hands whilst I am indisposed is a great help.' Her eyes rose to his, hope shining from their depths. Hope that withered at his next words: 'If you keep the children out of my way, all can continue as before.'

Shame spread through him again, along with irritation that he still felt such a sense of responsibility for Mary's happiness. Hadn't he been awake half the night, stewing over his growing distrust of both her and her motives? Why did she still affect him so very much?

He felt his knees sag. 'I think I need to rest now,' he muttered as he steadied himself against the wall.

Mary was by his side in an instant, placing his arm across her shoulders and her own arm around his waist.

'Well, Mary, this is cosy' he said, looking down at her.

She was so tiny against him. He recalled his parents with a shudder. His father had never allowed his mother's fragility to inhibit his aggression whenever his temper got the better of him.

'I can manage!' He tore his arm from Mary's shoulders and stumbled along the landing to the Blue Room, the memory of Mary's hurt expression burning into his brain. He heard a whispered exchange, then Robert followed him into the room and closed the door behind him, pacing around the room until Lucas had settled on to the *chaise longue*. As he lay back, relieved he had not passed out, Robert pulled a chair forward and sat down to face him.

'What was all that about, Luke?'

The unexpected use of his childhood name brought a lump to Lucas's throat. Gritting his teeth, he swallowed past it. He was a grown man now and entitled to behave as he wished in his own house. Why then did he feel guilty, as though it was he who was in the wrong? He was not the one colluding at secrets. He felt betrayed by the two people he had begun to trust.

'I never wanted children in this house. It isn't safe.'

'I actually meant why did you reject Mary's help in such an unforgivable manner but, as you broach the subject, what do you mean by *it isn't safe*? Why should the Hall be unsafe for children?' A puzzled frown creased Robert's brow.

'It is not the house that is unsafe. It is me. You, of all people, should know. You knew my father; he was a vicious tyrant.'

'But your father is dead.' Robert looked perplexed.

'I am his son. I have his temper. I will not subject any child to that.'

There was a protracted silence. Lucas avoided Robert's gaze. He had no need to look to know what he would see in his expression: pity, condemnation, disgust.

'You are not your father.' The words were quietly spoken, but none the less reverberated around the room. 'If you do not care to be governed by your temper, as he was, then you have the choice to be different.'

There was a further pause. Lucas continued to stare down at his own clenched fists.

'And my original question?' Robert continued. 'Why were you so antagonistic towards Mary? She has done nothing but help since she first arrived, yet you rebuffed her assistance as though she were made of poison. Is this what you have become? Is this how you repay the people who care about you, Lucas? The people who help you?'

The words hit Lucas like hammer blows. He had not meant to hurt Mary. He had thought to protect her. 'She reminded me of my mother.'

'Your mother?' Robert's voice was incredulous. 'She is nothing like your mother.'

'She's tiny, like Mama. She could never stand up to me.'

Robert gave a short laugh. 'Maybe not physically,' he said. 'But it's my belief she would give you a run for your money in every other way. She is a strong lady, despite her size. She has had a hard life, Luke.'

Lucas's feelings were in turmoil. He wanted her, so badly it was a physical ache, but when he looked into her eyes it resurrected memories of Julia. And, earlier, he had seen his mother, dwarfed by his father. He could not risk hurting her as his father hurt his mother. And now he had discovered the secret he had sensed was being kept from him by everyone around him.

The children.

Hers.

She was a mother. She was more distant than ever.

'Let me take a look at you, then,' Robert said. 'Turn over.' He examined Lucas's thigh. 'That's healed well. Now, how are you feeling in yourself?'

'I'm well enough, Rob. I want to go downstairs. I must see to my business.'

Robert looked at him, brows raised. 'You were very shaky just now, on the landing. Be rational, Lucas. Give yourself time. I understand you have been overseeing estate business from up here, with Mary's help. You know all is in hand. I fail to see any advantage in you being downstairs instead of up here. You are still weak…'

'I am tired of being weak. I need to—'

'You need to regain your strength. Mary—'

'I do not wish to depend on her any longer. She is going to her father's house.'

The words were a far cry from the truth. He was not ready to say goodbye to Mary. Not yet. *Or ever…?* He shook his head, conflicting thoughts crowding his brain.

'Is that where she is heading? I have not discussed her future plans with her. I shall be sorry to see her leave, she has uplifted everyone's spirits in the time she has been here.

'I would still advise you to wait a few more days before tackling the stairs, Lucas. Walk around this room; build up your strength gradually. Do not be too impatient, there is nothing you can do down-stairs you cannot achieve from here.'

'Is everything all right, ma'am?' Susan, face pale with worry, hurried up to Mary as she entered the kitchen. 'What did his lordship say about the bairns?'

Mary glanced around. The room was empty apart from Toby and Emily. 'He said we do not need to leave…'

Susan's face brightened. 'Well, that's good, isn't it?'

'…as long as the children are kept out of his way.'

Mary felt her temper simmer. How dare Lucas talk of her children as though they were vermin to be hidden from sight? She watched them as they played happily near the fire, all upset seemingly forgotten. How could any adult resent such innocent beings? What thoughts were inside his head? She could not begin to understand him.

She recalled the way he had snatched his arm from her shoulders, as though he couldn't bear to have physical contact with her. The abrupt rejection still stung. He hadn't felt that way when he kissed her. She felt as though the weight of the world was back on her shoulders—a feeling she hadn't experienced since her arrival at the Hall. She needed to get out of the house, to breathe in the clean, cool air, to feel the wind in her face and the earth beneath her feet.

'I shall take the children outside for some fresh air,' she told Susan. She raised her voice, 'Toby, Emily, come along. Fetch your coats. We are going for a walk.'

Outside, they headed along the front drive, lined with magnificent horse-chestnut trees, their leaves already painted golden and red by the shortening of the days. The afternoon was dry and mild, the light breeze whirling the few early fallen leaves in eddies beneath their feet. Mary strode along, tugging each of the children by the hand until Emily brought her back to the present with a heartfelt wail.

'Mama! Too fast!'

Guiltily, Mary stopped. She crouched down to give her daughter a hug. 'I'm sorry, sweetie,' she said. 'I wasn't thinking. I...'

'Mama!' Toby shook her shoulder. 'Mama, some-one's coming.'

Mary glanced back towards the Hall, expecting to see the doctor in his gig, but there was no one there.

'*That* way, Mama,' Toby said, pulling Mary's arm, pointing away from the Hall.

Mary glanced along the drive in the opposite direction, towards where she knew the big, iron gates that flanked the main entrance to the Hall opened out on to the road to the village of Rothley. A man astride a rangy bay horse rode towards them at an easy canter. Mary had wondered several times at the lack of visitors to the Hall, although she knew from Mrs Lindley that Lucas discouraged interaction with his neighbours. Quite why was yet another mystery, much like the reason he had banned children. In fact, he did not appear to care overmuch for anyone at all, she thought in disgust, although it seemed his neighbours were more forgiving than he deserved, as this was surely one of them come to enquire after his recovery.

She watched with interest as the rider came ever closer, slowing to a trot and then to a walk as he neared the small group on the edge of the driveway. As he came within hailing distance, however, a familiarity about the visitor sparked a flicker of unease. Mary viewed his approach with increasing concern. Rothley Hall was not many miles from the area where she grew up and she acknowledged, for the first time, the likelihood of meeting someone from her past whilst staying at the Hall.

Chapter Fifteen

The gentleman drew his mount to a halt and doffed his hat. With horror, Mary recognised him.

Sir Gerald Quartly!

Older than when she had last set eyes on him—he must be close on fifty by now, the same age as her father—and even heavier, the years of debauchery clearly having taken their toll. Nausea swelled her throat as she clutched at the children's hands.

'Good afternoon,' he said. 'I must confess this is quite a surprise. I had not thought Rothley had set up his nursery quite yet, or mayhap you are a visitor, madam? Sir Gerald Quartly, at your service.' He bowed, his sharp grey eyes glued to Mary's face. 'Enchanted to make your acquaintance, Mrs...?'

'Mrs Vale, sir,' Mary replied, grateful her bonnet shielded her hair and part of her face from his scrutiny. She thought he had not recognised her, but she felt the urgent need to remove herself and her children from his presence as soon as possible. 'We are visitors to the Hall, sir. Lord Rothley is—'

'Ah, yes, Rothley,' he interrupted. 'Rumour has it he has had an unfortunate accident. I do hope he is not seriously indisposed?'

'He is recov—'

'Have we met?' Quartly spoke over Mary's words once again. He was, she saw, quite as ill mannered as she remembered. She suppressed a shudder at the memory of the few times their paths had crossed at her father's house, times when those same grey eyes had raked her up and down, leaving her feeling as though she had been stripped bare before him.

She forced herself to hold his gaze. 'I do not believe so, sir,' she said with as much hauteur as she could summon. 'Now, if you will excuse me? I shall tell Lord Rothley you called to enquire after his health. I am afraid the doctor is with him at present, so I shall save you the futility of continuing as far as the Hall. Perhaps you would care to call another day?'

Quartly's face darkened at her words. 'I shall be sure to do that, m'dear,' he said, not bothering to conceal his irritation. 'You can give a message to your...' his eyes raked her insolently '...to Rothley for me. You tell him the Quarter Day is fast approaching. He will understand.'

Mary inclined her head, battling to keep her emotions from her face lest she inadvertently prompted a memory within him.

'Good day.' Quartly wheeled his horse round and set off for the gates at a brisk trot.

Mary, shaking, watched him go before turning the children towards the Hall. She scanned the honey-coloured stone walls ahead. The Hall might be rambling and shabby, but she had become fond of it in the time she had been there. She would be sad to leave, but could delay no longer. If Sir Gerald should remember her... She quickened her pace, hoisting Emily on to her hip when she wailed her protest.

Mary entered the front door with a heavy heart.

Trant accosted her almost immediately. 'Mrs Vale, his lordship is asking for you.'

Mary's stomach churned, nervy butterflies flitting through her.

'Did you tell him I was out for a walk?'

'I did, ma'am, but...'

'But...?'

'He seemed to believe, ma'am, that you might have left us. He became quite agitated...he was most insistent you attend him *the minute* you return.'

'Was he indeed?' Mary stripped her gloves off with a display of nonchalance that belied the tumultuous feelings flooding her mind and her body.

Her emotions had been in turmoil ever since Lucas's hurtful rejection of her and the unexpected meeting with Sir Gerald Quartly had increased her worries. One thing she knew for certain, she was in no state to face Lucas at the moment. Besides, after his treatment of her earlier, it would do him good to understand she was not at his beck and call. He must get used to it, for she was decided upon leaving in the morning.

She took off the children's coats. 'Where is Susan, please, Trant?'

'In the small sitting room, with Ellen and Mrs Lindley.'

Mary smiled, for the small sitting room was the new name she had given to the music room, the next on the list of rooms to be converted to a new, more practical use. Mayhap the servants were becoming amenable to her changes? The room had hardly warranted the title of music room when Mary first saw it. The single musical instrument it contained was a rather sad-looking, dust-covered pianoforte that had now been removed by Shorey and Hooper, to be stored in the drawing room under a dust sheet.

'Please convey my apologies to his lordship and tell him I shall see him in due course,' she told Trant. 'In the meantime, I shall be with Mrs Lindley in the small sitting room.'

It was exactly what she needed to take her mind off her problems.

Mary entered the old music room to find Mrs Lindley, Ellen and Susan hard at work. The cobwebs had been swept from the ceiling; the curtains had been taken outside and shaken until every speck of dust had been removed; the rugs had been beaten to within an inch of their lives; every surface was now being polished until it gleamed and Ellen was cleaning the windows, humming as she worked.

Mary felt proud she had injected some vigour and purpose into the servants. Susan took the children up to the old schoolroom that had become their nursery and Mary took over polishing the wall sconces until they gleamed.

'I'm thinking his lordship'll be right cosy in here, when he can tackle the stairs,' Mrs Lindley said after several minutes of silence.

Mary looked round from her precarious perch halfway up a ladder. The cook stood beneath her, gazing up.

'I hope so,' Mary said.

Mrs Lindley lumbered over to the window to point out a missed smear to Ellen. 'What d'you think, Ellen?'

Ellen finished rubbing the smear away before gazing around the room. Mary could see the satisfaction on her face. 'I'm sure you're right, Mrs Lindley. I dare say Mrs Vale had the right of it after all. It *will* be easier to keep nice now.'

She beamed across the room at Mary, who smiled back. 'I'm glad you are both content,' she said, happy she was again on good terms with the two women. Although that, she realised with a thud of her heart, would make it even more difficult to leave in the morning. She decided not to spoil the moment by telling them of her decision.

They put the finishing touches to the room, fetching a few specially chosen ornaments and paintings from other rooms to create a cosier ambience. While they worked, Mary listened with half an ear to Mrs Lindley grumbling about the hardship of managing with three less pairs of hands at the Hall since her ladyship had removed to the Dower House, taking her own maid, the housekeeper and the butler with her.

'Where is Lady Rothley now?'

'She went to London in the spring, to chaperon her niece until she gets wed. My, but I wish she hadn't gone, ma'am, and that's the truth. The old place ain't the same now, neglected as it is. Or was...' she added.

At her pause, Mary glanced at Mrs Lindley and

saw her gaze sweep the room, her expression brightening.

'Mebbe that's what's made the difference. Having a mistress again, I mean. Beggin' your pardon, ma'am, and no offence meant, but in the short time you've been here, it's breathed the life back into the old place. You and the bairns both, no matter what his lordship might say.'

'Well, I am flattered you should say so, Mrs Lindley, although I think his lordship might very well take exception should he hear you refer to me as mistress of the house,' Mary said with a laugh, even as a subversive corner of her mind plucked out that idea and, examining it, found it most appealing. Then she remembered that this time tomorrow she would be miles away from the Hall and her spirits tumbled back to earth.

When they had finished in the small sitting room, Mary climbed the stairs to the Blue Room. The more she mulled over her situation the more troubled she became. Discreet questioning of Mrs Lindley had elicited the information that Sir Gerald Quartly was still unmarried, news that filled Mary with horror. Despite Lucas's assertion that she need not leave, meeting Quartly had forced her hand.

'Trant said you would like to see me?'

Lucas was sitting at the table, an open ledger in front of him. The sight of him revived her fears about Sir Gerald. What, precisely, was the relationship between Lucas and Quartly? Sick apprehension swarmed up her throat until she feared she might choke. She swallowed several times, thrusting down the sense of dread, desperate to hide her emotions.

'Mary.' The relief in his voice was unmistakable. He pushed back his chair.

'Do not get up,' Mary said as she crossed the room to his side.

Lucas stood anyway. He smiled down at her.

'A gentleman always stands when a lady enters the room,' he said, his voice warm with suppressed laughter. 'I remember you once admonished me with the words: "I make no doubt you were raised as a gentleman." I should like to prove to you that I have not relinquished all my manners, despite my best endeavours to prove otherwise.'

Mary felt her forehead pucker as she thought over his words. 'Is that a convoluted attempt at an apology?'

'It is.'

'Could you not have just said *I am sorry*?'

'And make life easy for the two of us? Never! I need something—even if it only wordplay—to amuse myself. But I *am* sorry. I reacted badly.'

'I accept. Was that why you wished to see me or was there something in the ledgers you wanted to discuss?' She knew she sounded sharp and ungracious, but Mary was in no mood for teasing and fun. Her nerves were taut as a bowstring and she felt she might snap with even the tiniest increase in pressure.

'Mary? What is it?' Lucas pushed away from his perch against the table and placed his hands on her shoulders. His dark eyes were full of concern as they searched her face. 'Why are you shaking?'

Mary pushed at his chest, but he slid his hands down her upper arms and tightened his grip.

'You have nothing to fear, Mary. I am truly sorry about my earlier behaviour. I was unforgivably short with you. It won't happen again.'

Mary shook her head, her eyes riveted to his chest. He tucked his fingers under her chin and raised it. Not for the life of her could she meet his gaze. Nausea threatened to overwhelm her again. She should have stayed away from him, until she was more settled about Quartly.

'Mary?'

His gentle enquiry prompted the sting of tears and she blinked them away rapidly.

'Are the children the reason you are returning to your father?' Lucas asked. At Mary's mute nod, he said, 'Why did you not just say so? I am not an ogre.

I would not have sent you away had I known about the children. You do know that, don't you?'

The fear and tension created by her meeting with Quartly boiled over.

'No,' she spat. 'As a matter of fact, I did not know. How should I know? You never reveal anything about yourself, about your past. All I know is what others—yes, and you, yourself,—have told me. Children are banned from Rothley Hall. Even, apparently, the very *young children* of a person who has given up her time and plans to help you and your servants.'

Anguish roiled through her entire body, every muscle, every nerve set quivering as her hopeless situation again reared over her.

Lucas gathered her into his arms, holding her head against his chest. Great shudders erupted through her and scalding tears began to flow. Her legs, stringy and useless, could support her no longer and she slumped against him.

'Shh.' He rocked her, stroking her hair. 'It's all right. You're safe here. Nothing bad will happen.'

It already has! Her anguished scream echoed around her head. What was she to do?

Lucas moved suddenly and Mary was swept into his arms.

'No! Your leg!'

She stared blurrily at his set features as he deposited her on the *chaise longue*, then sat alongside in a reversal of their usual positions. Sweat had broken on his brow. Her guilt was enough to stem her tears. A clean handkerchief was thrust into her hand and she used it gratefully.

'Sorry,' she gasped. 'I shouldn't have…'

'Hush.'

He was very close, jet-black eyes full of concern, soft and tender. He smoothed her hair from her face as he twisted round to face her, his hip hard against her thigh. He was so close. His lips—smooth and sensual—entranced her as his breath fanned her damp skin. He was all she could see, feel, hear. His musky scent enveloped her. She must taste him. His eyes darkened as awareness flared.

Long fingers wove into her hair, dislodging her pins. It tumbled around her face and he smoothed it back once more, his eyes searching hers as his mouth lowered—achingly slowly—to hers. A tiny part of her—still cautious, still sensible, still shockable—clamoured at her to stop, but her heart and her body, every last fibre of her, refused to obey. She wanted this, had fantasised about it.

It is only a kiss. What could be the harm?

Mary shuddered with anticipation as their lips met and Lucas took control. Heat flushed her entire body as his lips opened against hers, hungry and demanding, his tongue sweeping into her mouth to explore and taste at will. His hand cradled her skull, holding her as his lips moved sensuously against hers. She savoured every moment, mirroring each caress of his lips and tongue.

His lips left hers and traced a scorching path along her jaw to her earlobe. Heat spiralled from her core and she tipped her head aside to ease his access. He licked and nibbled, sending waves of desire crashing through her. Beyond thought now, she pressed closer, ripples of excitement coursing through her. She brushed her fingertips along his jaw, savouring the roughness of his skin, and then tangled her fingers through his silky hair, her low hum of pleasure echoed by his visceral growl as his lips claimed hers once more.

His hands, sensually exploring, feathered her face, neck, back and the rounded tops of her breasts, raising heated yet shivery skin in their wake. Her nipples hardened and she felt that glorious, tugging sensation deep in her core, stoking her need.

Too soon, he lifted his head. They stared into one another's eyes, their breath mingling in erratic bursts.

'I shouldn't have done that, Mary. You were upset. I took advantage.'

Abruptly, Lucas stood. He tugged Mary to her feet.

'I could have stopped you. I should have. But I didn't.'

Mary touched her fingertips to his lips. Common sense—that curse of her nature—began to reassert itself.

'I am sorry. I must go.'

'Go? What do you mean? Not...?'

She did not elaborate. She wasn't even certain herself what she meant. She needed time to think.

Going back to her father was inevitable and mayhap the sooner she faced up to that, the better. She headed downstairs with new determination.

'Now the immediate crisis has past, I think we should leave.'

Mrs Lindley looked up from rolling out pastry for a pie for supper, her expression perplexed.

'But why the rush to go?' she queried. 'I thought you and the bairns were happy here. His lordship'll still need caring for, you know, and at least he knows about the children now, dear little souls that they are. He might disapprove, but there's no danger of his seeing them again until he's able to get down them stairs.

'I don't mind admitting what a help you've been to us all, despite our...um...difference of opinion.

I don't know how we would've coped without you. You've seen for yourself how stretched we are.'

'I know, Lindy,' Mary replied suppressing the panic looming inside. 'But we cannot remain here for ever, and the longer we leave it, the worse the weather will become. We have several miles to travel yet.'

'Mama?'

Toby tugged at Mary's hand. 'Yes, lovey?'

'I like it here. Em'ly does too.' He gestured to Emily, playing with a kitten on the rug before the kitchen fire. 'Why don't you like it, Mama?'

Mary regarded the children ruefully. Their time at the Hall had probably been the most tranquil the children could remember for a long time, if ever, in their short lives. Despite Mary's preoccupation with nursing Lucas, the children had wanted for neither love nor attention, having captured the hearts of all the servants. The last thing Mary wanted was to subject them to another long journey, with the added uncertainty of what kind of welcome they could expect at the other end.

'I do like it here, Toby, very much. But I am sure Lord Rothley will not want us to stay, eating him out of house and home,' she said as she tweaked her son's cheek. She took his hand, which clutched a half-eaten biscuit and shook it, trying to make a joke out of her words.

Then her heart broke as Toby pushed his biscuit into her hand, crying, 'I won't eat much, Mama, I promise. Don't let him send us away. I'm sorry I called him a bad man. I can work. Shorey said I can help with the horses.'

Mary crouched in front of Toby. 'His lordship isn't sending us away, Toby. We have to go. We are going to visit your grandpapa.'

Toby stared at her, wide-eyed. 'Who?'

'My father, lovey. We will live in the house I lived in when I was little. Won't that be fun?'

Toby hung his head. 'I like it here,' he repeated as Emily toddled over to him and put her hand in his. 'We want to stay. Pleeease, Mama.'

Mary gathered them both into her arms, gazing at Mrs Lindley, who shrugged. 'Out of the mouths...' she muttered as she finished topping her pie.

Trant slid into the room a few moments later.

'His lordship sends his compliments, Mrs Vale, and asks if you would do him the honour of dining with him this evening?'

'Dine? Where?'

'In the Blue Room, ma'am.' He turned to Mrs Lindley. 'He also said...' he coughed '...he doesn't want any more slops—those are his words, not mine—but a proper meal, if you please.'

'He must be on the mend, thank goodness,' Mrs Lindley said, beaming. 'I'm surprised it's taken this long for him to start making demands.'

Mary listened, mixed emotions of dread and anticipation coiling in the pit of her stomach as she remembered the last time they had met.

Chapter Sixteen

Mary.

She soothed his soul with her calm presence and her sweet nature. As he waited for her to join him for dinner that night, Lucas conjured up her image: her kind eyes, ready smile and the scattered freckles on her nose; her rosy lips, ripe for his kisses; her lush curves. Her children! Jolted out of his daydream, his muscles tensed and he stalked across the room to the window. Pain tore at his thigh in protest at his careless strides but he ignored it as he leaned his forehead against the cool glass.

Then he forced himself to pause and to think.

He considered the reasons why everyone had colluded to keep the presence of the children from him. His conclusions were not comfortable. He was in danger of turning into an autocratic curmudgeon. Like his father. He had announced his decree that children would not be countenanced in his household in order to prevent the constant speculation about when, and who, he might wed in order to beget an heir.

He would not wed, there would be no heir.

The sadness and reproach in his mother's eyes had haunted him. It was that, as well as his desire to hide his growing anxiety over the repayment of his father's loan, which had prompted his insistence she move to the Dower House. With the benefit of hindsight, that was not the best decision he had ever made but his pride—he now saw—had prevented him from changing his mind. Now Mama had been away for several months and he had been more lonely and isolated than ever.

Until Mary had entered his life.

When she walked into his room, the world seemed brighter. The impossible seemed possible. But now… his thoughts came full circle. She had concealed the presence of her children from him. His fault, yes, that nobody dared to mention their existence, but that Mary had lied felt like a betrayal.

But still he wasn't ready to lose her.

The more he had grown accustomed to her presence, the more he yearned for it, despite the unwelcome memories of Julia resurrected by her beautiful blue eyes.

Robert's words from that afternoon echoed

through his mind and Lucas recognised that, just as he was not his father, he must acknowledge that Mary was not Julia. In fact, he realised, he was reminded less and less of Julia every time he saw Mary.

But despite his growing feelings, a future with Mary was impossible.

A tap at the door jolted him from his reflections. The door opened and Mary stood silhouetted in the gap. He limped towards her, the increased pain in his leg reminding him of his foolishly abrupt movement earlier. His leg had been improving, getting easier every day, until now.

That's the result of your rash temper. It makes you act on impulse, without regard for the consequences. He resolved yet again to be more mindful in future.

'Thank you for the invitation,' Mary said.

She stood close, gazing up at him, her expression serious. He sensed the tension in her body, the control she exerted over her emotions. He drank in the sight of her silky skin, her luscious lips, her cornflower eyes with their long, pale lashes and the glorious soft gold of her hair, pinned back in her customary chignon. He itched to release those pins, to watch as her hair streamed over her shoulders, to gather great handfuls and bury his face in the sweet-scented mass. His gaze dropped and roved her creamy *décolletage*, enticingly framed by the lace-edged neckline of her dress.

'I am pleased you accepted.'

Her scent enveloped him. It infused every fibre of his being and he stepped back lest he yielded to the temptation to haul her into his arms. She glided across the room to the window. The curtains were undrawn despite night having fallen and Mary's image was blurrily reflected against the blackness of the night sky beyond the glass.

'I might as well confess I was tempted to refuse,' she said, her back to him, 'but we do have matters to discuss and, to tell the truth, I am somewhat tired of my own company at mealtimes.'

His eyes roved her figure, following the path his hands yearned to trace—the slender vulnerability of the back of her neck, the gentle slope of her shoulders, the feminine back, narrowing into her neat waist before flaring out into curved hips. The soft globe of her bottom was provocatively accentuated by the satiny fabric of her pale-blue dress: one he now recognised as an old gown of his mother's. Inadequacy swamped him. Mary deserved better than old cast-offs. She deserved new dresses and the fine fripperies the daughter of a gentleman ought to expect as her birthright. What would he not give to be able to provide her with such things? But he could scarcely provide for himself, let alone a wife.

Wife? Where on earth did that thought spring from? Unsettled, he forced his attention back to their conversation. He did not want a wife.

'Do you not eat with your children?' *And, most particularly, I do not wish for a wife with two children in tow.*

Mary glanced over her shoulder. 'No, they eat in the nursery. Mrs Lindley likes things done the traditional way and, besides, they are usually in bed by the time I have my dinner.' Her shoulders straightened. She turned around. 'I didn't say this earlier, but I *am* sorry you found out about the children in such a way. You were quite right; this is your house and you are entitled to know what is going on and who is living within its walls.'

'Had you intended to tell me?'

'Yes...well...that is, I would have told you, of course, had it become necessary.'

Lucas frowned. 'Necessary?'

'I had always intended to leave before you ventured downstairs. I knew you did not want children at the Hall. I could see no purpose in disturbing you without cause.'

Leave? He knew, of course he did, she must leave at some point—he had thought of little else since he had learned of the children—but to hear it from her own lips, uttered without, it seemed, any hint of regret, cut him to the quick.

He was not ready to say goodbye. The reasons why were complex. They were reasons he did not care to examine in too much detail.

'Robert is of the opinion—'

'We are leaving in the morning,' she blurted out.

'*The morning?* What…? Why?' Lucas was across the room in a fraction of a second, barely registering the further shriek of protest from his leg. He grabbed Mary by the shoulders as he stared into her face. 'You cannot!' The words ripped from him. 'The doctor…I am not ready to go downstairs yet. You are needed here.'

She can't go. Not yet.

She stared up at him, her eyes wide, darkened by the dilation of her pupils, her lips parted enticingly. He paused on the verge of kissing her, belatedly registering her gasp and recoil as he had grabbed her. He eased his grip and stepped back. When would he learn? So soon after his vow to be more mindful, he had acted once again on impulse. He eased back, stroking his hands up and down her arms before holding her shoulders again. He bent his knees, bringing his face level with hers.

'You have no need to fear me, Mary. Do you not

know that by now? My words are just that: words.'
He spoke the truth. The thought of using force
against her made him feel physically sick. Not since
his disastrous altercation with Henson over Julia had
he ever been tempted to lash out at anyone. Could
Rob be right? Was he less similar to his father than
he feared? 'I speak hastily, without thought, at times.
Please, you must not....'

There was a rattle at the door and Lucas swivelled
his head to see Trant, carrying a loaded tray, edge
into the room. He bit back a curse. Trant had always
possessed an uncanny knack of materialising at the
worst possible moment.

'Beg pardon, my lord. Dinner is about to be
served.'

Lucas straightened as Ellen followed Trant into
the room with another tray loaded with yet more
covered dishes and a bottle of wine. The servants
crossed the room to deposit their trays upon the
table and unload them. Trant pulled a chair away
from the table.

'Ma'am?'

Mary sat on the offered chair and Lucas took the
chair opposite before Trant had a chance to perform
the same function for him. He did not want formality. He had envisioned sharing an intimate dinner
with Mary: good food and wine and pleasant con-

versation; a chance for them to get to know one another better.

'Thank you, Trant. We will serve ourselves. There is no need for you to remain.'

Trant bowed. 'As you please, my lord. There is only the one course, plus dessert.' He indicated the dishes of nuts and sweetmeats clustered to one side of the table, next to the bottle of wine. 'With your leave, I shall serve the soup before I go.'

'Thank you, Trant.'

Trant set bowls of brown soup before them, then left the room, closing the door behind him. Silence reigned as their gazes locked, neither making a move to begin eating. Lucas cast around for the words to persuade Mary to stay.

'I beg you to reconsider,' he said, finally.

'Why?'

Why indeed? Because I need you. Because I want you. Because I cannot envision my life without you.

'I am still confined upstairs. As you have pointed out before, the Hall is understaffed. I do not wish to increase the burden on the servants.'

'It is to your credit you think only of their welfare,' Mary replied in a dry tone, concentrating on her bowl as she began to drink her soup.

'I do not believe you are so eager to return to your father's rule you will not welcome a few extra days' respite here at the Hall. As soon as I am fully recovered you may continue on your journey.'

Mary raised her head and stared across the table at him. Lucas picked through his words. *Selfish!* Did he truly expect her to conform to his whims? To stay until he was ready for her to go and then meekly go back to a life she clearly dreaded? And what of the children? What future awaited them?

It's not your problem. Let them go.

'I did not mean that as it sounded, Mary.'

She pinned him with a glare. 'Selfish and hard-hearted, you mean?'

'Exactly that. I am sorry.'

She bent her head to her soup once more. The candlelight highlighted the golden tints of her hair, illuminating the stray strands that encircled her head like a halo. Lucas drank in the vision, mesmerised, until she glanced up and their gazes locked. His heart leapt in his chest at the unguarded yearning in her expression. Did he…could he…dare to tell her how he felt? He must, for only the truth might change her mind.

'*I* do not want you to leave.'

His words hovered in the air between them. A light blush stained her cheeks as she shook her head. 'I cannot stay. I am sorry.'

'Why not? If it is the children…'

'It is not the children. I cannot stay here. I must go to my father's house.'

Not *I must go home*. She had run away, her father had not answered her letter after her husband had died and Lucas was well aware of Sir William Cranston's reputation. She could not be impatient to return to such a life.

'Why now? Why can you not stay longer? A few more days even?'

Mary shook her head; unshed tears pooled in her eyes, glinting in the candlelight. 'I cannot.'

Her fear was tangible. Lucas pushed his chair back and rounded the table. He knelt by her side and reached for her hands.

'What is it, Mary? Is it because of me? You must not fear me. I cannot deny I find you desirable, nor will I pretend I do not long to kiss you again, but I have promised you before and I mean it: I will take nothing you do not wish to give.' He tightened his grip on her hands. 'You do believe me?'

She tugged her hand from his and touched it to his cheek. 'Of course I do. It is not you, Lucas. I…I…' She swallowed audibly. 'The longer I remain here, the harder it will be to leave. Do you understand? Not only for me but, more importantly, for the children. They love it here. They are happy.'

'Then stay a while longer,' he urged.

Mary snatched her other hand from his grasp. 'No. You are not listening to me. We cannot stay. The weather is getting colder, the days shorter. We need to leave before...'

'I will take you to your father's house, when I am recovered.'

Mary remained silent, her lips tight, a crease furrowed between her fair brows as she stared straight ahead.

'Well,' Lucas said eventually, realising he was not going to get a response, 'can you promise me you will think about what I have said? For the sake of your children...'

'Do not—' she said, in a strangled voice as she speared him with a fierce look, '—use my children as a bargaining tool, for I know you have no care for their welfare. In fact, quite why you should concern yourself with my predicament is beyond my comprehension, for it can be of no concern to you what might happen to my family when we leave this house.'

Hurt by her outburst, although he had to accept there was an element of truth in what she said, Lucas rose to his feet and returned to his chair, marshalling his thoughts.

'I do care about you, Mary, you must believe me.'

'I know you care for what you see as an available

woman to slake your thirst.' Her bitter tone rocked Lucas to the core.

'No! You are wrong. That is unfair. I care about what happens to *you*.'

'Oh—' her eyes, now full of remorse, regarded him '—I did not intend…that is, I am sorry to lash out at you in such a way. I did not mean to throw your kindness back in your face in such a mean-spirited way. It's…no, I cannot say…I don't know what…' Her voice tailed away and she looked away again, but not before he had recognised her misery and, again, a hint of fear.

'Very well,' she said, after a pause, 'I shall stay for a few more days.'

Lucas wondered again at the cause of her fear. If it was not him—and he believed her when she said it was not—then what was she scared of? If it was her father, why would she insist on going back earlier than need be? He could reach no conclusion, but he longed to gather her into his arms and hold her close, to comfort her and erase her fear. To his astonishment, the impulse was almost impossible to resist. It held no element of desire and he could not recall ever feeling as protective towards any woman, other than his own mother. Mary looked so lost and vulnerable sitting opposite him.

'I regret you feel unable to confide in me, Mary,'

he said, 'but I am happy you are not leaving tomorrow. Please, finish your soup before it gets too cold.'

They each spooned some soup into their mouths and then they both grimaced.

'I think we are too late,' Mary said, with a smile. 'Mayhap the rabbit pie will have retained its heat? It smelled wonderful when Mrs Lindley took it from the oven.'

She rose from her seat and began to serve food on to two plates. Lucas pushed his chair back and started to rise. Mary held up her palm.

'Sit still, please. I can manage.'

'But...'

She fixed him with a rebuking stare. 'I am here to help and you still need to rest that leg.'

Lucas sank back into his chair. She talked sense, as ever. She placed his plate—piled with rabbit pie, pork cutlets with greens, calves foot jelly, green beans and apple loaf—in front of him. Before she could move away, he clasped her wrist.

'You are right, Mary. It is important I rest to regain my strength. Mayhap I need your help to eat my food?'

She bit her lip to hold back a smile, but her dancing eyes gave her away. Relieved to see her regain her usual good humour, he grinned up at her. 'Well?'

'I think not. The doctor has prescribed gentle

exercise for your leg and your shoulder. Lifting your fork should provide that very nicely.' Her smile was in her voice though she remained straight-faced.

Lucas released her wrist. 'Killjoy,' he said, with another grin.

They ate in companionable silence for several minutes, the tasty food commanding their full attention. Finally, Mary pushed her plate away.

'That was a lovely meal,' she said. 'Mrs Lindley is a very talented cook. You are lucky to have her.'

'I know. And now you are to stay a while longer, you will be able to enjoy her cooking all the more.' At his words, Mary's expression clouded over and he cursed himself for raising that contentious issue so soon after they had reached accord. She had agreed to stay—why could he not have let the subject lie?

'I *have* agreed to remain but, of course, it does depend...' She paused.

Lucas raised a brow.

'It will depend,' she continued firmly, 'on whether my children are made welcome in this house.'

'Welcome?' Irritation stirred. He had temporarily forgotten about the children, eager only to ensure Mary's continued presence in his life. The recollection of her deception shot to the surface of his consciousness. 'And what, precisely, do you mean by that, Mary? Am I to invite them up here to play at spillikins?'

'Do try not to be facetious!' Two spots of vivid red stained Mary's cheekbones. 'I shall endeavour to keep them out of your way as much as possible. I have no more wish for them to be exposed to you than you have to them. But I must have your word that if your paths do cross, you will not frighten them. They are too young to understand that you will not hurt them.'

Her tone revealed her uncertainty and, despite Lucas's belief that he was like his father, Mary's doubts hurt. Badly.

'I hope,' he said, with a calm he did not feel, 'you do not believe I would ever do such a thing?'

'How am I to know what you might do if pro-voked? I barely know you. I do know, however, you dislike children...'

'I do not dislike children. I have only ever stated I do not want children. It is not the same.'

'Is it not?' Mary looked away, staring towards the window at the inky void beyond. 'Why would you not want children, unless you dislike them?' She looked back, impaling him with her direct stare. 'You must want an heir—doesn't every nobleman wish to pass on his title and lands?'

'I have a brother. He is welcome to fulfil that obligation.'

'You have evaded my question, Lucas. Are my children welcome in your house? Will they be safe?'

Lucas clenched his jaw as he considered his long-held belief that children were not safe around him—he had never felt safe in his father's presence, never knowing when a blow might fall. Could he really, if provoked, harm a child? He had lived so long with the conviction he was like his father, but now...

His understanding of his character was in disarray. Contrarily, although he was aware Mary did not know the reason behind his ban on children, it still stung that she believed him capable of hurting one.

But he could at least give Mary the reassurance she sought.

'They will be safe. You have my word.'

Chapter Seventeen

'Thank you.'

Mary thrust aside her guilt at allowing Lucas to believe her reluctance to stay was driven by fear for her children's safety. She had formed her own opinion of Lucas in the time she had known him. His words—hasty and ill considered though they undoubtedly were at times—were, as he had said, merely words. She had enough experience of living with men who thought nothing of raising a fist to enforce their rule to recognise he was not of their ilk.

Lucas said the children would be safe and Mary trusted him, but still she vowed to keep them away from him as much as possible. She might understand his angry words would not result in a raised hand, but Toby and Emily were too young to make such a distinction.

But she still feared Sir Gerald Quartly: the real

reason she had felt compelled to leave the next day. And she had a message to convey.

'Sir Gerald Quartly called to enquire after your health this afternoon.'

'Quartly?'

'I told him you were not yet fit for visitors and he gave me a message to pass on to you.'

'Go on.'

'He said to remind you the Quarter Day is fast approaching.'

'And?'

'That was all. Is he a friend of yours?'

'He is a neighbour, from the far side of the village, an old acquaintance of my father's.'

That much she already knew. Lucas offered no further enlightenment and she could deduce nothing from his non-committal tone. Uncertain of his relationship with Quartly, she dared not confide her true fears to Lucas. She would stay close to the house and keep her wits about her. Surely that would be enough to keep her safe?

She watched Lucas through lowered lashes as he devoured her with brooding eyes, one long-fingered hand toying with the stem of his wineglass. Soon she must face the prospect of never seeing him again and the thought filled her with hopelessness. Every fibre of her being reached for him, but she fought the temptation. Not for the first time, she wondered whether it would it be more bearable to lie with him, to have the memory to sustain her through the hard years ahead. Or should she retain her dignity and resist the brief affair that was all she could expect from him? Either way meant heartache.

A tap at the door broke the silence and Trant and Ellen came in to clear the table.

'Would you care for brandy, my lord?'

Lucas pushed his chair back from the table. 'Not tonight, thank you. But you may bring the tea tray when you've finished here.'

Ellen, about to leave, said, 'Mrs Lindley's preparing it now, my lord. I'll bring it up directly.'

Lucas stood and held his hand out to Mary. 'Shall we sit by the fire?'

As his fingers closed around hers, Mary's heart lurched. His touch was warm, igniting her desire. Only the knowledge that Ellen would soon return kept her from turning into his arms and pressing her body against the solid strength of his.

Mary sat in one of the chairs by the fire whilst Lucas sat opposite.

'Is it not your custom to take brandy or port after a meal?' she asked, to distract herself from her desire.

'Not my custom, no,' Lucas replied. 'I do have the occasional glass, but that is all.'

'I remember stories, in the past…'

He grinned. 'Listening to gossip again, Mrs Vale?' Then he became serious. 'I hope I have matured somewhat since my salad days. I was a touch on the wild side in my youth, but that was a long time ago.'

His words did not relieve Mary. Quite the opposite, in fact, for the better she knew him and the more she learned, the faster the protective barriers she had erected around her heart were crumbling.

They chatted of this and that, Mary determinedly keeping the conversation mundane and, by the time Ellen came in with tea, Mary's pulse rate had calmed.

'Would you like me to make the tea?' she asked.

'Thank you, yes. My mother always…' His lips tightened, his words fading away.

Mary crossed to the table and busied herself, working by rote. She reviewed the events in his past about which she remained in ignorance: the reason for his ban on children; why he had forced his mother to move out of the Hall and, most important of all, who was Julia?

She handed him a cup of tea even as her mind churned.

Is he still in love with her?

'Tell me about Julia.'

As soon as the words escaped her lips she regretted them. She took her own tea and sat opposite him, silently berating her tactlessness. Could she not have phrased the question with more sensitivity? She could have asked him about the less contentious issues first and then eased into the matter of Julia. His eyes had shuttered, his lips firmed.

She could not take the words back. She might as well brazen it out.

'I apologise if the subject is painful, Lucas, but I am interested to know about your past.'

'Did we not have this conversation already today?' His indifferent tone matched his expression.

'We did, but we were interrupted before you had the opportunity of answering my question.'

Lucas set his cup and saucer on to the table by his side. 'You know precisely as much now as if there had been no interruption.'

If he had yawned, he could not have looked more uninterested.

'It was just before you met the children.'

'"Met"? Is that a euphemism for "found out about"?'

Mary pressed on. 'Will you tell me why you did not want children at the Hall?'

'*Did* not? Did I say I'd changed my mind?'

Did he know how infuriating he was? One peek at his poorly disguised amusement confirmed he was only too aware of the effect of his intransigence. She clenched her teeth.

'May I ask, then, what you were about to say about your mother?'

'My mother?'

'Yes. When I asked if I should make the tea, you said "My mother always" before clamming up. I should like to know what you were going to say.' Mary eyed the gathering storm in his eyes, although his expression remained one of mild amusement. 'Did she always make the tea here, before she moved to the Dower House?'

'Yes.'

Progress of a sort, she supposed. 'Why did you want her to move out?'

Lucas stood up and paced to the window, gazing out into the darkness. 'I may as well tell you, I suppose, as you already know something of the estate finances,' he muttered.

What he really means is he will tell me about his mother in the hope of deflecting my attention from other, more sensitive, subjects. Still, some information is better than none. And it was a useful distraction from the instinct to take him in her arms and soothe away the pain glimmering beneath the surface of his indifference.

'When my father died I discovered the estate was

deep in debt. My mother knew my father had borrowed, but not how much or, indeed, the consequences if I failed to pay back his debts.'

'But why did that necessitate her moving away?'

'I was protecting her.'

'She is a grown woman. Might she not have been able to help?'

'She has had enough trouble in her life. I did not wish to add to it.'

'Trouble?'

'My father. He was not an easy man to live with.'

'Will you tell me about him?'

'Mary!' With two strides, Lucas was in front of her. His chest swelled as he controlled his emotions with a visible effort. 'If this is the effect of drinking one glass of wine, I should hate to see you drunk,' he said, with a smile that did not touch his eyes.

Mary stiffened. 'You will never see *me* drunk,' she said. 'It is of all things the one I abhor the most.'

'How so?'

The conversation was finished, as far as Mary was concerned. Lucas did not trust her enough to confide in her. Indeed, he was growing ever more irritable at her questions. Why, then, should she trust him in return?

'Please excuse me,' she said, standing, 'but I am very tired. I think I shall retire now.'

'Mary?'

'Thank you for the lovely meal. Goodnight, Lucas.'

A pox on all women!

Three days after his supper with Mary, Lucas hobbled along the path towards the stable yard, a furious diatribe scorching his brain. Mary had become the elusive lady, never where he expected to find her and always—*always!*—either surrounded by members of his staff or off somewhere 'with the bairns'. How was he supposed to have a normal conversation with her when she was never to be found? Not once had he managed to catch her on her own. He should have saved his breath and let her leave. She might as well not be at the Hall, for all he saw of her.

The slowness of his progress further irritated him. His thigh and hip groaned with every step he took, despite the assistance of a stout blackthorn, but he gritted his teeth and kept going. He had started out with the intention of visiting the stable yard and he meant to do it. Finally, he reached the sandstone pillars that flanked the entrance. He rounded the nearest one and stopped to catch his breath, leaning against its rough surface to ease his leg. He surveyed the yard, enjoying the familiar scents of horse and leather and the sound of horses munching hay.

His initial pleasure was dampened by the number of closed stable doors around the square. In his youth, the yard had been full of hunters and carriage horses as well as the draught horses that worked the land, but now he kept the barest minimum necessary for the estate to function. His gaze alighted on Sultan's stable—situated to the immediate left of the entrance—and froze.

Perched precariously on an upturned bucket, his back to Lucas, was a small figure with a tousled mop of hair the exact same shade as Mary's, brushing Sultan's mane. The great grey's head drooped over the stable door, his eyes closed, one ear flicking intermittently in response to the boy's low crooning monologue. Neither Shorey nor Hooper was anywhere to be seen. Anger that the lad—*how old was he? Four? Five?*—should be there, alone, in such a potentially dangerous situation warred in Lucas's breast with the craven desire to retreat before he was spotted. He didn't want to deal with the boy. Why, he didn't even know his name.

And you wonder why Mary has been avoiding you?

He pushed away from the pillar, straightening. He was still undecided whether to advance or retreat when the decision was snatched from his hands. His abrupt movement startled Sultan, who threw his head into the air, knocking the boy, who seized a double handful of mane as his flailing feet kicked the bucket from underneath him. For an instant he swung in mid-air, then the horse started to back, eyes rolling at the weight hanging from his neck. Lucas sprang forward and grabbed the child before he could fall.

They tumbled to the ground in a tangle of arms and legs, Lucas twisting at the final second to avoid crushing the lad. He lay on his back, heart pounding against his ribcage, as he clutched the hot, solid little body to his chest. For an instant the boy was still and then he began to squirm. Lucas, instinctively, tightened his grip.

A muffled sniff sounded, followed by disjointed pleas. 'I'm sorry…didn't mean…please…didn't hurt him…'

'Lie still!'

Instantly, the lad stopped wriggling. The only sound was his ragged breathing punctuated by the occasional hiccupping sob.

'Please…' The whispered plea was barely audible, but the boy's dread was clear.

Lucas recalled the lad's fear the first time they had met on the landing. The Bad Man. No wonder he was terrified.

'If I let go, do you promise not to run away?'

A tremor shook the small body. 'I promise.'

Lucas loosened his grip at the same time as he worked his way to a sitting position. He put the boy from him, standing him on his feet, and looked him in the eye. 'I have your word as a gentleman, mind,' he said as he removed his hands from the boy's waist.

The boy nodded, his face pale and streaked with tears. But he had stopped crying. That must be a good sign. He had his mother's eyes and they regarded Lucas fearfully from beneath his shock of hair. Lucas reached out to brush the hair back and the boy flinched, but stood his ground.

'It's all right,' Lucas said. 'I won't hurt you. Why are you here on your own?'

The lad hung his head and scuffed at the ground with his boot. 'I thought Shorey would be here. He said I could help him.' His voice quavered. 'I didn't want to stay with Em'ly. She's a *baby*.'

Lucas bit back a smile. He remembered his own outrage when told he must stay in the nursery every day with Hugo, his younger brother.

'What is your name?'

'Toby. My...sir...' Toby eyed Lucas doubtfully.

Lucas smiled. 'Sir will do,' he said. The lad must call him something. 'Does your mother know where you are?'

Toby hung his head, then peeped up at Lucas. 'I don't *think* so.'

Which meant she had no idea and would no doubt be frantic with worry.

'Why did you not go back to the house when you saw Shorey wasn't here?'

'I wanted to brush Sultan. Shorey said I could.'

Lucas bent a stern look on Toby. 'You must know, Master Vale, that Shorey meant you to help only if he was around to keep you safe.'

Toby shrugged, pouting. Then he looked at Lucas, his eyes brightening. 'You called me Master Vale. I like that. Lindy calls me Master Toby sometimes, but that sounds like a baby.'

'It does indeed.' Lucas bent his good leg beneath him and, by grabbing hold of the stable door, he pulled himself to his feet. 'Who is Lindy?'

A gurgle escaped Toby. '*You* must know. She's yours. She makes bread and cakes and tasty things.'

Ah. 'How silly of me. Of course, you mean Mrs Lindley.' Lucas leaned forward to brush at his breeches. Toby moved behind him and Lucas felt his small hands batting at the back of his legs.

'There. Now Mama won't know you have been sitting on the ground,' Toby said as he came back into view and gazed up at Lucas. 'You must not sit on the ground. You will catch a chill.'

'She is quite right. Mothers usually are. Come...' Lucas held out his hand to Toby. 'Let us go and find your mama and put her mind to rest. I am sure she is worried about you.' He glanced over the stable door at Sultan, who was munching a mouthful of hay and seemed none the worse for being spooked. 'You can come with me to the stables another time and we shall groom Sultan together if you like.'

'I would like that 'cause if I work then you won't mind if I eat, will you?'

Startled, Lucas glanced down as Toby placed his tiny hand trustingly in his large one. 'Why should I mind if you eat, Toby?'

They walked out of the yard, making slow progress.

'Mama said we can't stay because I eat too much,' Toby said. 'I *try* not to eat much, but I don't like being hungry like before. I want to stay here. It's nice.'

'Were you often hungry, Toby?'

Toby's face screwed up in concentration. 'I *think* so,' he said. 'We walked a long way. I don't like dry bread.'

'What about your cottage, where you lived before? Did you like it there?'

'I didn't like it when that man made Mama cry.'

Lucas stiffened, his insides clenching at the

thought of anyone making Mary cry, even as he recognised his hypocrisy. After all, who had been the cause of all of Mary's tears since she had come to the Hall? He thrust that thought away.

'Which man was that, Toby?'

'Simon. He was Papa's friend, but he didn't like children.'

'Why did he make your mama cry?' Part of Lucas was appalled he would stoop so low as to question a child in such a way. The other part urged him on, too curious to let his gentlemanly scruples get in its way.

'She was sad because Simon's papa died and then Simon said, "You must do what I want," and Mama said, "Yes." But she told me she pretended and she really meant no.' Toby halted and pulled at Lucas's hand. Lucas looked down at Toby's upturned face. 'Mama always says I must not lie, but she lied, didn't she? She said it was to protect us and then we ran away in the dark. Do you think God will tell her off for lying?'

'I am sure He will understand, Toby. Your mama is a good person. God will see that.'

Toby smiled up at Lucas. 'She is a *lovely* person.'

'She is indeed, Toby, she is indeed.'

Toby ran ahead of Lucas, then stopped to examine the flowerbed that flanked the path.

'What is it?' Lucas bent down to see what had caught Toby's attention. A dead mouse, blood staining its fur, lay at the base of a clump of iris leaves.

'It's a dead mouse.' Toby announced. 'It's got blood on it.'

Lucas wondered if the boy might get upset, but it seemed he was more interested in how the mouse might have met its demise.

'It was probably one of the stable cats,' Lucas said.

'But you don't always die if you get blood, do you?'

'Er...no, not always. But mice are very small and fragile. They are no match for a cat.'

Toby stared up at Lucas with a serious expression. 'You are not small,' he said. 'What's fragile?'

Where on earth is he going with this? Lucas wondered. 'No, I am not small. Nor am I fragile—that means easily damaged.'

'Like Em'ly.' The satisfaction in the boy's voice made Lucas chuckle. 'That's why I have to be strong and be nice to her, Mama said, and not fight her.'

'Indeed.'

'I found your blood.'

'Yes, I know. You told me before.'

'You were cross.' Toby skipped a pace or two, then looked up at Lucas again. 'You're not cross now. Are you?'

'No, Toby, I'm not cross. Where did you find my blood?'

'On Sultan's neck. Only I didn't know he was called Sultan. I called him Cloudy in my head.'

'Cloudy? That's a good name for a horse.'

'It's my pretend horse, but you can call Sultan Cloudy if you like.'

'Ah, but he's used to me calling him Sultan. I don't want to make him sad.'

'Would he be sad?'

'Yes, I think so. Don't you think his name suits him?'

Toby frowned, then started towards the house again. 'Yes, I do,' he said, 'but I didn't think of it when I thought of Cloudy. You can call him Sultan, I don't mind.'

'Thank you,' said Lucas, battling the urge to laugh. He had never endured such a surreal conversation but, to his surprise, he was enjoying it.

'Have you got a mama, sir?'

'Why, yes, but she is away from home at the moment.'

Toby took Lucas's hand and squeezed. 'I bet you miss her.'

'I do…'

Lucas fell silent, his mind whirling, very much at ease in Toby's company. He could never remember having such a conversation with his own father. He had always been a stern, remote figure, likely to erupt into a fury at any time. Was this another pointer he was not the same? He shook his head. One short span of time in the company of a young child did not make a good father. But he had not felt angry with Toby at any time. Even when he had seen him with Sultan and feared for his safety, his anger had been directed at those who should have been caring for the boy.

'Toby! Toby!'

Mary, skirts hitched high, ran full tilt along the path towards them. Her face was flushed, her hair flying loose of the pins that normally held it in place. He stood still and waited, enjoying the glimpses of slim legs as she ran. She did not slow down, but kept up her speed until she reached them, then grabbed Toby by the shoulders, pulling his hand from Lucas's grasp as she dropped to her knees before him.

'Are you…all right…?' she panted, her bosom heaving. She turned him this way and that, anxiously scanning every inch of him, before raising her gaze to Lucas. 'What…why…? What happened? Have you…?'

Lucas lifted a brow. 'I have not touched him, if that is what you are afraid of.'

'No, of course you did not. I did not mean…'

Mary's words faded as her doubtful tone rang in his ears.

He frowned as she avoided meeting his eyes. Did she actually believe he might hurt her son?

Well, isn't that exactly what you *were scared of?* his inner voice taunted.

On the brink of returning to the house, leaving Mary and her son to it, Lucas felt a small hand creep into his and his heart skipped a beat. At least someone trusted him, he thought, conveniently forgetting it was his decree that had started the 'no children' rule.

'Me and sir, we're going to brush Sultan together next time. Sir said so,' Toby announced. He smiled up at Lucas. 'Didn't you, sir?'

'I did indeed, Toby. As long as your mama will give her permission.'

Mary gaped at Lucas, baffled. Lucas held out his other hand and helped her to her feet.

'I found him grooming Sultan, on his own,' he murmured into her ear.

'In the stable?' she gasped.

'No, thank goodness. He was standing on a bucket, brushing his neck. What were you thinking, letting him out of your sight? He—'

Mary spun to glare up at him, puffed up with indignation.

'Don't you *dare* to criticise my care for my son,' she hissed.

'Mary, I—'

'Mama!' Toby said urgently. 'Mama, I found a dead mouse. Come and see.'

There was a beat of silence during which their gazes remained locked. Then Mary narrowed her eyes at Lucas before speaking to her son. 'Toby, I have told you before. It is rude to interrupt grown-ups when they are talking. Please apologise to Lord Rothley.'

'I am sorry, sir,' a small voice said as Toby slid his hand from Lucas's grasp.

Lucas bent awkwardly, his leg too sore after his walk to attempt to crouch, to bring his face level with Toby's. 'I accept your apology, Master Vale,' he said gravely. He held out his right hand and Toby shook it, a wide beam spreading over his face as he looked up at Mary.

'Sir calls me Master Vale, Mama. That's 'cause I'm five. Can I show the dead mouse to Em'ly, Mama? Pleeease?'

As he straightened, a glance at Mary's face revealed dancing eyes and the corners of her mouth quirking as she struggled to remain stern.

'No, Toby, you cannot. You must not touch dead things. It might make you ill.'

'But it's got blood on it, Mama. Like sir. Only he's not small, or…or…' Toby's brow puckered. '*Frashile!*' he announced with satisfaction.

'I beg your pardon?' Mary turned bewildered eyes to Lucas.

'Fragile, Toby,' Lucas said.

'Yes, that is what I said: *fragile*. You are not *fragile* like the mouse, are you, sir, 'cause you didn't die.'

'That's right, Toby. I didn't die, thanks to you and your mama. Come…' Lucas held his arm out to Mary, who placed her hand on his forearm after a second's hesitation '…let us go back to the house. I think I've had quite enough excitement for one day.'

They began to stroll back towards the Hall, Toby skipping ahead of them. Lucas glanced down at Mary, who smiled.

'Only Toby could manage to compare you to a dead mouse,' she said, a gurgle of laughter escaping her, 'but he is quite right: you are not small. I am in danger of getting a crick in my neck looking up at you.'

Lucas covered Mary's hand and squeezed. Desire and need still bubbled away in his depths but there was another feeling dominating his emotions and it took him a few moments to realise what he felt was contentment. The simple act of walking in the autumn sunshine with Mary on his arm and he was consumed by peace. He glanced sideways, but an unaccustomed prickle behind his eyes made him return his attention to the path ahead.

'I did not mean to criticise your care of your children. I was…well, I was scared when I first saw him with Sultan. Toby looked so tiny and…well, *fragile*…beside him. Only do not, I beg of you, tell him I said so. I doubt he would ever forgive me.'

They laughed together.

'And I did not mean to bite your head off,' Mary said. 'You will find, when you are a parent…oh!' She stopped with a gasp and Lucas felt her fingers tense on his arm. 'I apologise. That was not meant to…what I meant to explain is that worry over children can sometimes result in an explosion of anger when they are found to be safe. It is a natural reaction.'

They had drawn level with the side door to the Hall and Mary pulled her hand from Lucas's arm.

'We have taken quite enough of your time this morning, Lucas. Thank you for your care for Toby. I shall ensure he does not bother you again.'

Lucas reached for her. 'Do not rush away, Mary. I have hardly seen you in the last few days. Why are you avoiding me? What are you afraid of?'

Chapter Eighteen

Mary stilled as long fingers wrapped around her upper arm. Toby had rushed indoors, leaving them alone on the threshold. She faced Lucas, her gaze fixed on a point in the centre of his chest. She *had* avoided him since their supper three nights ago, deliberately, for the sake of her sanity. But she could not avoid her thoughts and he had haunted her mind, day and night. And every time she had caught a glimpse of him she'd had to fight the urge to fling herself into his arms and allow him to soothe the ache in her heart and the need that burned between her thighs. She had grown increasingly disgusted by her wanton, wayward imaginings until a sudden insight had stolen her breath.

She was hopelessly, irrevocably in love with Lucas.

It should not have happened. Ever since their first meeting, she had battled his lure, knowing there was no hope of any permanence, knowing she could settle for nothing less. Yet, still, she was in love with this infuriating, secretive, stubborn man and the desire she felt was not sordid and disgusting, but beautiful and right and…impossible. And now, he had asked the question and she owed it to him to be honest, however embarrassing her admission might be.

She thrust aside her dreams, ruthlessly stamping out the ridiculous hope that had flickered into life when she had first seen Lucas with Toby. Fairytale endings did not happen to ordinary women with two children in tow.

'I will not dissemble, Lucas. We are both rational adults and I must behave as one and not as a simpering miss.'

Mary reached behind her and closed the door. She stepped around Lucas and walked a few paces back down the path they had already traversed. *If only it was as easy to turn back my feelings.*

'Mary? What is it?'

She stopped and faced him, gripping her hands in front of her, this time fixing her gaze on his unaccountably blurred neckcloth.

'This is hard for me to say.' Mary pinched the skin on the back of one hand, focusing on the pain, in a bid to prevent her tears from spilling. 'I *am* afraid of you. I am afraid of the way you make me feel.'

She risked a glance at his face. It was inscrutable

and she looked down again, lest she might lose her nerve. 'Yes, I have avoided being alone with you. I shall continue to do so until we leave.'

Silence reigned between them. Mary worried at her lower lip. 'You know—I can tell you know—I find you hard to resist. I have tried to deny it, but I cannot.'

She looked up into features as tender and yearning as she could wish. Her treacherous body swayed towards him, seeking his warmth and his comfort. She stiffened and stepped back.

'Go on.'

He was not helping, confound him. Why was it so very hard to say what she wanted to say? Could he not fill in the gaps himself?

'I am afraid of what might happen if we spend more time alone together and that I will regret it for the rest of my life. I do not want a brief liaison. I need more than that.'

'I have assured you, dearest Mary, that I will never take more than you wish to give. Is my promise not enough? I have missed your company.' He reached for her hands, pulling them apart and clasping them. 'What more can I say to persuade you of my good intentions?'

Say you love me. She choked back the words.

'Nothing, Lucas. It is me, not you. I have allowed

myself to be tempted, but I shall say it again—I do not want a brief liaison. Not with anyone.'

'You seek a protector? Another husband?' Brow wrinkled, Lucas gazed down at her. 'Is that what you want? You are asking me to provide for you?'

'No!' This was not going the way she imagined. Now he believed she was acting from mercenary motives. But she could not tell him she loved him. Not when there was no chance he reciprocated. She had stooped low enough; she would not demean herself further. 'You asked me a question, I have answered as honestly as I can. I am sorry, Lucas. I have no more to add.'

'Ooooh, ma'am, do come and see.'

Mary looked up from her sewing to see Ellen peering out of the window of the small sitting room.

'What are they up to now?' she queried, amused at the excitement in Ellen's voice.

The children were out in the garden with Susan and Ellen was helping Mary in her task of mending the worn cushion covers on the two small sofas that had been moved into the former music room to complete its transformation into a sitting room. Ellen, ever a fidget, kept glancing out of the window to see Toby and Emily at play, but now she was on her feet, leaning forward until her nose almost touched the glass.

'Hurry, ma'am, or he'll be gone.'

'He? Who do you mean, Ellen?' Mary jumped up and hurried to the window, spurred by the maid's urgent tone.

She gazed across the expanse of lawn to the magnificent oak tree, under which the children had been gathering fallen leaves into heaps and flinging handfuls at each other. She bit back a gasp at the sight of Lucas, a broad grin on his face, swinging Emily high, then swooping her down to drop her gently into a pile of leaves. No sooner had he let her go than she scrambled to her feet, arms stretched for more, as Toby clamoured for his turn. Their excitement was clear, even from this distance, and Mary could well imagine their squeals and giggles. Susan stood apart from the fun, her face wreathed in smiles. As Mary watched, Lucas picked up a handful of leaves and showered them over Toby, who dodged and then tripped, rolling and squirming on the ground as Lucas tickled him.

Full of wonder at what she had seen, Mary said, 'I thought his lordship was not due home until tomorrow?'

Lucas had left the Hall a few days before to travel to the autumn fair at Hexham market to see his sheep sold for mutton and lamb, and to find buyers for his highly bred breeding stock. Shorey and Hooper had left earlier than Lucas in order to drive the animals at an easy pace, in the hope they would not lose too much condition before reaching their destination.

'That is what we all thought, ma'am, aye,' Ellen said.

'He does not have the appearance of a man in the doldrums. Let us hope his early return signifies good news.'

Mary dropped her sewing on the table and headed for the door, itching not only to find out what had happened, but also, she acknowledged with resignation, desperate to see Lucas again. She had missed him. More than she liked to admit. The sight of him playing with the children raised an optimism within her she knew was foolish. She quashed the burgeoning hope. One frolic in the garden did not mean he was inured to the idea of children living permanently at the Hall.

'I will go and find out what has happened,' she called over her shoulder to Ellen as she hurried from the room.

She approached the cavorting group unnoticed and went to stand by Susan, reluctant to break up the fun and games.

'Do you know why his lordship is come home early?' she whispered to Susan.

'He said he had some good fortune, but I don't know any more,' Susan replied. Even more curious, Mary thought, laughing as Emily tried to kick leaves into the air like her brother and completely missed the heap. Lucas went to her, holding her steady as he encouraged her to kick again. This time, her foot swept through the loose pile and leaves swirled into the air, picked up by the breeze, before fluttering to the ground once more. Emily's happy giggle chimed through the air. Toby, a scowl on his face, muscled his way between Lucas and Emily, demanding attention.

'Steady, Toby,' Lucas said. 'You will knock Emily over if you do not take care.'

Toby pouted at Lucas, then shoved at Emily with both hands. She fell on to her bottom. For a split second she looked stunned, then her face began to pucker. Susan exclaimed and started forward, but Mary stopped her. Her own first instinct had been to rush to her daughter, but she could see Emily was not hurt and she was curious to see how Lucas would react—both to Toby's naughtiness and to Emily's distress.

Lucas didn't hesitate. He swept Emily up into his

arms and cuddled her close as he looked sternly at Toby.

'Why did you do that, Toby?'

There was no anger in his voice and Mary felt herself relax, although she had not until that moment realised how tense she had become. Lucas had not shouted at Toby or smacked him. Although that was good, it would make leaving him even harder. Her belief that Lucas hated children—fostered by his ban—had kept her feet planted on the ground during her time at the Hall. Now, that anchor had all but disintegrated and her flights of fancy could soar free.

Toby shrugged, stuffing his hands in his pockets as he shuffled through the leaves, kicking them up in vicious spurts. Lucas watched him in silence for a moment, then kissed Emily—who had not even cried, so quick had he been to comfort her—on her plump cheek and set her on the ground. He walked after Toby.

'Toby, I am speaking to you. What would your mama say if she saw you ignore a grown-up like this?'

Toby stood still, gazing up at Lucas.

'You are bigger and stronger than Emily, Toby. It is never clever to act the bully with someone weaker than you.'

'You played with her more than you did with me!'

Toby shouted his accusation and Mary readied herself to intervene should Lucas lose his temper. But he climbed another notch in her estimation as he cocked his head to one side and regarded Toby with raised brows, not a hint of anger on his face or in his voice.

'Is that true, Toby? Or could it be you wanted more of my attention for yourself?'

The corners of Toby's mouth twisted down. Lucas crouched down. He put his hands on Toby's shoulders.

'Come now, no sulking, or we won't be able to finish our game before your mama…ah…too late, I fear, Toby; we've been discovered.'

Lucas had finally caught sight of Mary. He stood up as Emily toddled over to her, arms aloft. Mary picked her up and hugged her. Toby approached at a snail's pace, dragging his feet. Mary smiled at Lucas, ignoring the customary swoop of her heart and the catch in her breath, before turning her attention to her shame-faced son, who had halted a few paces away.

'Why do you look so glum, Toby?'

'I was bad to Em'ly, Mama, but I didn't hurt her. Sir kept playing with her 'stead of me.'

'Well, it looked to me, young man, as if his lordship was playing equally with both of you. Are you sure you were not being greedy?'

Tears sheened Toby's eyes. 'He's a man, Mama. He *should* play more with me 'cause I'm a boy. Em'ly's just a *girl*!'

Mary froze at Toby's words. Was that truly how he felt? Inadequacy near overwhelmed her as she realised how Toby must miss the absence of his father, despite Michael spending barely any time with his son. Before she could marshal her thoughts to reassure her young son, however, Lucas stepped forward and put his hand on Toby's shoulder.

'Being a boy does not mean you are better than Emily because she is a girl, Toby. It simply means you are different.'

Toby pouted, looking mutinous.

'And when you are a man, you will understand the importance of never using your physical strength against those weaker than yourself. It does not make you important, Master Vale, it merely marks you out as a bully and those people whose opinions you value will lose their respect for you.'

Mary could see Toby's battle not to give way to tears. She recognised, in that moment, his desperation not to appear a baby in front of Lucas. She crouched down with Emily still in her arms. Reaching out, she said, 'Come on, Toby. You can help

Emily learn how to kick up the leaves. That's what big brothers do. There's no need to squabble.'

Toby rushed to Mary and allowed her to hug him hard for a few seconds before he squirmed free.

'Come on, Em'ly,' he shouted. 'Race you to the tree.'

He started to run fast, then slowed and turned, catching hold of Emily's hand. They ran side by side to the oak before starting a game, dodging each other around its massive trunk, their childish screams of excitement echoing around the garden.

'Thank you for your patience with them. It was lovely to see you all having such fun,' Mary said, smiling at Lucas.

Lucas brushed at his coat, removing the remnants of dried leaves. 'I didn't know I had it in me. Come—' he held out his arm '—Susan will watch the children. There is something I wish to ask you.'

Mary's heart missed a beat. What could he mean? *No!* She quashed her wild fantasy. Her dream of a proposal was impossible. It was more than likely some mundane matter such as what Mrs Lindley had planned for dinner tonight. She placed her hand on his sleeve, willing her fingers not to tremble, revelling in the now familiar rock-hard muscle of his forearm. She caught Susan's eye, who nodded.

'You go on, ma'am. I'll bring them in shortly.'

As they strolled towards the house, Mary said, 'You are in a very good mood, Lucas. I take it the sheep sale was a success?'

Lucas grinned. 'More than you know, my sweet Mary. Now, to my request...' He reached for her hand as he halted, turning to face her.

Mary's heart skipped another beat as her pulse jittered. She gazed up into dark eyes that sparkled with suppressed excitement. What was going on? What had happened whilst Lucas was away? Was he...?

Stop it! Stop wishing for the impossible and reading romantic intent into his every word and gesture.

She willed her features to show mere polite enquiry. 'Yes?'

'Will you do me the honour of dining with me tonight?'

Dinner! Mary battled against her disappointment. Foolish optimism: the triumph of hope over experience. She should know better. She pasted a smile on her face, but before she could answer, Lucas spoke again.

'I shall instruct Trant to remain in the room, if it will make you more comfortable. You see: no ulterior motive, merely the pleasure of your company.'

His eyes burned into hers as he stepped closer, his thighs brushing against her skirts. His chest was a hairbreadth from the tips of her breasts. If she inhaled deeply, she might soothe them with the brush of his coat. Her nipples peaked at her wayward thought. A familiar yearning ached deep in her belly. Seeing him with the children this afternoon had swept away any lingering doubts over his character.

She was in love with him, completely, utterly, hopelessly. This meal might be her last opportunity to spend time with him. No one could now argue he was not fully recovered. She could no longer pretend she was needed at the Hall. It was time to go.

'Thank you, Lucas. I shall be delighted to accept your invitation. And there will be no need for Trant to remain. Even you would not attempt to seduce me over the dining table.' She paused for effect, then cocked her head to one side and raised her brows. 'Would you?'

He grinned. Threw his head back and laughed. Then, before she knew it, his hands were at her waist and her feet flew out as he swung her in a circle, planting a kiss on her lips as he set her on the ground again.

'Now I can boast I swept you off your feet, Mary Vale,' he chuckled as he disappeared inside the house, leaving Mary staring after him in bewilderment.

Chapter Nineteen

Lucas hummed as he tied his neckcloth into an intricate knot. He had not felt this buoyant in a long, long time. Finally, the future was not to be viewed with dread, but with anticipation and purpose. It was a future where, he hoped, Mary would be by his side, as his wife. But he would not ask her to marry him.

Not tonight.

Not yet.

Not for two more days, in fact, for only then would Mary understand she had a viable alternative future. And only then would Lucas know for certain she stayed because she loved him and not because she had nowhere else to go.

Two days in which to woo her. Two days in which to build his relationship with the children and to prove to Mary as well as to himself he could be a father to them. That afternoon had shown him a glimpse of the future: joining in the children's game; having fun. Rob had been right. He was not his father and he chose not to be like his father. He felt as though a weight had lifted from his shoulders.

As he walked down the staircase he wondered how easy it would be to hide what he had discovered from Mary. Not easy at all, he suspected: she was very perceptive and already wondered at the change in him. He would look forward to her pleasure and surprise when she discovered his secret. He entered the new dining room and looked around with satisfaction. Mary had been right, it was cosy and intimate and it provided exactly the right ambience for a special evening with the woman he loved.

A light footstep behind him alerted him to Mary's presence a split second before her scent registered, permeating his senses. He turned, drinking in her calm beauty and her warm smile.

'Good evening, Mary. You look very beautiful tonight.'

He held out his arm. She smiled up at him as she placed her hand on his sleeve.

'I thank you for the compliment, Lucas, even though I know I am not beautiful.'

'You are beautiful to me. What other kind of beauty is there, other than in the eye of the beholder?'

'You look very fine as well, Lucas, if I may say so.'

'Why, thank you, although I dare say any old set of clothes would be an improvement on my nightshirt.'

Mary laughed. 'Indeed it would.'

As Lucas seated her at the table, she glanced over her shoulder. 'I do hope you intend to enlighten me as to what happened on your trip to Hexham, for I find it hard to believe all this bonhomie is solely due to receiving a good price for your livestock.'

Lucas took his seat opposite Mary and signalled to Trant to begin serving. He waited until he had finished and exited the room before answering.

'You have seen the state of the accounts, Mary, and I told you the other day a little of the reality of the estate finances.'

'I have.'

'I took a gamble...' He paused. Mary had stiffened, at his words. Mayhap she did not approve of gambling? He realised how much he still had to learn about the woman opposite. He wanted to spend the rest of his life exploring every aspect of her mind and her body. 'I do not mean I was literally gambling. It was an unfortunate turn of phrase.'

She relaxed, though her eyes were still wary. She gestured for him to continue.

'When my father died, I discovered not only had he run the estate into the ground, but he had taken a substantial loan on the most ruinous of terms. The loan was secured against a large tract of land on the far side of the village. That land is the most fertile, but is also the only unentailed land on the estate. If I were to lose it…well, it would mean disaster. The estate would not be viable without external funds to support it. And I do not have any external funds.

'It was a three-year loan, with one third of the capital repayable every Christmas. If, at any time, I cannot meet the repayment or pay the interest, I lose all that land.'

Mary frowned. 'When did your father take out the loan?'

'Nigh on three years ago, less than a year before he died. The final payment is due this Christmas, but I will soon have enough money to settle it and I will finally be clear. It has been like the sword of Damocles hanging above my head over the past two years. Hence my bonhomie, as you put it.'

He grinned at her across the table, but her expression was still puzzled.

'You cannot mean that if you are unable to make the repayment this year, you would still lose *all* of that land?'

'I mean exactly that. There is a clause in the agreement that forbids the sale of the land whilst it is indentured, so it has not been possible to sell even a small portion of it to raise funds.'

'But…you would already have paid back the majority of the loan. That cannot be fair.'

'I'm afraid it does not need to be fair, Mary. It is business. My father accepted the terms of the loan—presumably in order to gamble it away, for it was not used for improvements to the land or the house. Heaven knows what he did with it, or how he thought to repay it, or whether he even had any intention to repay it.

'Now, though, I can finally breathe easily. That gamble I spoke of has paid off handsomely.'

Mary raised her brows.

'Soon after I inherited the Hall, I travelled into Yorkshire to invest in some top quality rams and bulls to breed with our sheep and cows. Now, not only did we sell our fat stock for a good price, but the surplus breeding animals we took also sold well. It is the Quarter Day tomorrow, when the tenant farmers' rents are due, plus there is an interested buyer coming to see more breeding stock for sale the day after tomorrow.

'All of that should be enough to enable me to pay the interest that falls due tomorrow as well as the final instalment of the loan at Christmas, and I can then begin to rebuild the estate and improve the land. The few tenant farmers still with the estate have been patient with the delays in repairs, but I know they have suffered as well. I cannot tell you of my relief, to know all the hard work and worry is beginning to pay off.'

Lucas laughed, a touch shamefacedly. 'I am sorry, Mary, for boring you with business as well as talking about breeding animals. It is hardly the topic to discuss over dinner with anyone, let alone with a lady.'

'I do not mind,' Mary said. 'I am interested and it is good to see you relax and to hear you laugh.'

Lucas studied Mary's earnest expression and felt a wave of emotion so powerful sweep through him he almost gasped. She was everything he could wish for: beautiful, courageous, kind. Why had he ever thought he could let her go? He could no longer even contemplate life without Mary by his side.

'It *feels* good to laugh,' he said, speaking from the heart.

And it felt good to look forward to the future with pleasure. He would use every skill he possessed to ensure Mary accepted his proposal in two days' time. During the journey to market, he had reconsidered Mary's words the day he had found Toby at the stables. He believed he now understood what she had been trying to say. She was afraid of being alone with him because she wanted him. The knowledge hummed through every fibre of his being. She was wary of her own feelings, her own responses. He could possess her tonight; he knew that with the same certainty he knew the sun would rise every morning.

But he drew the line at seducing her into his bed. He could wait. He did not want her to accept his proposal out of shame, having succumbed to his seduction. Her acceptance must be because she loved him and for no other reason. The anticipation would sweeten the reward.

Lucas visualised the next two days. He and Mary would grow ever closer as she learned to trust him and to believe in his love. Then his secret would be revealed and he must hope that Mary would forgive his deception and accept his proposal. It was another gamble for, if Mary did not love him, there would be no further obstacle to her returning to her childhood home.

'What are you thinking, Mary?'

She looked up to find him scrutinising her face. She smiled and shook her head.

'A head empty of all thought, eh? Somehow, Mary, I cannot believe that of you.' He smiled: a slow, sensual smile that sent her heart racing.

'May I pass you the fruit? Or more wine?'

'No, thank you. I have had sufficient.'

Mary lifted her wineglass, drinking the final mouthful. She savoured the sweet fruitiness before releasing its warmth to trickle through her. It was very palatable, had complemented the desserts and it was helping her to relax—no mean feat with Lucas sitting opposite, hard to resist. She loved to see him relaxed and happy. He was optimistic over the future of the estate and—her heart leapt at the realisation—he had trusted her enough to confide in her about his business.

Lucas pushed his chair back and stood. She'd never seen him formally dressed before and she studied him, a flutter of anticipation deep inside. Oh, how she wanted him. He was so elegant and handsome, his white shirt and neckcloth in stark contrast to his black long-tailed coat, waistcoat and pantaloons. She felt shabby and unfashionable by comparison, in her borrowed dress.

He held out his hand. 'Come. We may as well warm ourselves by the fire in the sitting room.'

She placed her hand on his palm, revelling in his latent strength as he closed long fingers around hers. Her blood pumped faster as he raised her to her feet and pressed warm, firm lips to her hand before leading her to the small sitting room.

Every nerve in her body screamed *Danger!* but

she did not resist, even though she was filled alternately with dread and hope. She knew she could delay leaving no longer. This might be their last evening together but, at the same time, her foolish heart still dreamt of a happy ending, of a future where she and the children remained at the Hall as part of Lucas's life.

In the sitting room, he turned her to face him. Taking her face between his hands, he tilted her face and gazed down at her, his smile questioning. The musky scent of male enveloped her, interweaving with the faint tang of apple wood from the fire, where the logs burned with a steady glow.

Mayhap she could not voice her love but, as their eyes fused, she strived to communicate it without words. Surely a few kisses would not hurt? Could she convey her love and trust in such a way? There would be no need to go further.

Unless...? She played with the notion she had flirted with over the past few days. Why should she not do as her heart desired? She'd had her fill of Sensible Mary. Why should she not experience, even if only for the briefest of times, the passion and the thrill of loving Lucas? She was a widow, not a virgin. She had bricked herself in with rules of her own making. Why should she not break free of her self-imposed restraints and fly free?

She stepped close to Lucas and pushed her hands
beneath his coat. Felt him jerk as she unbuttoned
his waistcoat, then splayed her fingers over the solid
wall of his chest. The fine linen of his shirt was no
barrier to the heat radiating from his body or to the
fast, strong beat of his heart. Her own heart beat a
thunderous tattoo as it pumped hot blood around
her body.

'There is fire in your eyes, my sweet Mary,' Lucas
murmured. His eyes darkened until they were black
as coals. His gaze penetrated so deep it felt as though
it brushed her very soul. 'I wonder? Is there fire in
your belly, too?'

His words fanned the flame of her desire. It raced
through her veins, shrivelling any residual common
sense with its fiery heat as her body's needs surged
to the fore. Her insides seemed to swoop in anticipation as she pressed her body to his. Her lips parted
as his dark head lowered. He took her mouth, his
lips warm and firm, tasting of wine and his heady,
intoxicating flavour. Her soft curves moulded to his
hard, muscular body as she rose on to tiptoes, digging urgent fingers into muscular shoulders, then
winding frantic arms around his neck, revelling in
his stark heat.

A low groan sounded deep in his chest and reverberated through her body. His shaft was rock-hard

against her belly, intensifying her burning need. She pushed eager fingers through his locks, silky and slippery against her skin. Then she was arching over an arm of steel at the small of her back as scorching kisses trailed down her neck and seared her collarbone. Desire sizzled as her knees gave way, seemingly too weak to hold her weight.

Heavy breasts strained against the thin fabric of her dress, aching for release. His hand cupped her, moulding and squeezing, teasing. She gasped her pleasure, arching back even further, pressing into his touch. A hasty tug at her neckline and one breast sprang free. Her nipple was in his mouth and he suckled fiercely. She cried out and again as his thigh slid between her legs, parting them to press against her engorged flesh. She moved involuntarily against his hard muscle, needing him with an urgency that banished all else from her mind.

'Mary,' he groaned, holding her secure as her bones and muscles dissolved. 'Mary, I...'

She shivered as his mouth left her breast and his breath wafted over her damp skin.

'Nooo...!' She prised heavy lids open. Why had he stopped? She felt him tense.

'Quickly, sit there.' His voice was urgent; he was tugging her dress into place as he pushed her towards the chair by the fire.

She collapsed into the chair and watched, confused, as he took two long strides to gaze intently at a landscape on the wall.

What...?

Resentment swelled, until the rattle of cups outside the door penetrated the sensual haze that still enveloped her. She sat bolt upright, fingers clutching at the arms of the chair. What if Ellen—for it was she who had entered the room, carrying the tea tray— had had steadier hands? She would have come into the room to find... Heat scorched Mary's cheeks. Never in her married life had she lost herself in the moment quite so thoroughly.

Her whole body still vibrated with need. Unfulfilled, she wanted nothing more than to throw herself into Lucas's arms and beg him to take her. She stared into the flames and concentrated on breathing: in...out...in...out...

'What are you doing?' His amused voice broke into her near trance.

She looked up. 'Concentrating.'

The room behind Lucas was empty, the door closed. They were alone again.

'On...?'

Not throwing myself into your arms. 'I cannot do this. I must not. I am sorry. I...'

A dull ache spread through her as misery ripped at

her heart. Lucas knelt in front of her and she shuddered at the warmth of his touch as he clasped her hands and pressed his lips to each one in turn.

'I know.'

'I'm sorry...I don't know why...I want...but I can't...' Her throat was thick with despair.

'Mary!' He tightened his grip on her hands, shaking them in an effort, she dimly realised, to interrupt her disjointed attempts to explain. 'It is all right. I understand. You would not be the woman you are, the woman I...I *admire*...if you threw your principles aside on the strength of a few kisses. I know you do not wish a casual liaison and I have too much respect for you to encourage you to act against your own instinct and morals.'

Her tight muscles relaxed, but her blood still pumped hot. She could almost wish she had not been as honest with Lucas. Then she could... No. To think that way was surely madness. Could she live with herself were she to act with so little self-respect?

'Thank you for your understanding.'

He held her gaze, his ebony eyes clear and sincere. 'I do understand, Mary, though I—' His jaw snapped shut and he surged to his feet, reached out his hands. 'I must say no more or, despite my fine sentiments, I shall be in danger of trying to coax you after all.'

Mary took his hands and he pulled her upright. 'Would you like a cup of that tea?'

She shook her head, mute.

'Then I think it for the best if we both retire.'

Chapter Twenty

Lucas lay awake, restless and unfulfilled. He scanned the room, dimly lit by the embers of the fire, for the umpteenth time.

This is what you get for acting the gentleman!

He ached for Mary. His fingertips still tingled with the memory of her silky-soft skin; the taste of her lingered in his mouth. He closed his eyes and tried to lose himself in a fantasy of Mary in his arms, in his bed, but it was futile.

The bed was too lumpy; the pillow too flat; the room too hot.

He ripped off his nightshirt and cast it across the room. His skin felt too tight. His blood still surged. And he…he *wanted*. With a savage curse, he threw back the covers and strode to the window, hauled open the curtains and threw up the sash. The night air blasted over his skin. He sighed, staring mindlessly at the moonlit landscape. He shivered. Crashed the window shut. He had dealt with the heat, but…

'Can you not sleep either?'

He whipped round, stared, incredulous. Every sinew, every muscle, every cell locked tight. His heart thundered.

Mary.

Here.

Was she real? Or had his tortured imagination somehow…?

'I didn't hear you come in.'

Other questions, more pertinent, clamoured to be voiced, but he seemed incapable of forming the words. His heart leapt into his throat at the unbearably erotic glimpses of her naked feet beneath the hem of her full-length nightshift as she glided towards him with silent steps.

She stopped a foot away, eyes glimmering in the moonlight. Her scent enveloped him.

Mary.

He opened his arms and she stepped into his embrace.

'Why…? I thought…'

'Hush.' She leaned back, searching his face. 'I could not sleep either. I want you. It is as simple, and as complicated, as that.'

Tremors washed his skin as she curled her fingers

around his nape. Her other hand stroked his chest as she softly hummed her appreciation.

She was real. She was here.

He framed her beloved face with his palms, tilting it so he could read her eyes. 'Are you sure?'

She smiled, pressed closer. 'I am sure.'

He feathered kisses over her upturned face, then settled his mouth on hers, tasting her sweet, luscious lips as he explored with gentle hands, lingering over her delicate shoulder blades, tracing the elegant line of her back before settling, satisfyingly, on the round of her bottom.

Desire, passion, *need* urged him on. Ruthlessly, he reined them in. He was achingly aroused, but he resolved to take his time, to pay her the homage she deserved.

Slowly, he gathered up the fabric of her nightshift until he could lift it over her head. He stepped back, savouring the vision before him: her slender neck and the elegant sweep of her shoulders, the proud jut of her breasts above the curve of her ribs, the softly rounded belly and the barely visible fair curls at the juncture of her thighs.

He lifted his gaze to her face. Saw her hunger as her eyes swept his body. Felt the responding tug in his loins. Closed his eyes and tipped back his head as she stroked his neck, his chest, then trailed her fingers down his torso.

'Do you know how I have yearned to touch you like this?'

He gasped as her lips closed around his nipple, hot tongue flicking. Her hand drifted down, down...and then his reins snapped.

She was in his arms, all naked, writhing temptation. His lips devoured hers as he carried her to his bed and followed her down, fitting his hard lines against her lush curves. One hand tangled into the fragrant abundance of her hair and the other cupped her breast, kneading. Her nipple was a tight bud as he circled and teased. Her hands fluttered over his back and shoulders with butterfly touches, erotic, arousing. He was on fire. He tore his mouth from hers, pressed feverish lips to her neck, her collarbone, her breast. Sucked her nipple deep into his mouth, heard the catch in her breath, the low moan.

He skimmed the side of her body, following the dips and curves, caressed her smooth thigh, stroked the sensitive skin behind her knee. Then his fingers swept higher, seeking the moist heat at her core.

'Yes.' She arched, spread her thighs. 'Oh, yes, Lucas.'

He moved, settling between her legs.

'Please.'

Her whisper was the trigger. He buried himself deep inside her. Scalding hot, tight, she surrounded him.

Mary gasped her pleasure. Time stood still. He filled her, stretched her.

Lucas.

He was all she could see, all she could feel. He was all she wanted. She had made her decision. She had come to him, offering her body and her heart, knowing this might be her one and only chance to love him.

He had stilled, was poised above her—exciting, tempting. She reached for him, pulled him close, luxuriated in his weight, his heat, his hair-roughened skin. She wrapped her arms around his neck as he lowered his head and his lips took hers. She clung, kissing back with urgent need, stunned at the ferocity of her desire. The weight on her eased as he began to move inside her. Passion swirled and spiralled as a near unbearable tension built at her core. She clutched at his arms, fingers digging into the solid muscle as her legs wrapped around him, opening, tempting him deeper. She met each thrust, desperate to drive him on, but he slowed, tore his lips from hers. Frustrated, she cranked open heavy lids.

'Not yet, sweetheart.'

His deep voice reverberated through her. His

eyes, locked with hers, were dark and intent, his jaw set, as he began to move with tantalisingly slow, deep thrusts, driving her on until her back and neck arched, fingers clutched at the sheets, thighs strained.

'Lucas.' Her voice was a husky plea.

He slipped his hand between her thighs and stroked, and she finally, blissfully, shattered into a thousand sparkling pieces as wave after wave of ecstasy rippled through her. Hot tears, half-pleasure, half-agony, scalded her cheeks. He thrust faster, deeper, once…twice…and, with an exultant cry, reached his release. He collapsed atop her, chest heaving and she held him, smoothing his hair from his sweat-beaded brow. All too soon he withdrew, searching her eyes questioningly. She knew what he asked—words were unnecessary.

'No regrets.' She reached for him and their lips met in a long, slow, spellbinding kiss.

Towards dawn, Mary watched Lucas sleep, as she had done so many times before. But not like this. Not half lying across him, one leg thrown across his, exhausted after a night of lovemaking, their passion still scenting the air. His chest rose and fell under her hand, the crisp hairs rough against her skin. He did not stir as she eased away from him.

She slid from beneath the covers and found her nightshift where it lay discarded on the floor. She shivered as she pulled it over her head, the fabric chill against her skin. She must return to her own bedchamber before the servants stirred. It was the Quarter Day and she knew Trant would awaken Lucas early as he had a busy morning ahead, meeting with his tenants. She wondered what the day might bring. He had spoken no words of love, of a future; she had expected none. She had come to him last night with no purpose or hope other than to be with the man she loved.

She had spoken the truth last night.

No regrets.

At least, not yet.

She slipped out of the room and fled, silent-footed, back to her own room.

Chapter Twenty-One

The next afternoon, Mary took two steps into the library, pushing the door to behind her, and then jerked to a halt, breathless with shock. There was no time to retreat, for Sir Gerald Quartly, standing by the fire with his hands clasped behind his back, had seen her. He strode towards her. His expression, forbidding from the start, was positively glowering by the time he stood in front of her. That he now recognised her, she could not doubt. Her whole body trembled as he raked her with cold grey eyes, hard as granite. Then her brain scrambled to catch up and she whirled around, reaching for the door.

A hard hand encircled her arm and dragged her back against a solid chest.

'So, this is where you've been hiding, is it?' He spoke low, growling into her ear.

Mary froze. Harsh breaths rattled against her cheek as his grip tightened painfully.

'I should have recognised you before. I thought you looked familiar. And two brats, eh? The children you deprived me of: an heir, my future.'

Mary struggled to get free, but made no sound. She could not bear anyone—Lucas!—to find out what her father had done. That he had drunkenly gambled her life away as if she was worthless. That knowledge had almost crucified her. That her own father, once so loving and kind, had changed so much. That he had so little love for his only child, she had become a mere commodity to be traded upon the turn of a card.

Quartly dragged her away from the door and deeper into the room. Stumbling, she fought to stay on her feet. She spun around to face him, stomach churning. Her mind tumbled, snatching at options. Try to run? The door was impossible, with Quartly in the way. What about the windows? She glanced at them. No, she would never get them open in time.

Reluctantly, she looked back at Quartly. His arms hung by his side as his chest heaved, his breaths audible in the silence. His face was mottled with fury. Mary clenched her teeth and clasped her hands in front of her, willing them to stop shaking. Her only remaining option, although it went against her instinct, was to reason with him. Try to pacify him. Tell him lies, if necessary, to help her get away.

She stepped towards him. He stiffened. Good. She had surprised him, done the unexpected.

She tried a smile. He frowned—a puzzled frown, not angry.

Apologise.

'I am sorry, Sir Gerald. The way I behaved—it was thoughtless, but I was very young at the time. Did you not make mistakes in your youth?'

His eyes narrowed. Then he sneered. 'Next you will be telling me you wish you had wed me after all.'

Not a fool, Sir Gerald. Try another tack.

'No.' She strove to keep her voice level and her expression neutral, knowing instinctively he was the kind of man who would feed on any hint of fear. 'I do not wish that. But I regret my impetuosity. I should have stayed and talked to my father and to you. I am persuaded you would never have forced me to wed you against my wishes.'

That was exactly what he had intended, Mary's father had made that painfully clear. But she could act the *ingénue*.

'And now you are Rothley's lightskirt. How long have you been under his protection? Are the brats his?' He barked a bitter laugh. 'Your standards haven't risen much since that clerk you ran off with, have they? I should have thought a woman in your position would require a protector with more than a couple of farthings to rub together.'

'I am not under Lord Rothley's protection, as you put it. I have only been at the Hall a few weeks. I shall be leaving very soon, now his lordship is recovered.'

'Crawling back to your father? Do you imagine he'll be interested in you and your spawn now he's got a new family?'

He might as well have ploughed his fist into her belly.

Her father had remarried? He had other children?

'You didn't know, did you?' His voice came from far away. 'It is true. He remarried three years since. They have two boys. He has no need of you.'

Bile rose to choke her. What now of her plans? No wonder her father had not replied to her letter. Quartly was right. What need had her father of a recalcitrant daughter and two grandchildren sired by his erstwhile steward? Her whole world fractured and reformed a thousand times inside her head. She felt her knees sag and she desperately sucked in several deep breaths. Quartly grabbed her arm and dragged her to a chair by the fireplace, pushing her into it. A small, panicked portion of her brain clamoured to resist him, but her body seemed powerless to obey her will.

'It is a shock, I know, my dear. But never fear. Your father might be lost to you, but if, as you say, Rothley is nothing to you, you can come with me. You know I have always wanted you. And you have proved yourself fertile—I shall get my heir at long last.'

'No.' Her voice came out in a whisper. She licked at her dry lips and tried again. 'No. Thank you for the offer, but, no.'

Quartly knelt before her, clasping her hands. She battled the urge to snatch them from his sweaty grasp, pressing against the chair's back to try to widen the gap between them. He leaned towards her. The bulk of his torso pinned her to the chair as his belly squashed against her knees. She fought to conceal her revulsion, taking shallow breaths to avoid inhaling his foul breath as it fanned her face.

Her wits began to reassemble. She would reason with him and, if that failed, she would scream. Better Lucas knew the worst of her than she should endure much more of this.

'Come with me, Mary dearest. I will provide for you. You shall want for nothing. I am a wealthy man.' He sat back on his heels and released one of her hands as he gestured at their surroundings. 'You deserve better than this rundown old heap and a debt-ridden, ill-tempered recluse.'

Mary shook her head but, before she could speak, Quartly's face darkened as his eyes bored into hers.

'You owe me! I won you, fair and square. You are mine!'

His hand was around her neck, squeezing. Desperate, Mary scrabbled at his fingers as they dug in to her flesh. Panic set in as she struggled to draw breath, tears starting to her eyes. Dark shadows edged her vision. Wet lips smothered hers, a thick tongue probing at her open mouth. Finally, the hand loosened and he took his mouth from hers. Her breath rasped painfully along her bruised windpipe and into her desperate lungs. As her vision cleared, she saw his satisfied smirk. Hatred spiked through her, tempered by caution. She was still at his mercy.

Follow his lead. Say anything. Get away.

'I will take you to pack your belongings. That way, Rothley will not get the opportunity to change your mind.'

Sick dread pooled in her stomach. Where was Lucas? Trant must have shown Quartly into the library in the first place, then gone to inform his master. Where was he?

Please come.

'My…' Her throat was on fire, her voice a dry croak. She coughed. Forced down some saliva. Tried again. 'My children. What about…?'

'Oh, do not worry about them, my dear. Why, I shall treat them as my own.' He grinned as he grabbed her hand and pulled her to her feet, tugging her close. The other hand cupped her cheek. His abrupt change of mood frightened Mary more than ever. 'I shall provide generously for you and the children, you'll see. They shall have the best tutors money can buy and go to the best schools. Do you not want the best for them, my sweet Mary?'

Hearing that endearment—the same words Lucas had whispered the night before—spewing from Quartly's foul mouth nearly shattered Mary's fragile hold on her sanity. She summoned up a strength she had not realised she possessed in order to sustain her charade.

'Yes…yes, of course I do. They…they will have the benefit of a good education…and…and a father they can respect.' Those deceitful words almost choked Mary. 'What mother would not wish that for her children?'

'They will be a ready-made brother and sister for our son, when he is born, my darling.'

Mary stared at him, horrified. Did he actually believe the scenario he constructed? Was he mad, or simply deluding himself?

Chapter Twenty-Two

Lucas had heard enough. His blood bubbled with fury. Visions of Julia in Henson's arms crowded his brain. How had he been deceived again? Fallen for a woman who cared more for her material comfort than for the love he offered? Visions of Mary, her beautiful golden hair streaming around her naked body, taunted him.

Fool! Would he never learn?

He shoved the library door open with such venom it crashed back against the wall, shaking on its hinges. What a touching scene. Quartly—that money-grabbing, evil villain—and Mary: standing close together, gazing into each other's eyes.

He had delayed attending Quartly, wanting the satisfaction of handing over the interest due before it was demanded. He had counted the money into a pouch, anticipating Quartly's anger and disbelief when told the final instalment would be paid, on time, at Christmas. Now, his victory was as ashes. What did it matter? What did anything matter, now?

He had stood outside the library door and heard with his own ears yet another capricious female throw away love and happiness for pure greed. But on the brink of flying at Quartly and beating him to a pulp, Lucas hesitated. He would not give them the satisfaction. He was not his father.

'Good afternoon, Quartly. I see Mrs Vale has been entertaining you in my absence.' *Scheming witch!* 'I apologise for the delay in attending you, but I had a business matter to conclude.'

He crossed the library, his attention squarely on Quartly's face. He did not dare to even glance in Mary's direction for, if he did, he feared he might be unable to control his rage after all. He held out the pouch of coins.

'Your interest payment.' He indicated the table in the centre of the room. 'If you would care to count it out, verify it is correct…?'

'No need. I am sure it is all there.'

'Oh, but I insist, my dear fellow. I should prefer to rectify any shortfall now than to oblige you to come back should my reckoning have gone awry.'

It had happened before. Once. Quartly had returned to the Hall the day after the Quarter Day, claiming the full monies had not been paid when

Lucas knew very well they had. He had been left with no choice but to pay an additional sum, or Quartly would apply to the court to gain possession of the mortgaged land.

Quartly stumped over to the table and emptied the pouch, grumbling under his breath. Lucas felt Mary's eyes on him, but kept his attention on Quartly. He would not weaken. They were welcome to each other. But not until he had told Mary precisely what he thought of her.

As soon as Quartly had finished, Lucas said, 'Good. I am pleased all is to your satisfaction. You will be delighted to know the final instalment will be paid on time at Christmas, together with any further interest due.'

Quartly stared. 'Oh!' His frustration was clear to see. 'I see…well…I suppose I must congratulate you, Rothley.'

Lucas bowed. 'Thank you. Now, I have business with Mrs Vale, so I will bid you good day, Quartly.'

Quartly crossed the room in a flash, taking Mary by the arm. Lucas felt all his muscles lock in his attempt not to floor the man there and then.

'Mary is leaving with me.'

Mary twisted, pulling at her captured arm. 'Lucas, I have…'

Lucas spoke over Mary's words. He did not want

to know her reasons or her excuses. Not in front of Quartly. 'Not yet, she is not, and if you are not out of my house in the next two minutes, Quartly, I shall throw you out. Later, if she wishes to come to you, she may do so, with my blessing.'

'Now, see here...'

'Lucas, please...'

'Go!' Lucas roared, closing the gap between himself and Quartly, gaining some satisfaction from the sudden panic on Quartly's face. 'Or shall I throw you out after all?'

'Make sure you keep your side of our bargain, Mary,' Quartly said, his face dark with fury, before he stalked from the room, leaving Lucas to look directly at Mary for the first time.

'Oh, Lucas, thank goodness.' Mary rushed to him, reaching for his hands.

He snatched them from her grasp. 'Well?'

She eyed him uncertainly.

'Do you have nothing to say? Were you going to admit your deceitfulness, or were you thinking to sneak from my house without a word?'

'No, Lucas. You do not understand...'

'Oh, I understand very well. He can offer you more than I. And your sort will always take the idle solution, will they not?'

A frown creased Mary's brow. 'Offer? You made

me no offer, Lucas, other than that of becoming your mistress.'

'And you would rather stomach being his wife?'

'No! That is not what—'

'I heard you, Mary.' He took her by the shoulders. How could he convey his anguish? He felt his fingers dig into her and abruptly he put her from him. He would not risk hurting her, not physically. But he had his words and he lashed out. 'You were bargaining with him, like the strumpet you swore you were not. I thought you different, but I was wrong. You have betrayed me, just like her! You have no concept of the truth and I am all kinds of a fool for allowing myself to be taken in by your lies.'

He spun round and strode to the window to gaze unseeingly at the view. 'Go! Take your belongings and your children and leave this house. I don't want to see you ever again.'

'Lucas, no!'

He heard her move, sensed her approach. Felt her hand, hesitant, on his arm. He shrugged her off.

'Did I not make myself clear? You are no longer welcome in my house.'

'But…Lucas…last night…'

How long had they been planning this? Had she known, last night when she came to him? Every muscle locked tight as he fought the urge to grab her…shake her…kiss her…beg her…

'Go,' he roared. 'Now!'

'Please. Let me explain. I did not know…I knew him before…'

He did not want to hear any more. That she had known him in the past—somehow, it made it worse. It made her choice even harder to stomach. She must know what manner of man she dealt with. He could no longer bear to be near her. He strode for the door, knocking her aside in his haste.

In the hall, Trant hovered. 'Brandy, Trant. Now. In my study. And Mrs Vale is leaving. This afternoon.' He slammed the study door behind him and sank into his chair, burying his head in his hands.

Mary could not move. Lucas's words echoed as the door slammed. How could he ever believe she would go with Quartly? How could he even think… after last night…? She wrapped her arms around her waist, shivering, until the sound of Trant going into his master's study roused her.

What should she do? What *could* she do? Wait and hope Lucas would calm down and listen to her? But if she stayed, against his wishes, and Quartly came back? No, she could not risk staying.

Where to go? Her father… The shock of Quartly's

revelation still reverberated through her. Remarried? Where did that leave her? And Toby? And Emily? Tears scalded her eyes. She shook her head.

She must move; do something; take action.

She rushed from the room, almost cannoning into Trant in her haste. She mumbled an apology as she slipped past him, then ran up the stairs, seeking the sanctuary of her room.

One step at a time. She would gather their belongings. Then find the children. Then…?

Her thoughts slammed into the stone wall of her dilemma. They could not remain, not with Lucas so very furious. Why did he still not trust her? What had he overheard? He must have heard her trying to pacify Quartly, in order to escape him. He had accused her of betrayal.

'Just like her,' he had said.

Like Julia?

In her room, she leant back against the door, her breath hitching. She dug her nails into her palms to keep the tears at bay, but to no avail. An avalanche of grief swept over her and, before she knew it, she was face down on the bed, sobbing her heart out.

Some time later, a hand on her shoulder brought her back to reality. How long had she lain there? She was exhausted: her mind fuzzy, her body drained, her throat raw and her face hot and wet with tears. She lifted her head, to peer into the kindly, worried features of Mrs Lindley.

'Oh, Lindy,' she gasped. She sat up and felt the cook's arms go around her as a fresh bout of tears overwhelmed her.

'There, there, my dear.'

Mrs Lindley rocked Mary until she was all cried out. Then listened as she stuttered her story, telling her about her father and Quartly, and what Lucas had overheard.

'I have nowhere to go, Lindy. If it was only me, I could manage, but the children are so young. None of this is their fault. And if my own father will not help me, what can I do?'

'Come now, ma'am, don't you despair. We'll come up with some plan between us. We must, for the sake of those dear sweet bairns of yours. Maybe you can hide in the Hall? It is certainly big enough.'

Mary sat up, scrubbing at her face with her hands. She felt grubby and unkempt. Without a word, Mrs Lindley went to the washstand, tipped water into the basin and wet Mary's washcloth. Walking back to the bed, she came to an abrupt halt, her eyes on Mary's neck.

'What happened?' Her round face wrinkled with concern. 'Not his lordship, surely?'

Mary touched her neck, wincing. 'No, of course not. It was Sir Gerald. He is a brute. And that is why I cannot remain here. If he were to find me...' Her voice rose, hysteria close to the surface.

'He'll not find you, ma'am, not while I've got breath in my body.' Mrs Lindley fell silent, tapping her finger against her teeth. Then she grinned. 'I've an idea.'

Mary gazed at her, a seed of hope taking root.

'The Dower House.'

'But...'

'It's perfect. It's far enough away from the Hall that his lordship won't notice anything amiss and it's set well back from the lane, so there'll be no curious neighbours to wonder who's there when her ladyship's still away.' She fixed Mary with a knowing look. 'We have to keep you somewhere close, 'til his lordship comes to his senses.'

Mary stilled, the sound of her heartbeat ringing in her ears. 'What do you mean, Lindy?'

'Why, surely you won't deny what the rest of us have known this past week or more?'

The mattress sank as Mrs Lindley lowered her bulk on to the bed and began to wipe Mary's face with the washcloth.

'You were made for each other,' she said gruffly. 'Any fool can see it.'

'I had hoped...' Mary whispered, barely believing she was confessing even this much to the cook, 'but, now...oh, Lindy, you should have seen the way he looked at me. It was as though he could not bear the sight of me!'

'He'll find the truth. He's no fool, his lordship.'

Mary was wise enough to conceal her silent *hmmph* from Mrs Lindley. Lucas might be no fool, but he could be stubborn and blind, and impetuous, and...and...irresistible and loving and adorable. She wished she could share the cook's faith, but the vivid memory of his rage and pain did not allow her to believe. She forced her mind to more practical matters.

'What about the others? Will any of them betray us? Trant?'

'Trant won't know, not from my lips; although, to be fair to the man, it was him that sent me to you this afternoon. We can trust Ellen, mind you. I'll send her over there this afternoon to ready the house.'

Mrs Lindley grinned, rubbing her hands together. Mary suspected she would enjoy playing the conspirator.

'But for how long, Lindy? We cannot stay there for ever.'

'I don't know, ma'am, but we'll think of something. The most important thing is to keep you and the bairns safe for tonight.'

The children! Mary sat up with a jolt. What had she been thinking, wallowing in self-pity whilst her children were heaven knew where? She must find them, make sure they were safe. What if Quartly came back? He wouldn't hesitate to use her children to coerce her. Or what if Lucas came across them? In his current mood, how might he react? She recalled the bite of his fingers into her arms, how he had immediately slackened his grasp. No, he would not hurt the children, she knew. But she must find them and leave.

The sooner the better.

Chapter Twenty-Three

'*Emily!*'

Lifting his head from the intense scrutiny of the surface of his desk, Lucas listened.

There it was again. Frantic.

'*Emily!*'

What the …? Couldn't a man get any peace in his own house? Cursing, he shoved his chair back and stood up, swaying as the half-bottle of brandy he had drunk made itself felt. He steadied himself against the desk for a moment, breathing deeply, then headed for the door.

He was fine. Not drunk at all. Just betrayed.

Her perfidy ripped at his heart, fuelling his wrath. He flung open his study door, opened his mouth to bellow at them all to keep quiet, but the sound of running footsteps above stayed him. He listened. Something was wrong. He thrust his anger aside. He ran up the stairs, two at a time. At the top, Susan, her face drawn with worry, hurried from a bedchamber on the right.

'Susan? What is it?'

'The little girl, m'lord. Emily. She's missing.'

'How long?'

'I don't know, sir. We've been searching this past hour.'

Trant emerged from a different bedchamber, shaking his head.

'Where is Toby? Does he not know where his sister is?'

'No. He's with Mrs Lindley in the kitchen.' Mary had materialised beside him: eyes swollen and red; face pale; hair awry. He longed to take her in his arms, comfort her. He huffed a silent, bitter laugh at his pathetic weakness. She was a strumpet. She deserved no pity. The children, though. They had done nothing wrong. Their mother's character was not their fault. He pictured Emily's face and his heart lurched with fear. She was so young, so vulnerable.

'What happened? How can a two-year-old be missing? Was no one watching her?'

'I...' Her voice shook. He watched her take a steadying breath before she spoke again. 'I was packing our belongings. The children were playing in the old nursery. When I went to find them, Emily was gone. They were playing hide-and-seek and Emily went to hide from Toby and we can't… we can't…' A sob escaped her lips.

Susan patted Mary's shoulder. 'There, ma'am. We'll find her. She can't have gone far. She can't open the outside doors. She must be in the house somewhere.'

'What if…what if Sir Gerald has taken her?'

'Why on earth would Quartly need to take her? You will all be with him soon enough,' Lucas said bitterly.

'Don't worry about that, ma'am. I saw Sir Gerald off the premises myself,' Trant said, with an accusatory glance at Lucas. *Such insolence!* 'Emily was not with him.'

'Thank goodness,' Mary said.

'Where have you searched?' Lucas asked.

'Everywhere, my lord,' Trant replied. 'This is our second search. She's nowhere to be found. We must continue on this floor, as we intended. We must follow a system, or we risk rushing around in a disorganised panic.'

'Where is Ellen?'

'No one seems to know, sir,' Trant said.

'Well, there is your answer. Emily is off somewhere with Ellen.'

'No!'

He looked at Mary in surprise but she evaded his

gaze. 'I beg your pardon, I did not mean to snap. I understand Ellen has gone on an errand. She wouldn't take Emily without telling anyone. You are right, Trant, we should continue our search of this floor.'

Lucas watched as the servants and Mary hurried down the landing and vanished through various doors.

Where might a child hide? He frowned, thinking back to his own childhood and the games he and his brother had played—the sprawling old house a veritable playground when the weather had kept them indoors.

Why would Emily not come out when she heard people calling her? Mayhap because she was scared and—the answer came to him in a flash—because she was somewhere she should not be. Where was it he and Hugo had dared each other to go—the place they were not allowed and where they had quaked with terror lest he discover them? The answer was their father's rooms. And where might be Emily's equivalent of that forbidden place? Lucas spun on his heel and ran for his own bedchamber.

At the door, he turned the handle quietly and opened the door, peering around the edge. No sign of Emily. He slipped through the door and closed it again.

'It's all right, Emily. You can come out. No one is cross with you.' He kept his voice quiet and calm.

There was no response. Could he be wrong? He bent down and pulled the eiderdown up to peer under the bed. There was no one there. He looked around. The obvious hiding place was his wardrobe. He strode across, pulled open the door and was rewarded with a squeak of terror. A scared face stared up at him from the depths, eyes huge and fearful, brimming with tears.

He bent down and lifted her hot little body. 'Hush, now, sweeting. It's all right.'

Emily whimpered, but wrapped her arms trustingly around his neck and buried her face against his shoulder. His arms tightened around her, cuddling her close, his heart melting.

'Why did you not come when you heard your mama calling, Emily? She is very worried about you.'

Emily clung tighter, trembling. Lucas carried her to the door and opened it.

'Bad door.'

He pulled his head back and looked down at her. She was staring up at him. Her thumb stole into her mouth.

'What do you mean: bad door?'

She ducked her head against his shoulder again

and mumbled around her thumb. Lucas popped one finger beneath her chin and raised it.

'Tell me again, Emily. Which door was bad?'

She looked back over his shoulder, pointing to the wardrobe with her free hand, and Lucas understood. When he had looked in the wardrobe, the door had been latched shut. Somehow, Emily had gone inside and the door had closed behind her, trapping her.

'It was a bad door, indeed,' Lucas said. 'You must promise me not to hide in cupboards again. We were all very worried about you.'

His gut clenched as he said the words. He would never know if she did such a thing again. She would be gone from his life. His arms tightened involuntarily, hugging Emily's warm body closer. They would all be gone. They would go to live with Quartly and he would have to think of his Mary…

He gritted his teeth.

Don't think about it. Don't look back.

He strode along the landing. The sooner he returned Emily to her mother, the sooner they would be gone from his life and he could get back to normal. He refused to examine what that normality might be.

Standing at the head of the stairs, Susan saw him coming. She shrieked in delight.

'Emily! Oh, you're safe!' She raised her voice in a shout. 'Mrs Vale! Mrs Vale! Come quickly.'

Running footsteps heralded the arrival of Mary, who snatched Emily from Lucas. His gut clenched anew as he watched her hugging her daughter, who was now sobbing her eyes out in earnest.

'Where did you find her?' Mary asked.

'In my bedchamber, hiding in the wardrobe.'

'Your bedchamber? But Trant looked in there, I am sure he did.'

'I did. Twice.' Trant had arrived, beaming when he saw Emily was safe.

'Ah, but you didn't reckon on young Emily not daring to get caught in there. You did not look hard enough. And as the wardrobe door had latched shut, she was trapped in there.'

'Well, thank goodness she's safe,' Trant said. 'Come along, young Susan, we must go and tell Mrs Lindley and Toby the good news.'

Susan's eyes swivelled between Lucas and Mary. 'Shall we take Emily with us, ma'am?'

'Yes, please, Susan. I shall be down shortly.'

They started down the stairs, leaving Lucas and Mary facing each other. She lifted shining eyes to his.

'Thank you, Lucas. I'm so grateful. I…'

Her thanks tailed away as Lucas stiffened. He did

not need a mirror to know his expression was forbidding.

'Nothing has changed. I want you gone.'

He turned on his heel. There was half a bottle of brandy waiting for him in his study.

'Not tonight!'

He halted. 'I beg your pardon?' He turned back slowly.

Mary stood ramrod-straight in front of him, hands fisted by her side. 'It is late. It is near dark. I will not subject my children to a long journey when they should be in bed asleep.'

'Quartly only lives on the other side of the village. It is not very far. Hooper will drive you.'

Something like contempt flickered in her eyes, stabbing at his heart. Every muscle in his face ached with the effort of maintaining his expression.

'You will not even know we are here.'

Yes, I will. How could I not know you are here, under my roof, when every bone in my body remembers you and aches for you?

'We will leave at first light. You can remain in your bedchamber tomorrow, until Trant informs you we have gone, if it pleases you, but we will not leave tonight. Unless you intend to evict us with your own hands?'

He yearned to do precisely that. But if he touched

her now, if he felt her silken skin beneath his hands, how could he not take her in his arms? Try everything within his power to win her back from Quartly?

He banished his weak, foolish longings. 'I will leave word for Hooper to take you wherever you wish to go in the morning.'

Now he desperately needed that brandy. He sauntered towards the stairs in a show of indifference, despite every nerve he possessed screaming at him to run.

He could not bear her to suspect his heart had splintered into a million pieces.

Chapter Twenty-Four

Mary's bedchamber door flew open with a crash. Terrified, she sat bolt upright in her bed.

'What is it? What is wrong?' she gasped, before realising the figure framed in the open doorway, illuminated by a single flickering candle flame, was Lucas.

Sleep had eluded her since she had sought her bed at an earlier hour than usual. Her thoughts had chased round and round. Fear over what the future might hold for her and the children warred in her heart with the raw grief of unrequited love. Despite Mrs Lindley's assurances that Lucas would realise the truth once he had calmed down, Mary could not believe it. Mrs Lindley had not seen him or heard the things he said. But she was also angry he could believe her capable of behaving in such a despicable way, particularly after the night before.

Lucas clutched at the door frame with one hand

as the other lifted the candlestick. Mary's heart lurched as he released the frame and staggered into the room, coming to a swaying halt by the side of the bed.

'The tables are turned, sweet Mary, are they not?' he slurred, 'for you are in bed and *I* am here to minister to *you.*'

Brandy fumes wafted over her, catapulting her back to their first meeting in the woods, when she had dismissed him as a gentleman in his cups, until she had realised he was injured. He was not injured now, however. She grabbed at the bedcovers and tugged them up to cover her. He laughed, a mirthless sound.

'You must learn not to be shy, my sweet. You will be expected to expose more than that monstrosity of a nightgown to *Sir Gerald* once you are installed as his mistress.'

'You are wrong and you are insulting, sir, if you truthfully believe I would become any man's mistress. You should know that, of anyone, for I would have accepted your offer.'

He scowled. 'Ah, but I could not provide the lifestyle you crave, could I? There would be no luxuries to be had at Rothley Hall.'

Mary glared at him. 'I think you mistake me for a lady of your past acquaintance, sir. I have never sought riches and, if you took the time to consider events with a clear head, you would know it. But, no! You needs must seek solace for imagined wrongs at the bottom of a bottle!'

Lucas scowled down at her.

'You are drunk, Lord Rothley. I suggest you go to bed and sleep it off.'

'Hah! Nothing escapes you, does it, my dear?'

'Very little.'

He swayed again, then slumped on to the bed. The mattress sagged, causing Mary to tip towards Lucas. The second she touched him she pushed away, scrambling to the far side of the bed. He reached out, snagging her hand in a tight grip. She stilled, conscious of his strength, but she was not scared. Even drunk and angry, he would not hurt her. Unlike Quartly, she realised, who'd had no qualms about attacking her even though he was completely sober.

'Why?' Lucas banged the candlestick down on to the bedside table, causing the flame to dance. He flung her hand away as if her very skin was tainted, then leaned forward, his back to her. It was as though he could not bear the sight of her.

'Why, Mary? I thought...' He groaned as his head sunk into his hands.

'What did you think?' she asked after a couple of beats of silence.

'That you were different. I *wanted* you to be different. Mayhap that is my trouble. I wanted it so much I persuaded myself it was true.'

'Different to whom? To Julia? *I am not her.*'

Lucas turned to stare at her, his eyes glittering. The air crackled between them, sending a jolt of pure energy through Mary. Her pulse raced and her heart hammered in her chest. Even after all that had happened, she still wanted him.

He traced her lips with a tender fingertip, his eyes following the movement. Desire sped through her veins to pool—hot and urgent—between her thighs. The bed rocked as he shifted, pressing her back against the pillows.

She felt the bedcovers lift and cool air fingered beneath. He laid next to her, half-covering her, warming her. She stroked his powerful shoulders, revelling in his hard, muscular body pressed full length against her. Long fingers tangled in her hair as her kissed her, his tongue probing at her lips until she opened to him.

Mary drifted in a sensual haze as all her senses focused on the intense need burgeoning deep within her core. The neck of her nightgown was pushed aside and his mouth was on her nipple, his tongue flicking at the swollen bud as her body tensed with need, thighs taut, back arching.

Then his lips were at her throat and, as the pain of her bruises registered, reality burst in. She pushed her hands between them, at his shoulders, shoving against him.

'No!'

Lucas froze.

Bitter disgust at her behaviour flooded Mary, sweeping away her ardour. His words echoed in her head: *'I am here to minister to you.'*

And she had colluded with him, had led him on.

'No!' She shoved harder.

He reared back, eyes dazed, a puzzled frown on his face.

'What is it? What is wrong?' Then his eyes cleared. 'Why have you stopped? You want this as much as I do. You enjoyed it last night.'

Mary wriggled until she was no longer beneath him, tugging at her nightgown to cover her breast.

'I did. But this is different.'

Lucas scowled, turning away. 'I don't see why.'

'Well, I shall tell you why. You are meaning to punish me. That is not love. It is not right. I do not deserve that.'

Her voice wobbled and she dug her nails into her arm. She would not let him see her distress, only her anger and her disdain.

'You have it wrong, Lucas. I was not negotiating with Sir Gerald.'

He surged to his feet, spinning round to glare down at her. 'Don't lie to me! I heard you! You and Quartly! You were planning together. He was offering you everything I cannot give you. Things I cannot afford. You are only interested in money! Not in love! Not in my heart!'

Love?

'You have never offered me love! Not in the way I understand it. Physical love, yes, but your heart? When did you ever offer me that?'

Mary rose to her knees on the bed, reaching for him as he backed away. 'You are wrong! I do not want riches. I only ever wanted you.'

'I do not believe you.'

'What is love without trust?' Mary asked in despair, but Lucas had already gone and her words bounced off the closed door.

She slumped on to the bed. She was shattered. How could he imply he loved her, yet believe her capable of acting as accused? She could not bear another encounter with him, neither tonight nor in the morning. Mind made up, she got up and started to dress. She was already packed. Middle of the night or not, she would collect the children and leave immediately. But she would not go to the Dower House.

She had thought of an alternative and no one at the Hall would know where they had gone. It might provide her with a short respite during which she must search for a solution to her quandary: a solution that relied on neither her father nor Lucas.

She picked up the bag Mrs Lindley had loaned her and gazed around the room one last time. Setting her jaw, she shut the door behind her and headed for the children's room.

By the time he reached his bedchamber, Lucas had thrown off most of the effects of the brandy. He stalked across the room to the window, throwing it wide. He leaned out into the fresh night air and inhaled, forcing the cold air into his lungs, clearing his head.

Only to hear the echo of Mary's voice. 'You have it wrong, Lucas.'

Was he wrong? He scrubbed his hand through his hair. He'd been wrong before. Sincerity shone in her words, but could he still trust his own instincts, despite what he had heard? He pushed away from the window and strode across the room to the bed, where he sat, tugging his neckcloth loose as he picked over all that had happened.

The knowledge that Quartly was waiting, like a vulture, to pick over the bones of Lucas's failure had plagued his life ever since his return to Rothley and now, when the end was finally in sight, he was back to torture Lucas some more.

'You are meaning to punish me.'

Had he meant to punish her? No. He could never use the act of love to inflict pain. He had been determined to make her understand what she had thrown away with such thoughtless disregard. But once his lips touched hers, instinct had taken over and all he had felt was the overwhelming urge to make love to her, as gently and as skilfully as he knew how.

Mary.

He ached for her. The sound of her name brought conflict to his thoughts and his feelings. Longing, love—even trust—warred against rage, betrayal and pain in his heart.

He pulled his neckcloth from his neck and dropped in on the floor.

Doubts beset his understanding of what had taken place in the library. Had the snippet of conversation he had overheard given the true meaning of Mary's conversation with Quartly?

He scrubbed his hand over the back of his neck.

He had sworn he would no longer act without reflection, yet here he was again.

He began to unbutton his shirt.

Did he honestly believe Mary would become embroiled with a man such as Quartly for the sake of an easy life? She had known him before. Surely she would not willingly set up home with him, let alone subject her children to such a life?

As he stripped off his shirt he cursed his impulsiveness. Would he never learn? Why had he refused to listen to Mary, either this afternoon or tonight?

Impatient now to put matters right between them, Lucas shrugged into his robe and strode to the door. Another apology was due. He would go to Mary and he would listen to what she had to say. Hand on the door handle, he hesitated. It was late. If he went to her bedchamber now, she would be defensive, believing he had come for another quarrel or, half-undressed as he was, to seduce her.

He must wait until morning. He would beg her to stay. He would *make* her stay. His arms ached to hold her soft, warm body and his lips yearned to taste her again. What would he not give to be snuggled up to her right now?

Her final words echoed in his mind: 'I do not want riches. I only ever wanted you.'

It was time to tell her the truth of how he felt about her and the fear it invoked within him. It was time to tell her he loved her. He must hope she would listen with a more open mind than he had shown to her.

Chapter Twenty-Five

At first light, Lucas—fully dressed, for he did not want Mary to think he had any other purpose than talking in mind—knocked at her bedchamber door. He waited, but there was no response. He knocked again.

Louder.

Then turned the handle and walked in. Sick dread churned his stomach, chilling him. The house loomed silent around him.

She was gone. The bed was stripped. No item remained to suggest she had ever been in the room. He slammed out of the room, ran up the stairs two at a time to the children's room.

Empty.

He whirled on the spot and raced to the kitchen. Mrs Lindley and Ellen were both at the table, at breakfast. They scrutinised him with identical expressions of scorn. He barely noticed.

'Where is Mrs Vale?'

'Gone. And the bairns. As you ordered. My lord.'

'Where?'

Mrs Lindley shrugged her massive shoulders.

'No!'

He ran from the room. He would get Sultan. He wouldn't rest until he found her. He had thought he was being considerate, not going back to her room last night. Leaving her in peace. Instead, he had given her time to slip away and go to Quartly.

Didn't you decide you were wrong about her going to Quartly?

Where else would she go? To her father's? Linburgh? Yes! Well, maybe. But what if Quartly happened to see her on the road? He felt certain now that the words he had overheard had been Mary trying to appease Quartly. Dunwick Manor was *en route*. He might as well call in as he passed. Wherever she had gone, he would get her back. He *must* persuade her to come home. The Hall was colder and lonelier than ever. No children playing, no laughter, no prospect of bumping into Mary at odd times of the day, lifting his mood and heating his blood with her simple presence.

At the stable yard there was no sign of either Shorey or Hooper and there was no time to delay. He grabbed Sultan's saddle and bridle and tacked him up at record speed, then stepped into the stirrup and swung his leg across the horse's back. A protest from his recently healed thigh gave him grim satisfaction. He deserved to suffer.

As he rode through the gates of Dunwick Manor all appeared still and quiet. No sign of Mary or the children. A brisk trot up the drive to the front of the modern Georgian house elicited no response. He hesitated, then turned Sultan to ride around the back, to the stable yard.

As he reached the yard entrance, two dogs bounded into view, barking and snarling. Sultan spun round, presenting the dogs with his rear end, ears flattened as he lashed out. Lucas fought to calm him, smoothing his neck and murmuring to him. A shout from inside the yard gained his attention.

'Hi! Get back 'ere!'

The dogs stopped their snapping and snarling and Lucas turned his mount to face the owner of the voice. His hands tightened involuntarily on the reins, causing Sultan to back a step in response. Both dogs stood at the man's heels, but Lucas had eyes for only one of them.

A collie.

Slowly, unbelievably, parts of the puzzle began to slot into place. The half-black, half-white face, the distinctive merle ruff and, more tellingly, the odd-coloured eyes, propelled him straight back to the day he was shot. There was no mistake. It was the same animal. He looked at the man, who was staring at him with a belligerent expression.

'Will! Abel! Get out here now. Help me with these dogs.'

Lucas held his stare, feeling his eyes narrow and jaw tighten. The man did not need help with the dogs, which were now quiet. His reinforcements, one of whom held a pitchfork, emerged from the stables and flanked the first man. Lucas scanned all three. Were they his attackers? He could not swear to it. He had not seen enough of their faces to be certain, although their builds were about right. But the dog... The dog was all the proof he needed.

'Surprised to see me, boys?'

He watched them closely. The two older men brazened it out, but the youngest of the three stepped back half a pace, flushed and fidgety.

'Sorry, milord. Never seen 'ee before.' It was the first man who spoke, evidently the senior of the three.

'Yet you know to call me by my title? Try again.' Lucas nudged Sultan forward. 'My memory is sharper than yours, for I recall all three of you very clearly. You might like to know the magistrate is on his way. Will you claim to be doing your master's bidding that day, I wonder? If so, you might escape the hangman, but it will still be deportation for the lot of you.'

The first man snarled and stepped forward, snatching at Sultan's bridle. Lucas reined the horse around, freeing one foot from the stirrup, ready to kick out.

'Rothley? What are you doing here?'

Lucas glanced over his shoulder. Quartly strode towards them, his face mottled with anger. Behind him, Lucas could see Dr Robert Preece, medical bag in hand. Never had he been so pleased to see his old friend. He breathed a touch easier.

Quartly had passed where Lucas sat on Sultan and now stood between him and his men. He glared up at him. Robert had halted to one side, putting his bag on the ground. He looked on with a puzzled expression.

'Good morning, Quartly. I was merely renewing my acquaintance with your men here. And your dog.'

Lucas gestured at the collie, which was now snuffling around the doctor's bag. Robert glanced down at the dog, then stiffened, his eyes seeking Lucas, a clear question in them. Lucas gave a slight nod and Robert's lips thinned as his gaze switched to Quartly.

'Stuff and nonsense! Since when do you trouble yourself with stablehands?' Quartly blustered. 'Why are you snooping around?'

'Snooping? My dear man, I do not snoop. I rode up your drive quite openly—as will the magistrate, who is on his way.'

'Magistrate?'

'Oh, indeed. Did you actually think you would get away with it, Quartly? Stealing a man's stock? Murdering him?'

'That wasn't the plan! You weren't...!' Quartly's mouth snapped shut. He looked back at his men. 'Get him!'

Only the youngest of three stirred and that was to shuffle backwards again.

Quartly's complexion darkened, sweat standing on his upper lip. 'What are you waiting for? That was an order!'

The man in the centre hawked, turned his head and spat on the ground. 'In front of the doctor? After what you did to Molly last night? Keep your job. I'm getting out of here.' He looked at the others. 'And so will you two, if you know what's good for you.' He turned to go, passing the youngster, now frozen to the spot. 'Well?' He grabbed his shirt, tugging at him. 'What are you waiting for?'

All three melted from sight. Lucas frowned but,

with the imminent arrival of the magistrate a fallacy, he was not inclined to try to detain them. They were on their home territory and had already shown their disregard for the law and for human life. There was Robert to think of, as well as himself. Besides, Quartly was the real culprit and he was going nowhere.

And he still needed to find Mary.

Lucas dismounted and tethered Sultan to a ring in the wall. He faced Quartly, whose breath rasped loudly in the silence of the yard, his chest visibly heaving. From a deep red, his complexion had leached to sickly grey. Robert grabbed his bag and stepped forward.

'Let's get him to the house.'

One either side, they supported Quartly, walking him slowly to the house. As they arrived at the door, however, he shrugged them off.

'I can manage!'

Lucas and Robert exchanged glances as he lurched through the door. Rob tried to take his arm again, but it was snatched away. Quartly made his way slowly along the hall. Lucas and Robert followed.

'Mary! Bring us refreshments!'

Lucas slammed to a halt, but the face that peered around a door in response to Quartly's shout belonged to a round-faced, dark-haired woman in middle age. Not his Mary. Breath juddered from his lungs as he suppressed a shaky laugh. Just being in this house reinforced the impossibility of Mary ever colluding with Quartly. He was a fool for ever believing such nonsense. And now he was on edge, restless to get on his way. Every minute he delayed felt as though Mary was moving further out of reach.

He must deal with Quartly first, however.

'Why are you here?' he whispered to Robert as they followed Quartly into a drawing room.

Robert glanced at Quartly, who had flopped on to a sofa, taking no notice of the other two men.

'I was called for one of the housemaids. Molly,' he added with emphasis and Lucas recalled the stableman's words.

'Quartly beat her?'

'And the rest. Poor girl. I had quite a job to stop the bleeding.'

'Tell her she can come to me for a job,' Lucas said on impulse. 'She shouldn't have to stay here with him.'

'If he is still here, after the magistrate hears what happened.'

'Ah. That was not strictly true, I'm afraid. It was all I could think of to buy some time. I was never more pleased to see you, Robert, of that you can be certain.'

Robert frowned. 'But, if you did not come here to expose Quartly, why are you here?'

'I thought Mary might have come here.'

Robert's astonishment only served to make Lucas feel even more of a numbskull than he already did.

'Can it be she never told you?'

'Told me what?'

Robert jerked his thumb towards Quartly. 'It was Quartly she was meant to wed, when she was just seventeen. He is the reason she ran away from home with the steward. She was petrified of him. She confided in Jenny.'

'You!' Fury erupted and Lucas charged at Quartly. He snatch his lapels, hauling him upright. 'I ought to kill you!'

His face was a bare inch from Quartly's. Lucas froze. Quartly's eyes had not even flickered.

'Rob?'

Lucas lowered Quartly back on to the sofa. Robert felt Quartly's wrist, then put his fingers on his neck, sliding them beneath the man's neckcloth. He looked round at Lucas, who had stepped back to give him space.

'He's dead.'

'What?' It couldn't be. His temper! He had killed a man. Even a scoundrel like Quartly did not make that all right. 'I never meant...'

Robert straightened. He gripped Lucas's shoulders. 'It wasn't you, Luke. I swear. I saw him when you grabbed him. He didn't respond, not even a twitch. He was dead before you touched him.' He looked down at Quartly and shook his head. 'Maybe it's for the best. I doubt there'll be many to mourn his passing. Were you aware he attacked Mary yesterday?'

'He did what?'

'Almost throttled her, her neck is black and blue, poor...' Robert turned suddenly and strode for the door. 'There will be arrangements to be made. I must speak to the servants, if you will excuse me, Lucas.'

Lucas barely registered Robert's words. 'Of course,' he muttered, shame flooding him as he realised Mary *had* been trying to appease Quartly. If only his insight had come sooner. He called after Robert, by now halfway down the hall, 'Rob, do you need me to stay? Only I...'

'No, you go on home, Luke. There is nothing you can do here.'

As soon as Lucas mounted Sultan, the horse seemed to sense his urgency and he set off at a canter down Quartly's drive, ears pricked. For the first time that morning, Lucas recalled the visitor due at the Hall. A visitor calling not only to view the breeding stock Lucas had for sale, but to be re-united with his daughter and the grandchildren he had never met. Sir William Cranston had presented as a changed man when Lucas, quite by chance, was introduced to him at Hexham Market. Sober and upright, remarried and well respected, he had been thrilled to learn Mary and the children were safe at Rothley Hall and he was eager to meet them and make amends for the past.

The pressure to find Mary and the children multiplied. How on earth could Lucas even begin to explain he had mislaid Cranston's daughter and grandchildren?

As they reached the entrance gates to Dunwick Manor Lucas reined the big grey to a halt. Something niggled at his memory...something... He cursed fluently and looked back over his shoulder to Dunwick Manor, feeling a smile curve his lips.

'Robert Preece...you old scoundrel!'

The dread that had weighed so heavily, the fear he would never find her, eased. He knew where she was. On the brink of riding for the village, he hesitated. He ruffled Sultan's mane absently as he picked over his options. Mary and the children were coming back to the Hall. He would accept no other outcome. Ergo, he needed the carriage. He turned for home and gave Sultan his head.

He might not be at the Hall when Mary's father arrived, but he would leave a message and apologies for him. It would not do to offend the man: Lucas might have need of his support in persuading Mary to forgive him.

Again.

He quashed any thought of failure. He could not fail. It was unthinkable.

Chapter Twenty-Six

In dire need of solitude, Mary sought out a secluded bench in the Preeces' garden. Jenny was very kind, but she chattered incessantly and Mary needed to think. To plan. She had passed a restless night but had risen that morning with a new determination. Her daydream of a future with Lucas had been banished to a box marked 'Past'.

She swallowed past her grief.

Stupid, stupid, stupid! You have your health and you have two wonderful children. Concentrate on them, on the future you must provide for them.

Her lids drooped as the soothing warmth of autumn sunshine caressed her face.

'Why didn't you tell me?'

The voice was gruffly gentle. Mary started, eyes jerking open as she leapt to her feet, heart thudding against her ribcage. Fingers, feather-light, brushed her throat. Her skin erupted in goosebumps at his touch. Misery crowded her. Why had he followed her? There could be no happy-ever-after, not with all their differences on fundamental matters.

Like trust. And openness. And honesty.

'What are you doing here? *Why* are you here?'

'I came to bring you back home. You and Toby and Emily.'

Home? She hunched her shoulder, turning away.

'Why did you not tell me?'

She rounded on him. 'Did you afford me the courtesy of listening to *anything* I tried to say last night?'

A muscle leapt in his jaw. 'I regret that, more than you can know. At least I can set your mind at ease— you will never have to fear Quartly again.'

'You cannot guarantee…'

'I can. He is dead.'

Mary's heart missed a beat. Had she heard correctly? 'Dead?'

'He died this morning. Rob is over at Dunwick now.'

'Robert? But he was called out to one of the housemaids, Jenny said. What makes you think it was Quartly? Are you certain…?'

'Positive. I was there when he died.'

Fear snaked through her. 'Why did you go to Dunwick?'

A wry smile crossed his face. 'You are wondering if I went there to kill him.'

Mary felt her skin heat. 'No,' she said. 'Well…I did wonder if you may have been angry…'

'Angry? I was boiling mad. Not only about his treatment of you, but by the discovery it was his men, on his orders, who were trying to steal my sheep and who shot me.'

Mary gasped. 'Are you sure?'

'Quite, quite sure. Unfortunately, by the time Rob told me about Quartly and you, he had acted the gentleman for once in his miserable life and saved me the effort of killing him.'

'Oh.' She was appalled by the relief and delight that swept through her at the knowledge Quartly was dead. What poor excuse of a human being could rejoice over the demise of another, even one as despicable as Quartly?

'But…' Something still didn't quite fit, but she couldn't order her thoughts with Lucas standing so close.

Lucas reached for her arm and steered her towards the bench. 'Let us sit down, Mary. We need to talk.'

Mary pulled away. 'If you have something you wish to add to what you said last night, please do so without feeling the need to dissemble. I have nothing left to say.'

She ached with misery. She could have coped if he had stayed away, but he had not. He was here and all she could think was how she longed to feel his arms around her and his lips on hers. An involuntary shiver coursed down her spine.

'Very well. I owe you an apology for not listening to your side of the story last night. I leapt to a conclusion. Upon reflection, I realised how unfair I was.'

It changed nothing and she was in no mood to meekly forgive him in order to ease his conscience. His lack of trust in her had wounded her. Her future, although less desperate than before, still stretched ahead: grey, dull, interminable.

Why should she make this easy for him?

'Was that before or after the brandy had ceased to hold sway over your judgement?'

He raised one brow. 'Your perception is not unreasonable, although the imbibition of the brandy did, in fact, take place after the judgement.'

Mary felt her forehead pucker as she followed his logic. She eyed him with suspicion. Was that a hint of a smile on his lips? She tensed. 'You are mocking me.'

'I was teasing. It is not the same.'

Mary bit her lip. 'Very well,' she said. 'I accept your apology.'

She marched across the lawn to the back door of the Preeces' house.

'Wait!'

'For what purpose?' She halted. Spun to face him. 'You have made your apology. I have accepted it. There surely cannot be anything left to say?'

'There is a great deal left to say, Mary. Please. Will you come home? I have the carriage waiting. You *must* come home.'

'Must?'

'We have much to discuss, Mary. But, first, there is something…someone…waiting at the Hall to see you. I had thought to surprise you, but, then, everything went wrong.'

He stepped closer, stroked her cheek. She fought the urge to press into his touch. He gathered her into his arms and, despite her vow not to, her body softened and she relaxed into his embrace.

'Come home, Mary. At least listen to what I have to say. Then, if you still want to go, I shall not stop you.'

'Who is it waiting to see me?'

'Your father.'

The carriage ride back to Rothley Hall passed in a daze. Her father! At the Hall! So many questions clamoured for an answer, but she held her silence.

Thankfully, Lucas left her in peace, shielding her from the children's excited chatter as much as possible.

As they drew up in front of the Hall, Trant opened the front door.

'You have a visitor, my lord,' he murmured, flicking a glance at Mary. 'Sir William Cranston.'

Mary's breath seized. It was true. He was here. Her father.

'He is in the sitting room, my lord.'

'Thank you, Trant. Will you take the children to Susan, please? Ask her to bring them to the sitting room in about ten minutes.'

A hand settled at Mary's waist, urging her forward. 'No need to be nervous, sweetheart.'

Lucas opened the sitting room door and Mary stepped through.

'Papa?'

Her father looked up, then scrambled to his feet. Mary took two steps towards him, then hesitated, uncertain. She had persuaded herself he did not want her, that he was not interested in her or her children. How would he react? Tears welled as he held out his arms, but she blinked them aside and forced herself to approach him slowly. He appeared sober and clean, his spare frame neatly attired, unlike the wreck of a man he had been when she had left Linburgh. Did he still drink? And gamble? She glanced at Lucas. His expression revealed nothing.

She focused on her father. She wanted answers. 'How did you find me?'

Her father's beaming smile wavered. 'I met Rothley at Hexham...'

'Hexham?' Mary turned on Lucas. 'You have been back two days and you did not think to tell me you had met my father?'

'I—' Lucas snapped his mouth shut, his dark brows drawing together. 'I had my reasons. I will tell you of them later. In private.'

In private? Mary felt her nerves skitter at the prospect. She concentrated on her father.

'I was interested in the livestock Rothley had taken to Hexham and I arranged to call at the Hall on my way home to view some more animals for sale,' he said.

Animals? He had not come to find her, then. Her heart sank.

'Then Rothley told me you were at the Hall, with my grandchildren. Oh, Mary, I canna tell ye of my relief, to know ye were all safe.'

The knot loosened at his words. Hope stirred. Might she and the children be offered a home with her father after all? She banished any thought of Lucas, despite his brooding presence not three yards from where she stood. She must focus on the possible.

Her father continued, in a low, hurried voice: 'I bitterly regret my behaviour after your poor mama's passing, lass. *Bitterly* regret it. I know it is no excuse, but I drank to numb the pain of losing her. I ended up losing far more than I bargained for. If only I had realised the outcome of my actions. If I had not been so lost in my addictions, ye would not have been forced to take such desperate measures.

'Your leaving brought me to my senses and I gave up the drink, but it was too late. Can ye ever forgive me?'

How can he think otherwise? Mary's heart soared. Her dream had become reality. *One* of her dreams. She peeped through her lashes at Lucas—handsome, unreadable—as he stood apart. Their eyes met. Butterflies danced in her belly as her knees trembled. How could she have thought he was safely relegated to the past? She tore her eyes from his, clenched her jaw and concentrated on her father.

Who was gazing at her, hope and fear jostling for position on his face.

What was it he had asked her? *Oh!*

'Papa, of course I forgive you.'

His chest swelled as he inhaled. 'Well, now, that is splendid.' He took her hand and squeezed as his eyes grew shiny. 'I dare say I do not deserve it, but I am grateful ye have such a good heart, lass.'

As she sat with her father on one of the pair of sofas, Mary sneaked a peek at Lucas, seated opposite, as he sprawled at his ease. She envied him his nonchalance. What was he thinking? She could not begin to guess. His gaze was fixed on her face with an unfathomable expression. Was he relieved she was now reconciled with her father? That he need no longer be responsible for her and her children? She shifted in her seat, made edgy by his silent scrutiny.

'When I think of all those wasted years,' Papa was saying. He clasped her hand with his and squeezed. 'I searched everywhere for ye, Mary, but it was as though you had fallen off the edge of the world. The one good thing to come of it was it brought me to my senses. But it was too late. I am so sorry...'

Mary patted his hand. 'Papa, please. You have apologised a thousand times over. You were coping with Mama's death the best way you knew how.'

'Yes, and see how it got out of hand. Somehow, and I shall never fathom how, I allowed that scoundrel to corner me. Even in my cups, I knew it was wrong. I did not want to take his wager, but still I found myself agreeing to it. And then, when I had lost...och, my poor, poor girl. Quartly would brook no delay; he insisted on an immediate wedding. What I have put ye through… I shall regret it all my days.'

Lucas stirred. 'What do you regret?'

'Everything. It is to my eternal shame that I was the cause of her running away at seventeen, but Quartly played his role in it, too.'

Mary's father recounted the tale of how drink had almost ruined his life and had resulted in him wagering the hand of his only child to Quartly in order to settle his debts.

Lucas, face like thunder, paced the room. 'No wonder she was reluctant to continue her journey to Linburgh. At least you can rest assured Quartly can do no more harm.' He told Mary's father about Quartly's death. 'You were not the only man to find himself stitched up by him, sir—my own father, too, fell prey to his schemes. Listening to your story gives me a better understanding of what I used to think of as his crass stupidity. Quartly was a very cunning fellow. I doubt many will mourn his passing.'

He halted in front of Mary, his face softening. 'No wonder you have such distaste for drinking and gambling. How I wish you had trusted me enough to confide in me.'

He crossed to the other sofa and sat down again as

Mary tucked that idea away to examine later. Who was he to talk of trust?

'Your elopement finally brought me to my senses,' Papa continued, stroking Mary's hand, 'but it was too late. I never did succeed in tracing you. Until I received your letter, I had no clue where to look. I cannot tell ye what joy that simple letter brought to me.'

'But why you did not reply, Papa?'

'It took many weeks to reach me, lass. It must have travelled over most of the north of England before crossing the border to Linburgh. I travelled south that same day, but ye'd gone.'

'Did you see Mr Wendover?'

'I did. Nasty piece of work.' Mary felt his arm go around her shoulders and he hugged her close. 'Ye've had scant luck with the men in your life, have ye not?'

Mary was conscious of Lucas shifting in his seat. Was he bored? Now he had solved the mystery of her whereabouts and her past, was he restless to return to his old life and leave her to get on with hers? Cold dread dragged at her stomach. She must leave soon and return to Linburgh. She would never see him again. She forced her attention back to her father.

'I still owe Simon Wendover rent money. Do you think…?'

'It is all taken care of, don't worry. I paid him what

you owed, plus the interest he said was due. He will never trouble you again.'

It was one less thing to fret over. Why then did she feel so dreadful?

'Now, my bonny lass, what about these grandchildren I have yet to meet?'

Lucas sprang to his feet and went to the door. He spoke to Trant, then crossed to the fireplace and propped his shoulders against the mantelshelf.

There was a sudden commotion as a small body rocketed into the room.

'Sir! Sir!' Toby skidded to a halt in front of Lucas, gazing up at him with adoration. 'Can we go and groom Sultan?'

'Not today, Toby. Please, come over here, will you?' Mary said, as both she and her father stood up. 'Where is Emily?'

'She's coming.' He gestured disdainfully, back the way he had come. 'She can't run fast like me.'

Emily soon toddled into view, clutching tight to Susan's hand. Mary watched her father's reactions as he drank in every detail of his grandchildren.

'Toby, Emily—this is your grandpapa.'

Her heart swelled with pride as Toby bowed to her father. Emily, thumb in mouth, stared wide-eyed. Her father crouched down and held his hand out for Toby to shake.

'They are fine bairns, Mary.' He tweaked Emily's cheek.

'Papa?'

'Yes, Mary?'

'What about your new family? Will your wife not object...?'

Cranston threw his head back and laughed. 'Object? Of course they willna object. Matilda will be delighted to welcome ye back home and the boys will enjoy their two new playmates. I sent word from Hexham to expect ye.

'I suppose,' he went on, 'we must think about the practicalities? Might I impose on you, Rothley, and beg the use of your carriage to transport my daughter and grandchildren to Linburgh?'

'Delighted to be of assistance, sir,' Lucas said, still propped against the mantelshelf.

Mary felt her heart shrivel. Was he truly so indifferent to the knowledge she would soon be gone?

Cranston, wreathed in smiles, walked out of the room, saying, 'Come along, then, lass. Bring the bairns.'

Mary followed. 'Come along, Toby, Emily.' Pain stabbed at her until she could barely breathe. 'Let us...'

'Mary.'

The deep voice pinned her to the spot. Her stomach somersaulted. She turned to Lucas, battling to conceal her emotions, and raised her brows in enquiry.

'You and I—I believe we have some unfinished business.'

A statement of fact. Not even a question. As if his interpretation of events was the only valid one. She forced the recall of every false accusation he had flung at her. She pulled her shoulders back and lifted her chin.

'I believe all that needed to be said has already been…'

Her words faltered as he strode across the room. Strong fingers enclosed her upper arms. Heat flared through her body, radiating from his touch. Her breath stalled, her knees trembled.

'Mary?' Her father's voice came from the doorway. 'Is everything all right, lassie?'

Mary glanced up at Lucas. She did not care to listen to more excuses, or to yet more reasons why he could not offer her what she so desperately wanted, but the determination set in every line of his features persuaded her he would not rest until he had his say.

'It is all right, Papa. Would you mind taking the children? I shall be with you in a few moments. Lord Rothley will not keep me long.'

She heard her father's footsteps retreat down the passageway.

She was alone with Lucas.

Chapter Twenty-Seven

She sat on the sofa, folding her arms. 'What is it you wish to say?'

Lucas stared at her for one long moment, his chest rising and falling as though he struggled with some internal dilemma. Mary forced herself to sit and wait. Finally, he swept one hand through his hair, spun on his heel and strode to the window to stare out through the glass.

'I do not want you to leave. Please stay—you *and* the children.'

Her heart missed a beat. Was he saying what she thought he was? His words from the night before echoed inside her head. Words she had not dared to believe: *'You are only interested in money! Not in love! Not in my heart!'*

She fought to keep her voice low and steady. 'Why?'

He faced her, frowning. She did not relent. If he

had feelings for her and if he did not admit to them now, he might never do so. And Mary could not live with that. If she was to entrust her heart and her children to another man, she must be certain he truly loved her. And *he* must be under no illusion either. If he could not trust her enough to share his fears and hopes and his true feelings—as well as his past—what future could there be?

'I love you, Mary. You must know that.'

The words she had longed to hear. Yet still her heart was breaking. Nothing had changed from the night before. What *mattered* had not changed.

'But you do not trust me.'

'Of course I trust you, sweetheart. I told you I know I was wrong about Quartly. I acted in haste. I accused you without reason. I knew it last night, the minute I left your bedchamber. I knew I was wrong. You are an honest, moral woman. I am sorry, more than I can tell you. I allowed my past to taint my judgement of you. I was wrong.'

'You trust my moral judgement and my behaviour. Mayhap you trust that I would not cuckold you with another man. But do you trust *me*?'

Lucas cocked his head, a puzzled frown creasing his forehead. Mary stood, crossed the room to look deep into his eyes. '*Will* you trust me, Lucas?'

He took her by the shoulders. 'Of course I trust you,' he repeated, but she pulled away.

'I do not understand, Mary—' the words spilled out, his frustration clear '—what can I say or do to convince you? I *love* you. I want to marry you. I wanted to tell you days ago, but I decided to wait until your father came, until you knew you had an alternative if you did not wish to stay with me.'

'You wanted to be sure of me?'

He hesitated.

'Yes…well, no…I did not want you to say yes because you had no choice. I wanted you to know you had somewhere else you could be safe and make your home.'

His eyes searched hers. Not for the first time, Mary could see the vulnerability at his core. It was to do with Julia, she was certain, but she did not understand why. She needed to know what had happened, or he would retreat every time there was a difficulty or misunderstanding. She knew, intuitively, that if she could not coax him to bring his past into the sunlight it would continue to shadow their lives.

His uncertainty was palpable. Instinct almost took over. It took every ounce of her will not to comfort him.

'You said we had unfinished business, Lucas, but

what you meant was *you* had unfinished business with *me*. I, too, have unfinished business with you. For instance: Julia.'

His expression blanked. 'Julia has nothing to do with you and me.'

Mary held his stare in silence, before asking: 'Do you honestly believe that, Lucas?'

No reply.

'Is Julia not the reason you accused me of negotiating a future with Sir Gerald?'

Merely saying his name forced bile to her mouth. Mary swallowed convulsively. He was dead. He could not hurt or threaten her now. As she swept away her fear of Quartly, she watched Lucas pace the room, up and down. She moved to the sofa and sat down, transferring her gaze to the window, watching the clouds mindlessly, even as every nerve in her body screamed its awareness of Lucas: his agitated movements, the ragged sound of his breaths.

She gripped her hands together in her lap, waiting.

'You are right.'

The words were grudging, but at least he had admitted it. Hope stirred in Mary's breast.

'Do you still love her?'

It was probably an unwise question, at this point, but it spilled from her lips before she could stop it.

Lucas rounded the sofa and sat next to Mary,

clasping her hands in his. She drew in a deep breath, revelling in his unique, male scent. Desire coiled deep inside.

'No. But I thought I loved her, once.'

Mary waited, forcing herself to sit still, stifling the urge to move closer, to touch his face. She must allow him to tell her of his past at his own pace. Her future, so bleak one short hour ago, now held so much promise she was almost overcome. She blinked her suddenly prickling eyes. Happy tears, but she could not risk Lucas misinterpreting them.

'I was young. I was green. A wild youth, let loose on the town for the first time. I ran with a reckless crowd: gaming, drinking, up to any and every debauchery known to man. Julia was a widow—vivacious, fun, beautiful, with golden hair and blue eyes of the exact same shade as yours. I fear, in my confusion and fever, I might have mistaken you for her a time or two. But never, dearest Mary, in your character.'

Mary felt her brows shoot up. She bit back her smile. She could not resist her chance to tease. 'Never?'

Lucas shook his head at her, a slow grin stretching his lips. 'Minx! Yes, I have been an impulsive fool at times—acting upon judgements made in haste, without clear thought. I will admit I have found it difficult to place my trust in another woman, even though, in my heart, I *knew* you had none of Julia's selfish traits.

'At that time—with the single-mindedness of youth—I believed her encouragement to be based on deeper emotions. I lavished her with gifts. I was persuaded I was in love.'

He paused, staring down at their clasped hands, his thumb caressing her wrist, then looked up, his eyes searching hers.

'I have never admitted this to another living soul, Mary. I was too ashamed. But this is what you meant, is it not? When you asked if I trust you? You meant, will I—can I—trust you with my past? My secrets?'

Mary smiled. 'Yes.'

She freed one hand and smoothed his hair from his forehead, stroking his face with her fingers, feeling the scrape of his whiskers—unshaven, judging by the shadow on his jaw—against her skin. His eyes darkened and she leaned towards him, offering her mouth. He took her lips in a quick, bruising kiss, then drew back, a smile hovering.

'Do not distract me, wench, now I have finally worked out what you want of me!'

Mary laughed, light-headed. 'Then hurry up and finish telling me so I may kiss you again.'

'There's not much left to tell. One afternoon, I discovered her in the arms of another man. A married man. A man I had thought to be my friend. I blurted out my love for her, but she rejected as worthless the offer of my hand in marriage.'

Mary's heart ached for the naïve young man Lucas had been.

'Still I did not leave. I pleaded, protesting my love, but she laughed and I learned, for the first time, of my father's vast debts. I remember her exact words: "You are deluded if you believe for one minute I would countenance an alliance with a near bankrupt estate such as you will inherit." How could I believe her? My father still paid my brother and me generous allowances. And it was nigh on impossible to accept I had been so wrong about her love for me. I tried to change her mind. Then Henson, my so-called friend, joined in her mockery.

'I lost my temper and, in my rage, I near to killed him. Then I came home to Rothley, to take my place alongside my father, determined to prove them both wrong about his debts.'

He heaved a sigh. Mary squeezed his hand. She had seen for herself the state of Rothley Hall.

'My father rejected my help. He swore there were no debts, called me a no-account wastrel and told me to get back to my dissolute life as that was all I was good for.'

Mary lifted his hand and pressed her lips to his warm skin. She knew how parental rejection felt.

'Why should I doubt him? I returned to London. I will not give you a disgust of me by detailing my every debauchery and vice, but suffice it to say they were many. It served its purpose for a time and numbed my feelings. But mindless pleasure palls eventually and, in time, I vowed to change my lifestyle. I stayed in Devon with an old friend, learning about estate management and agriculture, then I travelled on the Continent.

'Two years ago, a letter telling me my father was gravely ill reached me in Italy. I travelled home straight away, but he died before I arrived.'

'I am sorry you did not make your peace with your father before he died. You must have found that painful.'

He smiled ruefully. 'It was not as painful as you might imagine. My father was a brutal man. I had no love for him.' He shrugged, grimacing. 'I respected him because he was my father, but I had no respect for him as a man. Hugo and I were petrified of him when we were boys.'

'It can be no wonder you rebelled as a young man in London, but you proved your strength of character in the end. You amended your ways and now you have used what you learned to save the Rothley estate. You can be proud of that.'

'You, Mary Vale, are a very wise woman.'

Mary glowed at his praise. 'Is your decree you will not allow children at the Hall because of your father and your childhood?'

'For a wise woman, that question was phrased badly.'

'What do you mean?'

'You should have said, *Was* your decree you *would* not allow children. It is consigned to the past, Mary. But you are right, it was because of my father. I heard the words "You are just like your father" so many times during my youth that I believed it.'

'You feared you might become a violent bully?'

'I was convinced of it, particularly after I attacked Henson. It is only recently I have questioned that blind belief and for that I have you, Toby and Emily to thank. I understand now people meant I *look* like my father.'

Mary laid her hand against his cheek. 'Your father must have been a *very* handsome man.'

Lucas threw his head back and his laughter echoed around the room. 'You shameless flatterer, Mrs Vale.'

He shifted sideways on the sofa to face her, holding her hands, his face now serious.

'I love you, Mary. Can you find it in your heart to forgive the way I treated you? My doubts in you? Can *you* trust *me*?'

Mary searched his eyes, elated by the intensity and the love that shone in their depths.

'I cannot promise I will never again jump to the wrong conclusion, but I *will* promise you—faithfully and wholeheartedly—I will always listen to you and try to keep an open mind. When I went to your room this morning and you had gone, I...' He paused, his hands tightening on hers. He smiled ruefully, shaking his head. 'I *never* want to feel that way again, Mary. I was so afraid...'

'As was I,' Mary whispered. 'So afraid I would never see you again. I could not bear that you thought so ill of me. My heart was full of lead, my future darker than I've ever known even though I have been through some dreadful times.'

Lucas gathered her into his arms, pressing her cheek against his chest. She could hear the fast, strong beat of his heart—comforting, secure.

'You need never be afraid again, sweetheart.' His voice was husky. He tucked one finger beneath her chin and tilted her head to gaze deep into her eyes.

'I love you with all my being, Mary Vale. Will you marry me?'

There was one question she needed to ask. 'The children?'

'Will be loved as my own, I swear. How could I not love them when they are part of you?' He stroked the wayward strands of her hair away from her face, his eyes full of tenderness. 'And when *we* have a child…'

Mary pulled her head back and stared, wonder coursing through her. 'You want *us* to have children?'

'Yes.' No hesitation in his voice or in his ebony eyes. 'As soon as possible. I have wasted too many years of my life being someone I was not, boxing myself into a corner, surrounding myself with messages from the past and the opinions of others. I have broken free. I am ready to live my life, with you by my side, if you will have me?'

'Oh!' Mary flung her arms around his neck, pressing her cheek to his. 'Yes, Lucas. My answer is yes.'

She felt his strong hands encircle her waist and then she was on his lap, his lips covering hers.

Mary braced her hands against his chest, pushing with all her strength. Lucas stilled. He drew his head back until he was gazing into her eyes, sudden doubt clouding his own.

'There is one thing I have not yet told you, Lucas.'

She kept a straight face, holding back her smile, as she let the silence stretch, relishing the chance to tease him for a change. His fingers tightened on her waist. A muscle bunched at his jaw.

She tilted her head, then let her smile fly free. 'I haven't yet told you I love you. With all my heart.'

She laughed joyously at the relief and delight in his expression.

'You *are* a little minx.'

His fingers tangled in her hair as he took her mouth in a scorching kiss. Her heart beat a hectic tattoo as fire sizzled in her veins and desire consumed her. The urgent thrust of his tongue rocked her to the core and she squirmed, his arousal beneath her bottom taunting the aching need between her thighs—a need that threatened to spiral out of control.

Oh, how she wanted him.

She met the challenge of his kiss thrust for thrust. Their tongues entwined as he stole the very breath from her body. She threaded her fingers through his hair, cleaving her body to his until she hardly knew where she ended and he began.

Finally, he tore his lips from hers, lifting her from his lap and putting her from him with a groan. Her knees trembled and she would have fallen but for his strong hands at her waist. She clutched at his fore-arms as dazed ebony eyes searched hers. Slowly, she emerged from the sensual haze enveloping her. Their mingled breathing was the only sound in the quiet of the room, until a child's distant squeal intruded, bringing reality into focus.

Lucas studied her, a bemused expression on his face.

'I need to make you my wife as soon as possible, Mary Vale, or you will be the death of me.'

She smiled, finally secure in his love. She leaned over him, bracing her hands on his broad shoulders. She nipped at his earlobe and blew gently into his ear, revelling in his sharp intake of breath and his involuntary shiver. Taking her time, she lowered herself back on to his lap and wriggled around until she was comfortable, savouring his pained expression.

'Yes, Lord Rothley,' she said, in her very meekest voice, then wound her arms around his neck and caressed his smiling lips with her own once more, tasting him, loving him.

* * * * *